mary-kateandashley

Sweet 16

NEVER BEEN KISSED

WISHES AND DREAMS

THE PERFECT SUMMER

*Three fantastic stories
in one big book!*

mary-kateandashley

Sweet 16

NEVER BEEN KISSED

Emma Harrison

WISHES AND DREAMS

Kathy Clark

THE PERFECT SUMMER

Kieran Scott

HarperCollins*Entertainment*
An Imprint of HarperCollins*Publishers*

A PARACHUTE PRESS BOOK

A PARACHUTE PRESS BOOK
Parachute Publishing, LLC
156 Fifth Avenue
Suite 325
NEW YORK
NY 10010

First published in the USA by HarperEntertainment 2002
Never Been Kissed first published in Great Britain by HarperCollins*Entertainment* 2002
Wishes and Dreams first published in Great Britain by HarperCollins*Entertainment* 2002
The Perfect Summer first published in Great Britain by HarperCollins*Entertainment* 2002
First published in this three-in-one edition by HarperCollins*Entertainment* 2003
HarperCollins*Entertainment* is an imprint of HarperCollins*Publishers* Ltd,
77-85 Fulham Palace Road, Hammersmith, London W6 8JB

Books for Real Girls TM & © 2002 Dualstar Entertainment Group, LLC

SWEET 16 books are created and produced by Parachute Press, LLC, in
cooperation with Dualstar Publications, a division of Dualstar Entertainment Group,
LLC, published by HarperEntertainment, an imprint of HarperCollins Publishers.

The HarperCollins website address is
www.fireandwater.com

1 3 5 7 9 8 6 4 2

The author asserts the moral right to be
identified as the author of the work.

ISBN 0 00 717309 1

Originated by Dot Gradations Ltd, UK
Printed and bound in Great Britain by Clays Ltd, St Ives plc

mary-kateandashley

Sweet 16
NEVER BEEN KISSED

Emma Harrison

■ HarperCollins*Entertainment*
An Imprint of HarperCollins*Publishers*

A PARACHUTE PRESS BOOK

chapter one

"Ashley? Are you ready yet?" I called out, barely able to hide the excitement in my voice.

"Just give me a couple of minutes!" my sister, Ashley, answered from the dressing room next to mine.

I stared at myself in the mirror. The store dressing room was completely littered with clothes, but I'd found the perfect outfit at last. I couldn't stop smiling. "Do I look great or what?" I asked myself.

The answer was yes.

The knit top I'd chosen brought out my blue eyes and looked killer with the short denim shorts. It was perfect for our sweet sixteen party.

"Ashley, hurry up!" I called. "I'm dying to see what you think of this outfit!"

"I've just got a few more dresses to try," Ashley called back. I rolled my eyes and sat down to wait on the little bench in my dressing room, pushing the pile of clothes aside. *Our party is going to be sooo great*, I thought. I let my mind wander off…

All of our girlfriends are hanging out on the beach and it's a sunny, breezy day. There's a DJ spinning in the sand while a bunch of people dance to the latest songs. A few people swim in the waves. The rest of the crowd watches as Ashley and I rule in a volleyball tournament. Dad mans the barbecue while Mom snaps pictures of our friends.

We hang out on the beach until the stars come out, dancing to our favourite hits next to a big bonfire. Our cake is huge and has tons of candles on it. All our friends gather around to sing to us. Everyone agrees that it's the most fantastic sweet sixteen they've ever been to.

And of course, there's a monster pile of presents waiting for us when it's all over. Can't forget about the presents…

"Almost ready, Mary-Kate." Ashley's voice snapped me out of my thoughts. The beach and the party all melted away. "Just give me two more minutes."

"No problem," I told her, smiling at my reflection in the dressing room mirror. After all, I could spend another half-hour just daydreaming about the presents!

Okay, Ashley, I said to myself, *you saved the best dress for last. Time to go for it.*

I hung up all the outfits I'd already tried on. Then I turned and took the last dress down from the hook on the back of the door. I had a feeling that this was going to be *the one*.

I slipped the long, flowy, light-blue gown over my head, and it fell perfectly on my frame. The dress looked like it was made for me – it was just the right length, fitted perfectly around the waist and its slim spaghetti straps were totally flattering. Plus, it sparkled when the light hit it just right.

Mary-Kate is going to love this so much, I thought. *She's going to want to get the exact same dress!*

I gathered up my long, wavy blonde hair into a twist and secured it with a clip. Then I stood up on my tiptoes and grinned at my reflection. I'd found it! The perfect outfit for our sweet sixteen...

Mary-Kate and I walk into a huge ballroom filled with people who are all dressed up in ball gowns and tuxedos. Elegantly dressed waiters circle the room carrying trays heaped with food and tall champagne glasses full of sparkling cider. The scent of flowers fills the air, and there are roses on every table. Hundreds of candles give the room a romantic glow.

The dance floor gleams, and two incredibly cute guys ask me and Mary-Kate to dance. Mom and Dad stand along the wall, watching us with proud smiles. One of the waiters wheels out a huge cake, and everyone sings to us. When we blow out the candles, the whole room bursts into applause.

It's the most amazing party anyone has ever attended.

I shook myself out of my daydream and smiled at my reflection once again. It was all coming together. *Our sixteenth birthday is less than two months away*, I thought, *and now I've found the perfect dress – an elegant dress that shows I'm not a kid any more.*

"Ashley!" My sister groaned.

"Okay, I'm ready!" I stood and smoothed the dress once more. "Let's both come out on the count of three."

"Right," Mary-Kate said. "Here goes. One…"

"Two…" I chimed in.

"Three!"

We both stepped out of our dressing rooms, took one look at each other and burst out laughing.

"Um… I think we may have a problem here," I said, taking in her shorts and tank top.

"Tell me about it, Cinderella," she joked. "Nice dress, though."

"Thanks, and those shorts are great. But..." I shuffled over to her dressing room and peeked inside, taking in the piles of casual clothes. There wasn't a single dress in sight. "Mary-Kate, what were you thinking?"

"Beach party, of course!" she replied.

"But...we live in Malibu, California," I said. "We go to the beach all the time."

"Exactly," she said. "What's the point of living here if you don't take advantage of it?"

I took in her shorts and tank top again. When it came to our birthday party, we were definitely not on the same planet. "Maybe we should go somewhere and start talking about this party," I suggested.

Ashley and I kicked back in the cushy corner booth at Starbucks with our coffees. "We've got to get serious about this sweet sixteen party," she said. "I know you like to be spontaneous, but—"

"Hey," I protested. "Even I know that great parties take planning. Give me a *little* credit, Miss Organisation."

She pulled out a glittery purple notebook and matching pen. "I'm no more organised than the average person," she insisted.

"Does the average person alphabetise all the books in her bedroom?" I asked. "Does the average person keep all of her drawers colour coordinated? I don't think so."

"All right," she said, sniffing. "So I'm above average. I just can't live in total chaos – like *some* people I know."

"Hey," I protested. "I don't live in chaos. I just…go with the flow." Though I have to admit the floor of my room is littered with shoes and I'm always tripping over them.

"Whatever." She tapped her purple pen, ready to work. "Back to the party. Where do we start?"

I zipped up the front of my dark blue hoodie and leaned my elbows on the table. "We've already been to a lot of sweet sixteens. Remember those goody bags from Sherra Cintron's party? With the CDs and the little disposable cameras? Those were cool."

"Yes! That *was* a good idea," Ashley agreed, making a note. "We could give out goody bags, too – something that goes along with our theme."

"Theme?" I flopped back against the velvety couch. "How are we supposed to find a theme that's got you wearing a ball gown and me hanging out in shorts and a T-shirt?"

"Okay, don't freak," Ashley said. "We'll just have to compromise, somehow."

"I know." I stirred my frappuccino with my straw. "I just wish we weren't born so late in the year. It's like there's all this pressure to top the parties that came before ours."

Ashley smiled confidently. "Hey, this is *our* party," she said. "It'll blow all those other ones out of the water." She glanced down at her notebook. "Who should we invite?"

"I've been thinking a lot about this," I said, sitting up again. "I think it should be an all-girl party."

"Really?" Ashley asked.

"Yeah. None of our friends has a serious boyfriend," I pointed out. "And I think everyone would have a lot more fun if they weren't worried about looking cool in front of the guys."

Ashley frowned. "I see your point. But we *are* turning sixteen. Wouldn't it be kind of...I don't know...unsophisticated to have an all-girl party?"

"Having guys there won't make it sophisticated," I said. "Most of our guy friends still think burping contests rule."

Ashley giggled. Then a movement by the door caught her eye. "Hey, there's Lauren and Brittany!"

Sure enough, our two best friends were making their way over to our table. Lauren and Brittany couldn't be more different if they tried. Lauren is tall with wavy brown hair, light skin and tons of freckles. She's always sweet to everyone and has an eternally sunny outlook. Brittany, on the other hand, can be sarcastic about anything – from breakfast cereal to biology class. She's African-American and has dark brown eyes and tight black curls that she never lets grow past her earlobes.

Brittany waved to us. "Mary-Kate and Ashley – at Starbucks? What a shocker!"

"Hey, I'm not the one with the frequent-customer card," I shot back.

Lauren glanced down at Ashley's notebook.

"Gift bags?" she read. "For what?"

"We're trying to plan our sweet sixteen." Ashley sighed. "Unfortunately we haven't got very far."

"Ashley's thinking royal ball while I'm thinking beach party," I explained. "I picked out shorts and she picked out a dress...and she wants to invite the guys and I think it should be just girls."

Brittany laughed and shook her head, her dangly earrings jingling.

"Another shocker!" she joked. "Anyone who knows you two could have seen this coming."

"Are we that predictable?" Ashley asked.

"Kind of – in a good way," Lauren said. "But whatever you guys decide to do, I'm sure it'll be the best party ever. Everyone's already looking forward to it. I overheard Rachel and Alex talking about it the other day. They can't wait to see what you're going to do."

"No pressure or anything," Brittany cracked.

Pressure? I wasn't worried. A wave of calm washed over me.

Working together, Ashley and I would plan a sweet sixteen to end all sweet sixteens – I felt sure of it.

"Hey, we love pressure," I declared, leaning back into the couch. "We *live* for pressure."

"Okay, let's talk about themes." Ashley flipped her notebook to a new page. "What were some good ones from parties we've gone to?"

Lauren's blue eyes brightened. "I loved the Paris theme at Melanie Han's party, with the Eiffel Tower replica and all the twinkling lights."

"Okay, so something international would be good," Ashley said, making a note. "What else?"

"Hey! What about a Broadway theme?" Brittany suggested. "Ashley loves acting, and you could have a city skyline and playbills and stuff like that."

"Good one!" Ashley said, writing it down.

"Or we could do a Hollywood thing," I added, ideas starting to flit through my head. "We could have a replica of the Hollywood sign, a red carpet—"

"Or what about a Hawaiian theme!" Ashley chimed in. "Hula skirts, leis, coconuts, sand…"

"Or we could do a music theme—"

"Or Mardi Gras—"

"Guys!" Brittany cried, holding up her hands.

The rest of us stopped our babble fest. "Look who just walked in," she whispered.

I looked up, and my breath caught in my throat. Jake Impenna was headed for the coffee counter. Jake is an incredibly cute seventeen-year-old junior who just moved to Malibu a few months ago. His brown, spiky hair was hidden beneath a well-worn baseball cap, and he was wearing a grey T-shirt that matched his amazing eyes.

Jake was on the basketball and baseball teams at our school, Bayside High, and everyone saw him as this total jock. But he was also in my creative writing class, and I could tell from his stories that he had a seriously sensitive side. I had a monster crush on him, and my friends knew it. I felt their eyes on me while I stared at him.

"Are you gonna talk to him?" Brittany asked.

I blushed. "I don't feel like making an idiot of myself today."

Brittany raised her eyebrows. "Since when do you have trouble talking to anyone?"

"Since whenever Jake walks into a room," I answered. "I need at least half an hour to practise before I can even say hello to him."

"Well, start practising," Ashley said.

My heart raced and my mouth went dry. Jake was weaving through the café with his coffee... and heading right for our table!

chapter two

"Hey, everybody," Jake said. He leaned his free hand on the back of an empty chair. "Mary-Kate," he added.

"Hi, Jake." My tongue felt dead inside my mouth, but I don't think Jake noticed.

"Have you finished that creative writing assignment yet?" he asked me.

"Not yet." I relaxed a little, glad that I didn't have to come up with something to talk about. "We have to write a poem about ourselves," I explained to my friends. "It's harder than it sounds."

"Seriously," Jake agreed. "I keep trying different things, but they all come out embarrassing. How about you?"

"Yeah…exactly." I gave a nervous little laugh. I didn't want to admit that every time I tried to write my poem, I thought of Jake. What if I had to

11

read it out loud in class? What would he think of it? The idea totally paralysed me.

An awkward silence fell over the group. My friends stared at me. I could tell what they were thinking. Their eyes practically screamed *Say something, stupid!*

I know! I wanted to shout back. But I can't think of anything! Where are my jokes? Why can't I talk?

"Whatever," Jake said. "You've probably never done anything embarrassing in your life."

"Uh...thanks." Was he kidding? Wasn't he witnessing my total lack of conversational skills?

"Well, good luck with the poem," Jake said. "I'll see you guys later."

He started to walk away, and Brittany widened her eyes at me. *Say something!* she mouthed.

"Like what?" I whispered back.

"Um, Jake?" Lauren piped up. "We were just wondering if...you're going to Todd Malone's beach party this weekend."

Nice save, Lauren! I thought.

Jake turned back to us. "I'm not sure I want to go. I'm getting a little beached out lately, you know?" He shrugged.

I sagged with disappointment. Todd's party would definitely be a lot less interesting without Jake.

"Oh, but you *should* come," Ashley insisted. "Todd always throws the best parties."

"Yeah!" I broke in, finally finding my voice. "Ashley and I never miss them." *Great*, I thought. *That was impressive*.

Jake smiled slowly and looked directly at me. For a split second, it felt as if everyone else disappeared.

"In that case, I'll be there," he said.

My cheeks burned, but I managed to sound cool when I said, "See ya there!"

Jake lifted his coffee cup to say goodbye, then pushed his way through the door of the shop.

"Aaaaaa!" As soon as he was gone, we all squealed in excitement. I'm not normally a squealer, but I couldn't help myself.

"Did you hear that?" I cried.

"He *so* likes you," Brittany said.

"No!" I protested, waving her off, even though I was grinning so hard my face hurt.

"You know he does," Ashley put in. "He was practically drooling."

"And he *is* going to the party for you," Lauren said. "That was totally obvious."

I bit my lip as a little shiver went down my back. "It was, wasn't it?"

"Totally," Ashley confirmed. She took a sip of coffee, then pulled her notebook towards her. She loves to get things done. "Now, let's get back to our party. Where should we have it?"

Brittany and Lauren started to spout out

different ideas for places to hold our sweet sixteen. I zoned out a little, thinking ahead to Todd's party. Suddenly I couldn't wait for the weekend!

"Mary-Kate, are you all right?" Mom asked me that night. "You've got the funniest expression on your face."

Ashley elbowed me. We were sitting down for dinner with our parents, and I knew what Mom was talking about – this ridiculous grin that just wouldn't go away. All I could think about was Jake. I kept playing his words over and over in my mind and coming to the same, undeniable conclusion. Jake definitely liked me! Or, at the very least, he wanted to see me at Todd's party, which was almost as good.

"I'm fine, Mom," I assured her. "I'm just in a good mood."

"I'm glad to hear that," Dad said as he sank into his seat at the head of the table. He pulled at his tie until it was loosened and then unbuttoned the top button of his shirt. "Because I have great news."

His blue eyes twinkled with excitement. It wasn't often that Dad came home from work looking psyched. He's an executive at a big music company, and he always has to deal with people who have "big attitudes and even bigger egos" (or so he says), and it sometimes wears him down. He's been extra stressed lately because of this huge summer music festival he's been helping to plan. It was good to see him looking happy for a change.

"Don't keep them in suspense, honey," Mom laughed, tucking a few stray strands of her blonde hair behind her ear.

"Well, I was meeting with this band called Rave today—"

"Wait a minute, *Rave*?" Ashley interrupted him, her eyes wide. "When did you guys sign Rave? They're one of my favourite bands! Dad, *please* tell me you're going to let us meet them."

I held my breath. Even though our father had access to all these incredibly cool people, Ashley and I had never met any of the musicians his label represented. He had a strict policy of keeping business separate from the family.

Of course, his policy didn't keep me and Ashley from begging every chance we got.

"No, honey," my father said slowly. Ashley's face fell. "But listen, girls, they had their party planner there with them. His name is Wilson Miller, and he's worked with a lot of our bands over the last couple of years. Great guy."

He paused to take a bite of his pasta. Ashley

and I watched him chew, waiting to hear more. He chewed, and chewed, and chewed...

"And?" I prompted when my father finally swallowed.

"And he owes me a favour, so when he heard you and Ashley had a sweet sixteen coming up, he offered to plan it for you," Dad announced. "Free of charge!"

"Isn't that great, girls?" Mom asked.

"I don't believe it!" Ashley exclaimed. "Rave's party planner working on *our* sweet sixteen?"

"That's incredible!" I flashed back to the fabulous pictures from swank celebrity parties I'd seen in fashion magazines. "This could be the biggest party of the year!"

"Thank you so much, Dad," Ashley said. "This is going to be so cool!"

"I'll set up a meeting for all of us." Dad smiled. "You girls are going to love Wilson."

I dug in to my food and realised my perma-grin had actually widened. But this time it wasn't because of Jake. Now I was imagining a Hollywood-worthy sweet sixteen!

Breathe, Ashley, I coached myself.

A few days later, Mary-Kate and I were in the back seat of Dad's car on our way to Wilson Miller's office. A bunch of nervous butterflies were holding a dance party in my stomach. After all, this guy had worked not only with Rave, but with a bunch of other bands at Dad's label. He'd hung with the coolest people on the planet! What if Mary-Kate and I didn't measure up?

Wilson worked out of his home – a huge, Spanish-style stucco ranch house that was built into the side of a hill. It was surrounded by palm trees and tropical flowers, and was totally secluded. I almost gasped when Dad pulled the car into the driveway. It was so beautiful! We made our way to the front door. I couldn't help imagining the star-studded parties Wilson had probably thrown there.

"Welcome to my abode!" Wilson said brightly when he opened the door.

I smiled the moment I saw him. Wilson was young and totally down with the latest trends. His hair was hidden under a burgundy and blue ski cap, and he was wearing a black T-shirt and seriously faded jeans. He was definitely cute, in a post-college-guy kind of way, and he had a mobile in one hand and a pager in the other.

"Just give me one sec," he said as we stepped into the foyer. He held the phone to his ear while scrolling through messages on his pager. "Yeah...yeah, Carlos. I will definitely be in Grand Cayman tonight, but I have to leave for Aspen on

Monday. Yeah...right. Looking forward to it. I have some people here, so I gotta go. Okay...later." He looked up at us and gave a casual shrug. "So many plans, so little time. You know how it is."

Mom and Dad laughed, and Wilson turned to Mary-Kate and me. "So you're the infamous Mary-Kate and Ashley," he said, pretending to give us a once-over. "I've heard all about you from your father."

Mary-Kate groaned in mock horror. "I hope he didn't break out the baby pictures," she joked. "Because if he did, watch out. America's snooziest home videos are next."

Wilson laughed. I wished I could be more like Mary-Kate – she always knows just what to say to break the ice.

"Okay, we've got a lot to do, and I gotta get out of here in less than an hour." Wilson checked his watch. "So come on in."

We followed him into his office. Mary-Kate and I settled into the two soft chairs across from his desk. Mom and Dad took the couch in the back of the office, behind us.

"Okay." Wilson leaned his elbows on his desk. "The first thing I want to make clear is that I'm working for you. That means that my job is to do whatever you want me to do, and to do it right.

18

I'm going to help you realise the party of your dreams."

I grinned at Mary-Kate, impressed. Talk about saying exactly what we wanted to hear!

"We're sold. Where do I sign?" Mary-Kate joked.

"Well, hold on." Wilson chuckled. "First let me show you some pictures from other parties I've thrown."

He opened a drawer and pulled out a thick, suede-covered photo album. I lifted myself up from my chair a bit so I could see the photos better.

I couldn't believe my eyes. I was looking at pictures from Jenna Rodenberry's wedding! There she was herself, cutting the cake! Jenna was one of the biggest movie stars in the world, and Wilson Miller had done her wedding!

"I can't believe it." I gasped.

I turned to Mary-Kate and saw her staring down at the page as if she couldn't tear her eyes away.

"Oh, but that's a wedding. You don't need to see that," Wilson said.

He turned to a page full of pictures taken at a dance club, all decked out for Hallowe'en. The decorations were unreal. Every inch of wall was covered with cobwebs and fake spiders. Hanging from the ceiling were yards of black-and-orange crepe, and along the floor sat fat pumpkins carved so intricately they looked like sculptures.

"You are *seriously* detail oriented," Mary-Kate said.

Wilson laughed. "That's my job. Let me show you an example of something more understated."

He flipped the page and smoothed the book down in front of us. These pictures were from a much simpler party. It was a tropical theme with fresh flowers strewn all over the tables and colourful umbrellas ruffling in the breeze. Leis made of real flowers were draped over the backs of bamboo chairs. The waiters were wearing Hawaiian shirts with khaki shorts and sandals.

My skin tingled with excitement. Wilson Miller could be the secret weapon we needed to make our sweet sixteen the coolest one yet!

Mary-Kate raised her eyebrows, I nodded, and then we both looked at Wilson.

"No joking...you're hired!" Mary-Kate announced.

"Great!" Wilson exclaimed. He looked over our heads at our parents. "That was easy!"

Mom and Dad laughed. "We're glad to have you on board," Mom said.

"So, let's get right down to it," Wilson said, closing the book and pulling it away. "What kind of party are you two thinking about throwing?"

I thought about the brainstorming session

we'd had earlier in the week. I'd made about five pages of notes, but we had no clear idea of what we wanted.

I bit my lip. "Well, we haven't really decided on a theme yet," I said slowly.

"Let's just say, decision-making isn't our strong point," Mary-Kate added.

"That's all right," Wilson said. "A theme is a tough thing to settle on. It can make or break your whole party."

Tell me about it, I thought.

"I have a suggestion." Wilson stood up and walked over to a packed bookcase in the corner of the office.

He slipped out a thick album and brought it over to the desk. This one was filled with invitations.

He thumbed through the pages. "Take this home with you and try to pick out an invitation." He flipped through a huge array of different invites. "Sometimes the kind of invitation you choose can be a good jumping-off point for a theme."

"Great!" I said as he handed the book to me. I hugged it against my chest. "I can't wait to go through this."

"Yeah, thanks, Mr. Miller," Mary-Kate said, standing up. She offered her hand, and he shook it.

"Call me Wilson," he offered, letting go of Mary-Kate's hand and grasping my free one. "Call me as soon as you've decided, and we'll go from there. Your party date is only eight weeks from now – that's not as far away as it sounds. So let's try to settle some of the details this week. I'm never in one place for long, but you can always get me on my mobile."

As Wilson walked our parents to the door, Mary-Kate and I practically ran to the car with the invitation book.

All I could think about was getting home and getting to work on the party. Soon Mary-Kate and I would have an invitation and a theme, and now that we had Wilson working with us, we were going to have the coolest sweet sixteen in history.

chapter three

"Another quiet Saturday night in Malibu," I joked as music blasted up to us from the beach.

I followed Ashley, Lauren and Brittany around the side of Todd Malone's house towards the wooden staircase that led to the beach. We could see that the party below was already in full swing. There was a huge bonfire with tons of people crowded around it. Todd was barbecuing with some of the guys at an open grill. Dance music blasted from speakers placed around the fire, and a couple of dozen kids were dancing near the water.

"Now this is cool," I said.

"Todd's outdone himself this time," Lauren agreed as we picked our way carefully down the stairs.

Brittany flashed me her devilish grin. "So, do you think he's here yet?"

I felt a nervous twinge in the pit of my stomach. "Who? Todd?" I asked, hoping to throw them off the subject of Jake Impenna. As if that were possible.

"No! Jake!" all three of them shouted in unison.

I stopped in the middle of the staircase. "Say it a little louder!" I told them. "I think there are a few fish out there who didn't hear you."

"Sorry." Ashley bit her lip. "No more Jake talk. We promise."

"Thank you!" I said as we continued down the steps.

Of course, as soon as we were close enough to see everyone, I found myself scanning the faces of the party-goers, looking for Jake. It took me about five seconds to spot him standing with a few guys over by the food.

He looked up and caught my eye. Then he smiled, and I instantly blushed. I was glad that I was so close to the bonfire. I could pretend I was just flushed from the heat.

"Hey, there's Tashema and Melanie." Brittany grabbed my hand and started to pull me towards the water. "Let's dance!"

"Okay! I'm coming!" I laughed, grabbing Ashley and Lauren as well. Brittany could not control herself if there was a dance floor nearby.

The music mixed with the sound of crashing

waves and made it a pretty loud scene. We shouted our hellos to Melanie and Tashema and started dancing.

"This is a great set up!" I said to Ashley, leaning in close to her ear so I could be heard. "It's kind of like what I was thinking about for our sweet sixteen."

"I can see that." Ashley frowned as she looked around. "Maybe we should compromise and—"

I grabbed Ashley's wrist and froze. She stopped mid-sentence. She followed my gaze and saw what – I mean, *who* – had paralysed me.

Jake Impenna was cutting across the dance floor and honing in on us. I had no idea what to do. What should I say to him? Should I act happy to see him? Should I be aloof? Should I panic and run away?

Ashley gave me a little shake. "Snap out of it!" she whispered. "Dance!" She started dancing again. I tried to dance, but my feet felt like lead.

"Hey!" Jake called as he slid past a couple of people to dance with Ashley and me. "I'm glad you showed!"

"Yeah! Me, too," I said. "I mean...you, too." Oh, no! I was making no sense again! Why did Jake have such a weird effect on me?

Maybe because he's older, and gorgeous and athletic and smart and...perfect! I thought.

"I mean, I'm glad you showed, too," I added, finally getting my point across.

"Thanks." Jake laughed.

We all danced together, and, after a few minutes, I relaxed a bit. Then, when Jake had his back turned, Ashley tapped my arm and whispered, "I'll be right back."

My breath caught, and I tried to grab her hand, but she just waved and disappeared. My pulse pounded like crazy. How could my sister leave me on the dance floor with Jake? What if he thought I wanted to dance alone with him but he didn't want to dance alone with me?

I was going to have to kill her.

Then, out of nowhere, the hip-hop song that was playing cut off and one of my favourite slow songs came on. Everyone paused for a moment, but soon the crowd started to pair off, and couples dotted the dance floor, swaying slowly to the music.

Jake raised his eyebrows. "Wanna dance?"

My heart melted. He was too cute for words!

"Sure." I reached up and wrapped my arms around his neck as he put his around my waist.

Before I knew it, we were moving together to the perfect, romantic slow song. Me and Jake Impenna! Slow dancing! I couldn't believe it. Over his shoulder, I spotted Ashley standing by the stereo. She waved, and I realised what she'd done. Oh, my gosh. She'd changed the song just so that I could dance with Jake! Suddenly, I didn't feel so much like strangling her any more.

Ashley flashed me a thumbs-up sign. I shook my head. What would I do without her?

When the song came to an end, I reluctantly pulled away from Jake. People began to walk away from the dance floor, heading for the barbecue. I hesitated for a second. I didn't want this part of the night to end.

"So…" Jake said.

"So…" I laughed nervously. *Say something*! I told myself, but my brain refused to cooperate.

"Listen, I know this is kind of out of nowhere, but do you think…I mean, would you like to go out with me sometime?" he asked.

I forced myself to look into his grey eyes. I had to make sure he wasn't joking. No, I realised. He meant it.

I felt like blurting out "Yes!" at the top of my lungs. Stay cool, stay cool, I warned myself. I took a deep breath and smiled up at him.

"Sure," I said. "That sounds great."

A huge smile lit his face.

"Excellent," he said. "How's Friday? I was thinking dinner and a movie or something like that. Can I pick you up around six?"

"That would be perfect," I replied.

"Perfect," Jake repeated. "Then I guess I'll... talk to you later." He turned and started up the beach, following the rest of the crowd.

"Yeah! Later!" I said, lifting my hand. I didn't even know what I was doing or saying. All I knew was that Jake Impenna had actually asked me out!

When he was a safe distance away, I scanned the crowd for my sister and spotted her hanging with a couple of people by the fire. I half ran, half skipped over to her. I could barely contain my excitement.

"What happened?" Ashley said.

"He asked me out!" I whispered, grasping her arms. "We're going out on Friday!"

Ashley let out a squeal and hugged me. "I knew it!" she cried. "I knew he was going to!"

"Thank you so much!" I said when we pulled away from each other. "You totally set the mood with that slow song."

Ashley grinned. I could tell she was happy for me. "Hey, that's what sisters are for."

A little while later, Mary-Kate and I were getting ourselves a couple of sodas. Mary-Kate was still completely giddy over Jake.

"You don't understand," she said, all

starry-eyed. "He's not just a super-jock. You should hear the stuff he writes for class. He can be totally mushy."

"He sounds really sweet," I told her, taking a sip of my soda. "I'm so psyched for you!"

"I know! Me, too," Mary-Kate said. "So where's Brittany?" she asked, looking around. "I haven't seen her since he asked me out and I already told Lauren, Tashema and Melanie. If Brittany hears this from someone else, I'm a dead girl."

"She's over there, shamelessly flirting with Michael Gelb." I pointed her out to Mary-Kate. Brittany stood by the stereo, sorting through CDs with Michael and giggling like crazy. "You tell her. I'm going to go get some food."

"I'll be right back." Mary-Kate took off down the beach.

I spun around to head for the barbecue and smacked right into someone. I managed to stay on my feet, but the poor, unsuspecting guy was sent sprawling on to the sand. A bunch of people standing around us laughed.

"I am so sorry!" I cried. My victim sat up and dusted the sand from the front of his black concert T-shirt.

"Hey, no problem," he responded, smiling up at me. "It's not a party until someone lands on their butt."

I didn't mean to stare at him, but I couldn't help it. This guy was cute. Incredibly cute. His shaggy brown hair fell into his eyes - the warmest brown eyes I had ever seen. I reached out to help him up. When he grabbed my hand, my heart gave a little extra thump.

"Are you okay?" I asked, letting go of his hand.

"No harm done," he said, waving me off. "But I am gonna warn my friends to keep a safe distance from you," he joked.

I just kept staring at him. His smile...it was kind of mischievous. Kind of sly.

What's wrong with me? I thought. Say something, Ashley! Something funny like Mary-Kate would. But I couldn't. I was totally speechless.

"Uh...right," I mumbled. "Good idea."

"I'm just kidding." The guy stared at me like I was insane.

"No! I know. Of course you were. I just...I *am* a klutz so it would probably be a good idea for you to...you know...."

Stop talking, Ashley! Just stop talking!

"Warn my friends?" he supplied, putting me out of my misery.

"Yeah," I said with a laugh.

"Okay. Well, I'll see ya." He jogged off and joined a group of people who were down by the DJ, getting the dancing going again. I opened my mouth to call after him. I wanted to ask him his name, but he was too far away.

Instead, I searched the crowd and found Lauren at a table over by the barbecue, chowing down on cheeseburgers with Melanie and Tashema.

"What's up?" Lauren asked.

"Not much," I told her, glancing at the dance floor. Mystery Boy was hamming it up with a few of his friends.

"Do any of you know who that guy is?" I asked, tilting my head in Mystery Boy's direction. "The one in the black T-shirt and the green cargos?"

Tashema slowly shook her head, her beaded braids clicking together. "No clue," she said. "Why? Are you thinking that both twins are going to get lucky in love tonight?"

"Yeah, right," I scoffed.

"I've never seen him before," Melanie added, putting her fork down and wiping her fingers on a napkin. "But he is seriously cute – if you go for the just-this-side-of-grungy type. Maybe he's from Harrison High."

"Yeah! Todd does know a lot of people from Harrison, remember?" Tashema said. "He lived over there until seventh grade, and he stayed friends with a lot of those guys."

Harrison High. It wasn't a lot to go on, but it was definitely a place to start.

I pulled out the plastic chair next to Lauren's and sat down, watching Mystery Boy, who was still dancing. Who did Todd know from Harrison High? I had to admit I had absolutely no idea.

But when I pictured Mystery Boy's lopsided grin, I knew that somehow, I had to find out.

I never felt so attracted to anyone so fast! That had to mean something, I thought. And after all, maybe Tashema was right. Now that Mary-Kate had a date with a really cute guy, I was starting to think I should have one, too!

chapter four

I crossed my legs Indian style on Mary-Kate's bed as she sat down next to me. "Okay, so...what do we want our invitation to say?" I asked, opening Wilson's big book of invitations next to my party-planning notebook.

It was late on Friday afternoon. We'd decided to figure out the whole invitation issue before Jake picked Mary-Kate up for their date.

"The usual," Mary-Kate said absently. She stared off into space, fiddling with her rings. "Date, time, place..."

I laughed as I picked up one of Mary-Kate's grey flannel throw pillows – and whacked her over the head with it.

"Hey!" She scowled at me. "What was that for?"

"I know what we want it to *say*, I mean what kind of message should it send?" I clarified. "You know, is this a *cool* party, a *casual* party, a *dressy* party... What planet are you on, anyway?"

"Planet Jake," Mary-Kate admitted, shaking her head at herself. "Sorry. I'm going to focus now, I promise."

"That's okay. I totally understand," I said. "Let's just get this done. Then we can concentrate on picking out something for you to wear on your date."

"Deal," Mary-Kate agreed.

We paged through the book past invitations that were too frilly, too plain, or too cute. None of them were quite right. Finally, Mary-Kate turned the page, and we both paused.

"Ooooh," I said. *"This* I like."

Right smack in the middle of the page was the perfect invitation. It was a real CD with a sample photo of a girl and the details of her party printed on it. It was made to look as if the girl was a pop star and recorded the CD herself. A note beside the disk said that it was a real CD – you could burn any song or message you wanted on it. The lettering and design were totally funky and said exactly what I thought our invitation should say. *"This party is going to be fun and completely hip."*

"I love it!" Mary-Kate said. "Even the envelope is cool!"

The envelope was a cardboard CD sleeve – just like the ones record companies used when they were promoting a new band.

"I think we found our invitation," I said.

"Definitely," Mary-Kate said. "And you get to scratch something off your to-do list!" she added, teasing me.

"Ha, ha," I said flatly, even though she was right. I loved getting things done! I pulled my planning notebook over and carefully copied down the item number from the invitation book. "Everyone is going to love these!"

"One problem," Mary-Kate said, squirming her way up into a seated position. "Wilson said our invitation would be a...what did he call it again?"

I frowned and looked down at the invitation. "A jumping-off point."

"Yeah," Mary-Kate said. "And this would be good for any kind of party. I mean, we'll have music no matter what."

I sighed, realising Mary-Kate was right. It was a great invitation, but it didn't get us much closer to deciding on the theme.

"Oh, well." I shrugged. "We'll just have to figure out the theme another time, I guess."

I reached over the side of her bed, grabbed my backpack and pulled out my planner. Wilson had called with a few deadlines the other day, and I'd written them all down in my date book.

"We're doing fine," I told Mary-Kate. "We've got six weeks until the party. We'll call Wilson tomorrow with the item number so he can order the invitations, and that'll be done on time. We'll get him the theme next week, and he doesn't need the guest list until a few days after that."

I scanned the calendar to see if there was anything else we had to do and noticed a big star on Monday.

"Drivers Ed starts next week," I reminded Mary-Kate. "Our first step toward total freedom!"

"I can't wait to see you behind the wheel," Mary-Kate joked. "People of Malibu, run for your lives!"

"Hey!" I protested. "I may be a klutz on my feet, but I know I'll be a great driver."

"It'll be so cool," Mary-Kate said. "We'll be able to go wherever we want, whenever we want."

I flopped back on the bed, staring up at the ceiling. I pictured the two of us cruising the coast in Dad's SUV. (It was a totally parental car, but at least it was better than Mom's Volvo.)

I twisted a few strands of hair around my finger. "We'll go to the beach by ourselves, go to the mall without Mom looking over our shoulder. Where do you think we should drive ourselves first?"

There was no answer.

"Mary-Kate?" I prompted.

Nothing.

I sat up and looked at her. "Mary-Kate?"

"What?" she asked, snapping out of a blank-faced stare. The girl had obviously been off on Planet Jake again.

I hit her with the pillow one more time for good measure, then pushed myself off her bed. "I think it's time to start picking out your clothes for tonight."

"How do I look?" I asked, stepping in front of the full-length mirror that hung on the back of my door.

Ashley and I were standing in the middle of my bedroom with clothes scattered everywhere – on the floor, the bed, my desk chair, the dresser...Some of the stuff was mine, some of it was Ashley's. We'd even swiped a couple of sweaters from Mom's closet.

"You look amazing." Ashley stepped up to admire me in the mirror. I was wearing my favourite lavender halter top with Ashley's favourite slim black jeans. How could I go wrong?

I turned to check myself out from the side. "Not too overdressed, right?" I asked.

"No. It's perfect for dinner and a movie," Ashley said.

A nervous chill crept down my back. In a few minutes Jake and I would be out alone together!

"What if we don't have anything to talk about?" I asked, my pulse starting to pound. "I don't even know if we have anything in common."

"Of course you do!" Ashley said. "You go to the same school, you know all the same people, you both take creative writing—"

"Yeah, but how long can two people talk about a class?" I asked, swallowing hard.

"Mary-Kate, it's going to be fine. It shouldn't be too hard to make dinner conversation. Especially for you."

"Right." I sat down on my bed and breathed deeply to calm my nerves. "But I really like him, Ashley. I want everything to be perfect. And you saw me go wordless when he talked to us at Starbucks the other day."

"Mary-Kate, you have nothing to worry about," Ashley promised. She sat down next to me and put an arm around my shoulders. She gave me a little squeeze. "Jake already likes you. If he didn't, he wouldn't have asked you out."

"True," I said slowly, staring down at a pile of clothes on the floor.

"All you have to do is be yourself," Ashley assured me.

"Okay, be myself," I said. I took another deep breath. "It's going to be fine. My first real date with an older, totally gorgeous guy is going to be perfect, fun and totally mistake free." For a split second, I felt better. Then I remembered what I was *really* nervous about.

"Ashley?" I said. "What if he tries to kiss me?"

"Then you'll kiss him back." Ashley shrugged.

"Come on!" I stood and started to pace. "Jake's older. He's probably gone on lots of dates. Kissed tons of girls! What if he wants to kiss me like...I mean...a *real* kiss?"

Ashley grabbed my shoulders and looked me right in the eye. "Mary-Kate! Chill!" she said firmly. She pulled me over to the mirror again, and we both got in real close, standing next to one another.

"Now, if he goes in for the kiss, this is what you do," Ashley said, shaking her hair behind her shoulders. "First, you tilt your head just a little like this." She tilted her head just to the right, so I imitated her.

"We look ridiculous," I said.

"Shhh!" she said. "Now, pucker your lips a little. Like this." Ashley demonstrated, pursing her lips. I did the same, but then I cracked up laughing.

"Come on!" Ashley said, grabbing my hand and pursing her lips again. "This is important."

"Okay! Okay!" I stifled my laughter. I took a deep breath and mimicked her.

"Mary-Kate! Jake is here!" Mom called up the stairs.

"I'll be right down!" I shouted back, happy to hear that my voice didn't crack from nervousness.

"Just be yourself and have fun," Ashley advised me.

I nodded and smiled, but then I realised I was holding my breath. My nerves were totally fried, and "be yourself" seemed like pretty basic advice. Could it really be that easy?

"Thanks, Ashley," I said.

I grabbed my bag, tossed my hair back, and strode out of my room, making sure to hold my head up high. Easy or not, I was about to find out.

chapter five

I sprawled out in the big cushy chair in our living room with a bowl of popcorn on my lap. "I wonder how Mary-Kate is doing on her date," I muttered. "What time is it?"

"It's eight-oh-four," Brittany replied. "Exactly one minute after the last time you asked. Now pay attention to the movie, Ashley – this is the best part!"

Brittany and Lauren had come over, and we were watching *Always a Bridesmaid*, one of my all-time favourite movies. It had everything – cute guy, beautiful girl, romance and lots of wedding dresses.

I was having a hard time concentrating, though. I couldn't stop thinking about Mary-Kate's date with Jake. They were probably finishing up dinner...unless they had to wait for a table. Where did Jake take her for dinner? What did she order? She was so nervous before she left!

I really hoped it all went well. No, not just well. I wanted it to be absolutely perfect!

I glanced at the movie. It was the scene where the bridesmaid accidentally messes up her friend's wedding. "This is Mary-Kate's favourite part," I noted. "She knows these lines by heart." I felt a quick pang in my chest. "You know, I wish she were here with us. I miss her."

Brittany snorted. "You miss Mary-Kate? You guys must spend twenty hours a day together. She's only been gone for two hours."

I laughed. "I know. It's silly."

"I think it's sweet," Lauren put in. "I wish I was as close to my sister as you and Mary-Kate are."

When the movie ended a little while later, Lauren clicked the T.V. off and leaned back in her seat. "I love that movie," she said wistfully. "The wedding at the end is so beautiful. It's like the party of my dreams!"

Brittany pushed herself up in her seat and brushed a few popcorn crumbs from the front of her sweater. "Speaking of parties, what's up with your sweet sixteen? Have you and Mary-Kate been able to agree on anything yet?"

"Well, we picked out an invitation tonight," I told her. I set the popcorn bowl on the table. "We didn't have any trouble agreeing on that. Want to see it?"

Lauren's eyes brightened. "Totally!"

"I'll be right back." I jumped from my seat and jogged upstairs to my room to grab the invitation book. I ran back downstairs again, and Brittany and Lauren both scooted over, making room for me on the couch.

"I love it!" Lauren exclaimed when she saw the CD.

"We've already picked out the photo we're going to use," I said. "And the party planner is going to have Rave record a message for us! When you play the CD, it'll be like Rave is inviting you to our party!"

"Rave?" Lauren asked. "You mean the real Rave? The girl group?"

I nodded. "Wilson's pretty close with them. He said he could get them to do it, no problem."

"Wow! That is totally amazing!" Brittany said. "Even the guys will like it – if you're inviting guys. Are you inviting guys?"

I shrugged. "We haven't decided yet, but Mary-Kate seemed pretty set on an all-girl party. The more I think about it, the more I think it might be okay. It could be fun."

"Definitely." Lauren nodded. "Who needs guys to have a good time?"

"Speak for yourself," Brittany protested. Then she broke into a grin. "Just kidding. We all know that guys have their uses, but girls rule!"

My thoughts turned back to Mary-Kate. I hoped she was at least having a good time with the guy she was with tonight! I checked my watch again, wondering what time their movie started. I couldn't wait for her to get home so I could hear all about her date!

"Great choice, Jake! I've been dying to try this place, ever since it opened," I gushed.

The two of us were settled at a cosy table at Giovanelli's, the newest, most romantic Italian restaurant in town. I hadn't stopped smiling since Jake pulled into the parking lot. It was as if he knew exactly where I'd want to go.

I'd often dreamed of going on a date to a romantic restaurant just like this. But now that I was there, my nerves were on edge. There were so many potential disasters just waiting to happen! I could knock over a water glass or burn myself on the candle. I snatched a breadstick and bit it. It deteriorated into powder, spraying crumbs on the tablecloth and all over my lap.

After that, I was afraid to touch anything. I sat still with my hands clenched together in my lap.

"Now that you're here, what do you think of it?" Jake asked me. "Because if you don't like it we can go somewhere else."

He raised his eyes from his menu. He looked

cuter than ever in the candlelight. He was wearing a blue shirt and chinos, and he'd done something different to his hair. Gel or something. Did he realise how great he was? And did he know that he could date almost any girl at Bayside High?

"No – it's great!" I lifted my hand to wave off the suggestion – and knocked my spoon clear off the table. It landed somewhere across the room with a loud clatter. "I mean, I love this place," I said, trying to act as if nothing had happened. Inside, however, I was shrinking to the size of a peanut from embarrassment.

Jake glanced in the direction of my projectile spoon, then smiled.

"Good," he said. "It was either this or the Burger Shack, so…"

"Good choice," I said with a little laugh.

He sipped of his water and examined his menu. I watched him, amazed at how cool and collected he seemed. Why wasn't he as freaked out and nervous as I was?

Calm down, I told myself. I picked up my menu and tried to study the different dishes, all of which were written in Italian. *If the spoon thing is the worst that happens tonight, you'll be fine.*

"Are you ready to order?" the waiter said, coming up to the table with his pen and pad ready.

"Mary-Kate?" Jake prompted politely.

I'd barely had time to read the menu. Flushed and confused, I scanned it quickly and ordered the first thing I recognised.

"Spaghetti?" I blurted, looking up at the waiter.

"Of course, miss," the waiter said. "Would you like that with bolognese, marinara or primavera?"

"Uh, primavera," I answered.

I lifted the menu to hand it to the waiter. It clipped the side of my water glass and the glass tipped over! Water splashed across the tablecloth and all over the waiter's apron, shirt, and right in his face!

"I'm so sorry!" I gasped. I wished the earth would open up beneath me and swallow me whole.

Jake pulled his napkin from his lap and handed it to the stunned waiter, who thanked him and used it to wipe his face.

"It's no problem, miss," the waiter said kindly. "Happens all the time."

I laughed nervously, but I knew he was just trying to make me feel better. This couldn't happen all the time! If people were always messing up like this on first dates, there would be no couples in the world!

Jake placed his order, then looked across table at me. "You okay?" he asked.

"Yes," I said. "You'd better watch out, though. Who knows what I'll do next?"

"Thanks for the warning," Jake teased. "So, how's the whole poem thing going?"

"Don't even ask." I rolled my eyes. "I haven't had much time to work on it. How about you?"

"I'm just hoping Ms. Trauth doesn't make us read them in front of the class," he said. "I hate that."

"Really?" I asked, surprised. "You'd never know it. You always look totally comfortable up there."

"Are you kidding?" Jake shook his head. "I'd rather have to make a million game-saving penalty shots than get up there and read for five seconds."

I smiled, amazed. Here I thought Jake was this totally together, popular jock who always knew the right thing to do, but it turned out he got nervous just like everyone else.

I sat back in my chair, waiting for him to say something else, but a silence fell over the table and stayed there for way too long. I realised with a start that it was actually my turn to speak.

Just think of something, I thought. *Anything!* I glanced at Jake, who was obviously as freaked as I was by the lack of conversation. He looked away, took another sip of his water, and cleared his throat.

My hands were actually shaking. Why was this happening to me? I could make conversation with anyone from the little old lady who worked at the grocery store to the five-year-olds at Mom's daycare centre. And I'd always been fine on dates I'd had in the past. Why was I at a total loss now when it was so important?

Maybe it's because *it's so important*, I realised.

"Here you go!" the waiter said, arriving with our meals and finally breaking the silence.

He placed a huge bowl of spaghetti in front of me. It was still steaming from the kitchen, and it smelled incredible. Then he served Jake his chicken and pasta dish. I took a deep breath and picked up my fork as the waiter added a basket of freshly baked bread to the centre of the table and refilled my water glass. I was so glad the food had arrived. At least we had something to concentrate on besides the silence!

"This looks great," Jake said, digging in. He cut a piece of his chicken and took a bite, smiling the moment he tasted it.

"Good?" I asked, twirling my fork around in my spaghetti.

"Awesome," Jake answered after he swallowed. "How's yours?"

"I'm about to find out," I said, picking up my fork. Yikes! All but one strand of the spaghetti slipped right off and fell back to the plate. *Stay calm*, I told myself. I tried once more, twirling the fork in one of the thickest parts of the hill of pasta. The fork was loaded, with long strands of spaghetti still dangling on to the plate. I sighed. *There's no good way for me to eat this*, I realised. *It's going to be a mess!*

I glanced at Jake, and he was watching me, waiting to see what I thought of my dinner. I plastered a brave smile on my face. Then I brought the fork to my mouth and hoped for the best.

I took as big a bite as I could, but three or four long pieces of spaghetti hung awkwardly from my lips. I quickly slurped them down. It was *definitely* not ladylike.

"How is it?" Jake asked.

"Great!" I murmured, nodding, my mouth still full. And it was. Unfortunately I wasn't going to be able to eat any more of it. I couldn't spend the whole dinner slurping and wiping, slurping and wiping. Ugh! Jake would be disgusted!

"I thought we could try to catch the eight-thirty show of *Off the Hook*," Jake suggested. "What do you think?"

I glanced at Jake to see if he was joking, but his beautiful grey eyes were entirely serious. I couldn't believe it. *Off the Hook* was supposed to be the stupidest movie of all time.

"Off the Hook, huh?" I repeated, stalling.

"Yeah! I've been waiting for it to come out forever," Jake said. "I love the director."

The director! I thought, a little shocked. *The same guy who did* Pigs in a Blanket? *The worst movie I've ever seen?*

Be open-minded, I decided. *Who knows? Maybe the movie won't be so bad.* "Ummm... I guess it could be funny," I said with a shrug.

"Great!" Jake said. "Maybe we should skip dessert here and just go crazy at the snack bar."

"Now you're talking." I started to relax a little. "I'd rather have a tub of popcorn and some gummy bears than a piece of cheesecake any day."

Jake grinned. "Gummy Bears and popcorn, huh? That's exactly what I get whenever I go to the movies."

"Really?" I said. We had the exact same taste in junk food! I knew I liked this guy for a reason.

I buttered a piece of bread, feeling a bit more comfortable. Maybe this date was going to shape up after all. Of course, I couldn't help glaring down at my spaghetti.

I made a mental note: Never order pasta on a date!

I sat in the dark theatre next to Jake, munching hungrily on Gummi Bears. As predicted, the movie was truly horrible.

Jake laughed at the film, then shifted in his

seat. His arm brushed mine, sending a little shiver of excitement over my skin. *He's so good-looking*, I thought. *He even smells good!* He glanced over at me, and I smiled.

You can do this, I told myself. *You can sit through this movie. It's for a very good cause... Jake Impenna!*

I started to slouch, so I moved back in my seat, trying to sit up straight. My Gummi Bear box hit the armrest and slipped from my hand. I held my breath as it clattered to the floor. The guy in front of us turned around and glared at me.

"Sorry!" I whispered.

I bent down to retrieve the box, but at that moment, Jake did the same, and we knocked heads – hard.

"Ow!" Jake moaned, bringing his hand to his forehead. "Sorry," he whispered.

"It's okay," I whispered back, my head throbbing.

Jake stared into my eyes, and I froze. He looked really serious all of a sudden. Was he going to try to kiss me now?

"Let's leave," Jake whispered.

My jaw dropped open. He wanted to leave? Was he having that bad a time?

Of course he is, I thought. *All night I've been nothing but klutzy, messy and dull. Why wouldn't he want to cut the night short?*

I was totally mortified, but there was nothing I could do. I wasn't going to *make* him sit there.

"Oh...okay," I said quietly.

Jake stood and led the way out of our nearly deserted row. It was all I could do to keep from bursting into tears behind his back. I'd wanted to go out with Jake Impenna from the first time I saw him. Now that I finally got my chance, what did I do?

I totally blew it.

chapter six

"Mary-Kate, did you have a bad time tonight?" Jake asked. He had just pulled his Jeep up in front of my house. He sounded as tense as I felt.

"No!" I blurted kind of loudly. The word hung in the air for a second and then I laughed uncertainly. "I mean, I was kind of nervous and everything, and, to be honest, I wasn't really into the movie...but I liked...being with you."

Oh, smooth, Mary-Kate, I thought.

"I liked being with you, too," Jake said.

"Well...good." I laughed. "Glad we cleared that up."

Jake glanced at me out of the corner of his eye. "I feel like an idiot for picking that movie. It was so bad!"

"Wait a minute." I was confused. "I thought you liked it!"

He shook his head. "I was faking it. I just

laughed when the other people in the theatre did because I didn't want you to think *I* was having a bad time."

I smiled, relieved. "And I just sat there with a smile plastered on my face so you'd think I was having a good time."

For a moment, neither of us said anything. Then Jake spoke up. "Hey, I'd like to hang out with you again. How about after school some time?"

A second date! I thought. *He wants a second date!*

"How about Monday?" I blurted out.

Jake frowned. "Actually, that's not good for me. I take my little brother and sister to the park on Mondays. It's really important to them – we do it every week, so I can't cancel."

"Well, I love kids. Why don't I just come along with you?" I asked.

Jake frowned. "Are you sure? It wouldn't be anything big—"

"Absolutely! It sounds like total fun!" I insisted.

Jake grinned. "You know, I think Caitlin and Tristan would really like that."

Amazing. Jake wasn't just cute. He was so sweet that he made time to play with his little brother and sister!

"I'll be there," I told him.

"Great," Jake said. "We'll leave right from

school, if that's cool with you."

"Definitely." I unbuckled my seat belt. "So... thank you so much for tonight. Dinner and half a movie."

"No problem." Jake started to climb out of the car. "Let me walk you to the door."

The second he started to move, I realised that the whole kiss question was back on. Nervous butterflies flittered through my stomach.

As we walked towards my front door, I landed on my high heel wrong and stumbled. Jake had to reach out to steady me.

"You okay?" he asked, gripping my arms.

"Yeah...fine." I pulled away slightly and stood up straight.

I glanced up at the house and spotted Ashley at the window, peeking through the curtain. I quickly waved her away. The curtain dropped, and Ashley's face disappeared just before Jake could see what I was looking at.

"You really don't have to walk me up," I said. "I've done it on my own a million times."

Jake chuckled. "Okay," he said. "Then I guess, if you don't mind, I'll kiss you goodnight right here."

The direct approach! I liked it! He leaned in to kiss me. My heart pounded so quickly I was sure I was going to pass out right there.

This was it! Our first kiss!

Just as his lips met mine, something moved in the window. I turned my head and saw Ashley's grinning face again. Jake's kiss landed on my earlobe.

"Whoa! Uh, sorry," I muttered nervously as he pulled away.

I turned my eyes towards him. He was blushing as hard as I was! We both cracked up laughing.

"I'll see you Monday," I said through my giggles.

"Right...Monday." Jake nodded.

I turned and started up the path to the house, but stopped midway and turned around.

"Thanks again, Jake. Tonight really was... interesting."

"Yeah. It sure was." I could tell by his grin that he meant, *interesting in a good way*.

I turned around and jogged into the house.

The moment Mary-Kate came through the front door, I grabbed her arm and pulled her into the living room. I was ready to burst. "So? How was it? Did he take you to a good restaurant? What movie did you see? Details! I need details!"

I couldn't wait a second longer to hear all about my sister's first date with the guy of her dreams.

We flopped down on the couch. Her eyes were

shining brightly. I knew everything had gone perfectly. Why else would she be walking on air?

"Well, let's see, we went to Giovanelli's and I got spaghetti, which was a mistake," Mary-Kate began. "Every time I slurped up a piece, the sauce splattered everywhere. Oh! But that was after I dumped my water on the waiter and flung my spoon across the room."

"You what?"

"Not on *purpose*," Mary-Kate assured me. As if that explained everything. "Then we went to see the worst movie ever – *Off the Hook*. So bad. I dropped my candy, we knocked heads, left early, came back here, and when he tried to kiss me I turned my head and he ended up kissing my ear."

I stared at my sister. She sighed and leaned into the back of the couch, gazing off into the distance as if she was replaying a wonderful romantic memory in her mind.

"Um…Mary-Kate?" I started.

She snapped out of her daydream and looked at me. "Yeah?"

"What are you so happy about? Everything on your date went wrong," I told her.

"That's just it!" she exclaimed, whacking my leg to make a point. "Everything went wrong and we still had a great time! There were one or two awkward silences, but the rest of the night, we totally connected. He even asked me out again!"

It was great to see her so happy. "Well then...I'm glad you had such a bad date!" I exclaimed. "Jake sounds like he's a really great guy."

"I know!" Mary-Kate agreed. "I can't wait to see him again." She leaned over to the coffee table and grabbed one of the nearly empty bowls of popcorn. "Did you have fun with Brittany and Lauren?"

"Yeah, we watched *Always a Bridesmaid* and gorged ourselves on junk food. You know, the usual." I shrugged. "Oh, and I showed them the invitation. They loved it!"

"Good!" Mary-Kate said. "I can't wait to send them out." She twisted in her seat and put her feet up on the table, crossing them at the ankles.

"Lauren and Brittany are jealous that we're going to be getting our driver's licences before them," I told her. "I promised them we'd drive them everywhere until their birthdays. I can't believe we're starting Driver's Ed on Monday."

"Oh, no!" Mary-Kate slapped her forehead. "I totally forgot about Driver's Ed. I told Jake I'd go to the park with him on Monday."

"So? Just call him and tell him you'll do it another time," I suggested.

"I can't!" Mary-Kate said, dropping her feet to

the floor with a thud. "I made a really big deal about going to the park with him and his little brother and sister! After all the craziness on our date tonight, I don't want to call him and cancel our second date! He'll think I'm nuts."

"So what are you going to do?" I asked her, baffled. "Not take Driver's Ed?"

Mary-Kate munched on her popcorn, mulling it over. "Wait a minute!" she cried. "Isn't there a Tuesday/Thursday class? Let's switch to that one!"

"I can't," I said. "I have drama club on Tuesday afternoons. That's why we signed up for Monday/Wednesday in the first place, remember?"

Mary-Kate squeezed her eyes shut and groaned. "Right," she said. "Well, then I guess I'll switch by myself. It's no big deal, right? We'll just take Driver's Ed on different days."

She grabbed some more popcorn. I sat beside her, stunned. We always did *everything* together, and now that we were about to take what was basically the most important step of our lives, she wanted to split up?

"Ashley?" Mary-Kate eyed me. "That's okay, right?"

No, it's not okay! I wanted to shout. But I couldn't. Mary-Kate was so happy about Jake, I couldn't make a big deal about this. I didn't want to bring her down.

"Sure!" I said with a hollow smile, forcing myself to sound cheerful.

"Cool." She flicked on the television. "When you get home on Monday you can tell me all about it so I'll know what to expect."

"Yeah. That'll be...great," I said.

I leaned back into the couch and slouched way down. I wanted to be enthusiastic, but I just couldn't. I was totally nervous about learning to drive, and the idea of doing it without Mary-Kate by my side made it ten times worse. Plus, Mary-Kate had already been behind the wheel a couple of times with Dad, but I'd never had a chance to try it. She was supposed to help me out. I didn't understand how she could bail on me so easily.

I was about to say something, but she had that far-off look on her face again. Mary-Kate was so obviously happy there was no way I could stay upset. This thing with Jake was really important to her. I sat up again and decided to think positively. I was sure there were plenty of people who took Driver's Ed without their best friend by their side. I was going to be fine – absolutely, totally fine...

chapter seven

I woke up on Saturday morning thinking about Driver's Ed. I couldn't believe Mary-Kate had bailed on me. But instead of getting angry, I decided to put it out of my mind.

Time to start organising the guest list for the party! I thought. Just the idea of the party – and having something to organise – made me feel better.

I crawled out of bed on Saturday morning and pulled on my favourite fluffy pink robe. I picked up my purple notebook and pen and opened the door to my bedroom. Across the hall, Mary-Kate opened her door at the very same time. Her hair was sticking out on the right side, and she had a pillow crease across her face. She still looked half asleep.

"I smell French toast," she said with a huge yawn.

I inhaled and realised she was right. My stomach growled when the scent hit my nostrils.

"What are we waiting for then?" I said.

We hurried for the stairs, knocking into each other and laughing as we scurried down to the kitchen. We ran in and took our regular seats at the kitchen table. Mom looked at us over the rim of her coffee cup and smiled.

"Hungry?" she asked.

"How could you tell?" Mary-Kate answered.

"I knew I'd get you up if I made this," Dad said, bringing a plate of steaming hot French toast over to the table.

I grabbed a couple of slices and passed the plate to Mary-Kate. Then I opened up my notebook to a clean page.

"Let's talk guest list," I said, taking a sip of my orange juice. "Who are we going to invite to our party?"

Dad sat down at the head of the table and piled some food on his plate. "Well, Lauren and Brittany, for starters," he said.

"Obviously," I answered. I took a bite of my breakfast and wrote down Lauren and Brittany's names. "Who else?"

"Diana, Marci and Rachel," Mary-Kate said.

"And we have to invite everyone whose parties we already went to," I added. "That's Tashema, Krista, Melanie and Sherra."

"Wait a minute," Mom interrupted. She placed

her coffee cup down on the table and turned my notebook towards her so she could scan the list. "These are all girls," she said. "Don't you want to invite some boys, too?"

"Well... " I began, glancing at Mary-Kate. "We haven't actually decided on that yet."

"I don't think we should," Mary-Kate declared. "Boys can be so...immature. Plus, some of our friends act different when boys are around. All they think about is who's looking at them, who thinks they look cute, who *they* think looks cute... If we have an all-girl party we'll be more comfortable."

As Mary-Kate made her case, I started to see he point. Our friends weren't the only ones who focused on guys whenever they were around. Mary-Kate and I could be like that, too. Take Todd Malone's party. Mary-Kate had started obsessing about Jake from the moment we got there, and I'd spent half the night trying to find out who that mystery guy – the one I'd hip-checked into the sand – was.

I sighed and thought about his lopsided smile. I wondered, what was he doing right now?

I shook my head. What was wrong with me? I never felt this way about a guy before.

But there was something special about Mystery Guy...

If we *did* have boys at our party, I would love him to be my date. But obviously that was never going to happen. I mean, I couldn't even find out what his name was!

"Hey!" Mary-Kate suddenly cried, snapping me out of my thoughts. "We could even make girl power the theme!"

"Girl power..." I flipped to our list of possible themes so I could write it down. "I like it. We could have a lot of bright decorations, pictures of strong female characters—"

"Wait a minute!" Mom said. "You don't even have a *theme* yet?"

Mary-Kate and I looked at each other guiltily. "We haven't really had time to nail that one down," Mary-Kate admitted, suddenly becoming very interested in sopping up all the syrup on her plate with her last bit of French toast.

Mom leaned back in her chair and shook her head. "Girls, you'd really better get cracking on some of these bigger things. The party is only six weeks away, and there's a lot of work to do even *after* you send out invitations, pick a theme and a location—"

"Wait!" Mary-Kate yelped. "We've already decided on a location, right, Ashley?"

"Yeah." I smiled at my parents. "We talked about it before bed last night, and we decided we'd like to have the party here...at the house."

Mom's face softened. I could tell that she was

touched that Mary-Kate and I thought our house was cool enough for the biggest party of our lives.

"Yeah! If we have it here, we can party all night!" Mary-Kate grinned from ear to ear.

"All night?" Dad repeated. "I don't know how the neighbours would feel about that."

Mary-Kate laughed. "I mean, we won't have to end it at a certain time, the way we would if we rented a place out."

Mom and Dad exchanged looks. "What do you think?" she asked. "Want to open our house to a bunch of crazy teenagers?"

"Mom!" Mary-Kate and I blurted in protest.

"I'm kidding!" She raised her hands in surrender. "Of course you girls can have the party here."

"So, back to the boy-girl thing," I said to Mary-Kate. "I understand your point, but are you sure that you want to leave all of our guy friends out? What about—" The phone rang, cutting off my sentence.

"Hello?" Dad answered the phone. Then he glanced at Mary-Kate. "Sure. She's right here." He handed the phone to my sister. "It's Jake."

Mary-Kate's face lit up. She jumped from her seat and grabbed the cordless phone from my father.

"Hi!" she said into the receiver, as she walked

into the living room.

I slumped back in my seat, suddenly irritated. Hello? Weren't we in the middle of a discussion here?

"You know what?" I said, staring after Mary-Kate. "I think a girls-only party is a great idea."

"Good," Mom said. She cleared away a few dishes. "Mary-Kate will be happy you decided to go with her plan."

"Let's call Wilson right now and tell him." I picked up my plate and walked it over to the sink.

"Okay. Use my mobile," Mom offered.

"Thanks, Mom." I grabbed her purse and pulled out her phone, then went back to the table to look up Wilson's number in my notebook.

As I was dialling, I felt nervous. I hoped Wilson liked the idea. And I couldn't wait to tell Mary-Kate that we were going with girl power. She was going to be so psyched…*if* she ever got off the phone.

"You've already been out for a run, fed your dog, *and* changed the oil in your Jeep?" I asked Jake, amused.

"Yeah! Why? What have you done this morning?" Jake asked, a laugh in his voice.

"I've…uh…yawned a lot and eaten some French toast," I admitted. I sat down on the couch and shifted the phone to my other ear.

"Busy girl!" Jake joked.

"Wait!" I said, snapping my fingers. "Ashley and I also started the guest list for our sweet sixteen party."

"Oh, really?" Jake asked, obviously intrigued. "Am I on that guest list?"

I bit the inside of my cheek, remembering something Ashley had said the other day – something about all-girl parties being unsophisticated. If I told Jake that I wanted to invite only girls, he might think I was a big baby.

"I'm...not...sure," I said, stalling for time.

Jake laughed, obviously taking my answer as a flirty joke instead of the honest truth.

"Well, in that case, I'll just have to spend all my time being nice to you so that you'll decide to invite me," Jake said. "Of course, I was planning on doing that anyway."

My heart melted when he said that. Maybe, just maybe, Ashley was right. Maybe a boy-girl party wasn't such a bad idea. Not if Jake would be my date.

In my mind I saw myself with Jake, walking into the party together hand in hand. Jake looked amazing all dressed up in a suit and tie, and I was wearing that beautiful blue dress Ashley had picked out at the store the other day. We'd dance in the middle of the dance floor while everyone else looked on, sighing over what a perfect couple we were. Somehow, with Jake in the picture, Ashley's sophisticated party plan seemed like the right way to go.

Maybe I'd been a little bit too quick to decide about this all-girl concept...

"I'm really looking forward to seeing you on Monday," Jake said. "Let's meet in the lobby after last period."

"Sounds like a plan!" I agreed.

"Okay," Jake said. "'Bye, Mary-Kate."

"'Bye."

I hung up the phone, and I let out a little squeal of excitement. Then I walked back to the kitchen and found Ashley on Mom's phone.

"Yes, Wilson, we definitely want an all-girl party," she was saying, gripping the phone in one hand as she doodled in her notebook with the other. "And the theme is girl power."

Uh oh, I thought. *What is she doing?*

Ashley glanced up at me in the middle of a sentence and smiled. She dropped her pen and gave me a little thumbs-up, obviously thinking I was totally thrilled.

"Mary-Kate?" Mom said, a crease of concern on her face. "What's wrong?"

I walked over to the sink where my mother was

68

standing and turned my back to Ashley so she wouldn't be able to hear us.

"It's just...I'm kind of surprised that Ashley would call Wilson without me," I said. "I mean, we hadn't *definitely* decided on girl power."

"I thought you'd be pleased," Mom whispered. "I think Ashley really wanted to have boys at your party. It was very thoughtful of her to let you have your way."

Right, I thought. *But it's not my way any more.* Of course, Ashley had no way of knowing that I was going to change my mind.

"Thanks, Wilson," Ashley said. "'Bye!" She clicked off the phone and turned around in her chair to look at us, a bright smile on her face. "He loves it!" she told us. "He's never done a girl power party before, but he's already got tons of ideas!"

I forced myself to smile. "That's great."

Ashley stood up and gave me a big bear hug. "Isn't this awesome?" she cried, holding on to my shoulders as she pulled away. "We're on our way!"

"Yeah," I said. "It's awesome."

As Ashley grabbed her stuff and headed upstairs to take a shower, I trudged over to the table to clean up my dishes.

My thoughts drifted back to my daydream, then drifted away. In with girl power, out with romance. I just hoped Jake would understand.

chapter eight

Monday afternoon, Ashley and I stood in line at the cafeteria checking out the food. A lunch lady refilled one of the silver steam trays with a greyish substance. She looked up at us and smiled, the steam from the food fogging up her glasses.

"Want to try the meat loaf?" she asked, digging a huge spoon into the mush.

"That's *meatloaf*?" I said, shocked.

We took some macaroni and cheese and inched along towards the cash register. "Listen, I brought a few magazines with me," Ashley told me. "I figured we could go through them for ideas on what to wear to the party."

"Good plan," I agreed. "I don't think the gown-slash-shorts thing is going to work."

"Hey, guys!" Ashley called as she approached our regular table. Brittany, Lauren, Melanie and

Tashema were already there. Everyone said hello as we slid into two empty chairs across from each other.

"We were just talking about going over to Lauren's tonight to watch that *'very special episode'* of *Spencer Academy*," Brittany informed us.

"Yeah. Do you guys want to come?" Lauren asked, taking a bite of her grey meatloaf. I couldn't believe she'd actually ordered that. Brave girl.

"I'm in." Ashley shrugged off her pink sweater and hung it over the back of her chair. "I've been dying to see that episode. Possibly because they've been showing the ads every five seconds for the past week," she added with a laugh.

"Ashley – you promised to help me study for geometry, remember?" I didn't want to burst her *Spencer Academy* bubble, but I definitely needed her help. Geometry isn't exactly my best subject, but Ashley, somehow, totally gets it.

"Oh, right!" Ashley said without even blinking. "Sorry, I forgot. Looks like we're not going to be able to make it, Lauren."

"Thanks, Ashley," I said.

"No problem." Ashley opened her backpack and pulled out a couple of magazines, placing them in the middle of the table. "Okay, I figured we could just go through the fashion spreads and—"

"What's up with this?" Tashema pointed at the magazines with her plastic fork. "We're so boring you need to bring reading material now?"

Everyone laughed as Ashley blushed slightly. "No! We're just going to look for something to wear to our sweet sixteen," she answered. "We went shopping the other day and I picked out a gown..."

"And I picked out a shorts and a tank top," I finished, explaining the situation to Tashema and Melanie. "We figure that's not exactly going to work."

"Why don't you go with something in between?" Melanie suggested.

Ashley took a bite of her mac and cheese, thinking it over. "You mean like semi-formal? I guess that's an idea."

"Yeah, like really nice trousers and some kind of fancy top." Melanie picked up one of the magazines and flipped it open. "Maybe something beaded or sequinned. Or you could just wear short dresses instead of long ones."

Melanie was probably the most fashionable of our friends. Her sleek, dark hair was cut in the latest style. Her father's job took him all over the world, and he always brought back the coolest fashions from Paris, Milan and Tokyo for his only daughter. Ashley and I trusted our own sense of style, but if there was ever a question, we consulted Melanie.

Brittany opened one of the magazines to a fashion spread and held it up. "What about this stuff?" The picture showed a bunch of girls all dressed up, laughing and talking in a party setting with balloons and streamers. There were a few guys pictured, too, wearing trendy, semi-casual suits. One of them even looked a little bit like Jake, and I couldn't help thinking how gorgeous he would look all dressed up.

"Yes, these are perfect!" Melanie exclaimed, taking the magazine out of Brittany's hands and passing it to us. "You guys would look great in that purple dress. Or that red one on the end."

"Oooh! I *love* that!" Ashley said, pointing at the red dress. It had an overlay made out of a black gauzy material and it fell just above the knee, so it wasn't as formal as the gown she had picked out earlier.

"This one's awesome." I showed her a light-blue dress with beaded straps.

"That's perfect for you," Ashley said. "This is a great idea. Everyone likes to get dressed up once in a while."

"Well, girls do, anyway." Tashema leaned over Ashley's shoulder to get a look at the magazine. "But if we wear dresses like that the guys are going to have to wear suits like these guys are... or at least nice trousers and shirts."

Brittany smirked. "They'll *love* that," she said sarcastically.

"We don't have to worry about the guys," Ashley announced. She snapped the magazine shut and put it back in her bag. "It's going to be an all-girl party."

The second she said it, my face fell. I still had to break the news to Jake. I was looking forward to seeing him that afternoon, but whenever I remembered the conversation we were going to have to have, my stomach twisted into knots.

"Really?" Melanie asked. Her face scrunched up into a confused frown. "Why?"

"Don't sound so disappointed," Brittany said. "We'll live without them."

"Of course we will!" Ashley agreed. "It was Mary-Kate's idea, actually. She just thought it would be more sophisticated without the guys... you know...being guys."

Don't remind me, I thought, sitting back in my seat and staring at my plate. I couldn't believe that it was all my fault that Jake wasn't going to be at my sweet sixteen – only the biggest night of my life.

"That makes sense," Tashema said. "I think it's a great idea."

"So… semi-formal dresses?" Ashley asked, raising her eyebrows as she grinned at me.

"Semi-formal dresses it is," I agreed. I even managed a convincing smile. "We should start shopping A.S.A.P."

I caught a glimpse of Jake, who was just walking into the cafeteria. My breath caught for a second when I realised he was headed straight for our table.

"Hey, everybody," Jake said when he reached us.

My friends grinned knowingly at each other before calling out, "Hi, Jake!" in unison, then breaking into giggles.

Jake chuckled as he glanced down at me. "Are they like this all the time?"

"They're all on too much caffeine," I joked.

Yes! A good joke in front of Jake!

"That explains it." Jake shoved his hands into the front pockets of his jeans. "So, my brother and sister are totally excited about meeting you."

Ashley let out a sigh. Jake and I both looked at her as she pushed her macaroni around on her plate. Weird – just two seconds ago she was all excited about dresses. Now she suddenly seemed to be in a bad mood.

"I can't wait to meet them," I told Jake.

"Cool. So what were you guys talking about, anyway?" Jake asked.

"Actually, we were just figuring out some sweet sixteen details," Ashley said, fiddling with the heart pendant she was wearing on a chain around her neck.

I noticed that she barely looked at him when she spoke. Was Ashley nervous around Jake for some reason?

"Oh, the infamous sweet sixteen, huh?" Jake said. "Well, Mary-Kate, I was going to ask you if you wanted to sit with me and my friends, but if you guys are busy..."

I felt my face light up at his suggestion. Jake Impenna was asking me to sit at his table! If I went over there, everyone would know we were dating! I looked at my friends and they all grinned back at me, obviously thinking the same thing.

"No, that's okay," I said, standing up. "I'd love to sit with you. Ashley and I can talk later."

"Okay," Jake said. He picked up my tray as I slid out into the aisle between tables. "See you guys later," he said to my friends.

"'Bye, Jake!" they all sing-songed.

"'Bye, guys." I turned to my friends and caught Ashley's eye. She smiled, giving me a little wave. A rush of relief washed through me. Whatever was bothering her couldn't be that big a deal. I'd have to remember to ask her about it later.

When Mary-Kate stood up to go over to Jake's table, I thought I was going to lose it. Here we were talking about our sweet sixteen, and once again she was bailing. And once again it was because of Jake.

This was supposed to be the most important night of our lives, and we hadn't even had much time to talk about it. Didn't she care about the party at all?

"Are you okay?" Lauren asked, glancing at my full plate.

"Oh, I'm fine." I waved my hand. "I wasn't very hungry – and the cafeteria food didn't exactly help."

"Mary-Kate's meeting Jake's brother and sister? I guess he doesn't like her much," Brittany teased. "When is that happening?"

"This afternoon." I leaned my elbows on the table and forced myself to smile.

"Wait a minute," Brittany said, her forehead creasing. "I thought you guys were starting Driver's Ed this afternoon."

I tensed up again. I'd been dreading Driver's Ed all day. That morning I woke up way too early and stared at the ceiling, imagining what it was going to be like to take the course in a strange school where I knew no one. Then I spent most of my time in class wondering if I was going to look like a big loser taking Driver's Ed all by myself.

"Ashley? Are you in there?" Brittany tapped her knuckles on my head. "Are you guys starting the class today or what?"

"We were. I mean, I still am." I shook my head. "But Mary-Kate transferred into the Tuesday/Thursday class." I shrugged as if it wasn't eating me up inside. "So I'm on my own."

Melanie pushed her chair away from the table and looked at me. "Wait a minute. Mary-Kate changed her Driver's Ed class just so she could hang out with some guy for one afternoon?"

"It's not that bad," I insisted. "She's still going to learn to drive. She's just going to do it on different days."

And without me, I added silently.

"Well, it's great that Jake asked her out again so quickly," Tashema said.

"Absolutely!" I said, pulling my food towards me again. "It's fantastic."

And it was...kind of.

chapter nine

"You are so good with them," I said to Jake. I watched Caitlin and Tristan, his sister and brother, playing together in the park. Eight-year-old Caitlin was pushing five-year-old Tristan on the swings. The four of us had just finished a silly, no-rules basketball game, girls against boys, with ice cream sundaes promised to the winners. Jake and I made sure it ended in a tie.

"Yeah, well, I have the mentality of a five-year-old, so that makes it easy," Jake explained. "What's your excuse?"

"Well, I'd say I'm about eight, so I guess that's why I bonded with Caitlin," I deadpanned.

"I'll make sure she invites you to her next slumber party," Jake joked.

"I am *so* there," I said. "I've been looking for a reason to break out my Snoopy sleeping bag."

Jake bounced the basketball in front of him.

"Speaking of parties...have I locked in an invitation to your sweet sixteen yet?"

All the blood rushed out of my face. How could I tell him he wasn't invited? *Think, Mary-Kate*! I told myself. *Think*! But I didn't come up with much.

"Yeah," I said finally. "I mean...yes, of course you're invited."

"Great." Jake gave me a wide smile. "I knew you'd come around."

I laughed, my pulse racing. So I'd gone with my heart. So what? Ashley had always wanted boys at the party, I told myself. I was sure I could get her to change her mind again with no problem.

"You're late," a not-so-kind-looking lady barked at me as I hurried into the Driver's Ed classroom. She had frizzy brown hair and crooked glasses. She stood at the front of the room with the name "Ms. Junger" scrawled on the board behind her. She was my Driver's Ed teacher. "What's your name?"

"I'm Ashley." I flashed her an apologetic smile. "I'm sorry I'm late." Mom and I had got stuck in traffic on the way to Columbus High, where I was taking the class.

"Don't let it happen again," Ms. Junger snapped. She nodded at the only empty desk, right smack in the middle of the front row. "Have a seat."

I swallowed hard and made my way over to the chair, feeling everyone's eyes on me as I slid into it. Some of the kids already had bright yellow books on their desks. I really was late.

"As I was just about to explain," Ms. Junger said, looking down her nose at me, "we don't have enough books to go around, so you're going to have to share."

I gazed around to see if anyone was partnerless, but it seemed as if everyone had a friend. Finally, I glanced to the right and caught the eye of the guy sitting next to me. I froze. It was *the guy*! The mystery guy from Todd Malone's party!

"You!" he exclaimed, with his lopsided grin.

"You!" I said right back.

I was about to ask him if he had a partner when the teacher announced that she was going to call the roll. She read a list of names, and I sat back in my chair, waiting until she got to my mystery guy. I was finally going to find out his name! The afternoon was suddenly looking up.

"Ben Jones?" Ms. Junger called out. Mystery guy raised his hand, and I tried not to smile. Ben Jones. Nice name.

When she was done, I looked at Ben again,

ready to ask him if he wanted to share a book, but he was already pulling his desk over to a boy on his other side. I frowned, disappointed. So much for me getting to know the mystery guy.

Meanwhile, I still didn't have a book, and Ms. Junger was about to start class.

"Do you have a partner?" a voice asked behind me.

I turned around and my eyes fell on a nice-looking guy who was behind me to my left. He had buzz-cut brown hair and wore a Star Wars T-shirt. But most importantly, he had his own book. He held it up in front of him and smiled.

"You can share with me if you want," he whispered. "I'm Evan."

"Thanks," I responded. "I'm Ashley."

Ms. Junger started with chapter one – "All About Safety." Taking a deep breath, I told myself, once again, that everything was going to be fine. It couldn't get much worse.

Then Evan let out the loudest sneeze I've ever heard. Everyone in the room laughed, and Evan sniffled loudly. Ben turned around to look at us, and when he caught my eye, he smiled. I almost melted. Could he *be* any cuter?

"Sorry" Evan said. "Bad cold."

"Just try to keep it down," Ms. Junger told him.

From that point on, Evan did nothing but

sniffle, sneeze and blow his nose. I felt bad for him, of course, but it was no fun sitting right next to him while he made all that noise. It was hard to pay attention to what Ms. Junger was saying. Towards the end of the class, the teacher decided to go over everything she'd lectured on. She picked up her book and walked to the front of her desk, leaning back against it.

"What's the first thing you should do when you sit down in your car?" she asked.

A few hands went up, and she called on a red-headed girl. "Janine?"

"Put on your seat belt and check your mirrors," Janine answered.

"Right," Ms. Junger said, glancing down at her book again. "How far from a corner should you be when you turn on your signal indicating that you intend to turn?"

I raised my hand, but Ms. Junger called on someone else. At that point, Evan started to blow his nose again. This time, it was so loud, all the people around us either turned to look, or started to shift uncomfortably in their chairs. I leaned slightly to the right to avoid getting sneezed on. I didn't want him to think I was trying to get away from him, but I couldn't help it. I didn't want to get sick.

I watched as he crumpled up the tissue and

stuffed it in the back pocket of his backpack with a bunch of others. I wrinkled my nose and turned away. Ugh! Colds could be so icky...

"Ashley?"

I sat up straight when I heard my name. Ms. Junger was staring right at me, and she did not look pleased.

"Are you going to answer my question?" she demanded, crossing her arms over her chest.

Question? What question? I hadn't even heard the answer to the last one. "Ummm . . ." What was I supposed to say? I had to answer something, or she'd know that I wasn't paying attention.

Think! I told myself. *What would be the next logical question after the blinker thing*? I looked at my book. The topic right after signaling was stopping. Maybe she'd asked how long you're supposed to wait at a stop sign. I took a stab in the dark.

"Five seconds?" I said, raising my eyebrows with hope.

The whole classroom burst out laughing. I wanted to sink into the floor.

"Very good, Ashley." Ms. Junger smirked. "That's exactly the amount of practice time you have to spend behind the wheel before they'll test you for your licence. Five whole seconds."

Everyone laughed even harder. I glanced over

at Ben, who was practically falling out of his chair. Why did this have to happen to me?

I stared down at the book, wishing Ms. Junger would move on to the next question. Where was Mary-Kate when I needed her? She always knows exactly what to say to make awkward situations better. She would definitely be cracking some perfect joke right now – something that would make everyone forget my lame answer.

When I looked up at Ben again, he was gazing at me sympathetically. I managed to crack a small smile. At least I'd finally found my mystery guy. And now that I knew who he was, Driver's Ed was going to be a whole lot more fun!

chapter ten

"Ashley, I can't believe she actually said that to you!" I exclaimed, flopping back in my chair at the dinner table. "A whole five seconds,'" I repeated, mimicking Ashley's imitation of Ms. Junger. "I hope I have a different teacher."

"For your sake, I hope so, too." Ashley glanced up from her plate and half smiled. "Anyway...I've been thinking about our sweet sixteen, and I have an idea. What if we rent a karaoke machine? We could do a whole divas thing, you know? Everyone's going to be all dressed up, and we can take turns belting out girl power songs to go with our theme."

"Girl power songs?" Dad repeated. "Like what?"

"You know, like 'I Will Survive', 'R-E-S-P-E-C-T', 'Survivor'. Stuff like that," Ashley said. "What do you think, Mary-Kate?"

Now's your chance, I thought. *Tell her you want to have boys at the party before she comes up with a ten-mile-long list of girl power songs.*

"Karaoke would be great!" I said brightly. "And our invitations are perfect for it." I paused, searching for a smooth way to bring boys into the conversation. Karaoke...boys...karaoke ...boys...

"Hey! You know what would be *so* funny?" I began, trying to seem casual. "If our guy friends had to sing karaoke."

Ashley scrunched up her nose. "Yeah...I guess that would be funny."

"I mean, imagine Todd trying to sing some Glowstick song," I said, laughing awkwardly. "Or Mike and Brian doing those hip-hop songs they love to imitate."

Come on, Ash, I thought, holding my breath. *Take the hint.*

Ashley giggled and pushed her hair behind her ears. "Ugh! Thank God we're not having guys there," she said. "I don't think I could handle Mike and Brian in stereo surround sound. They're bad enough when they do that routine in the lunchroom."

"Yeah," I said slowly. "Thank God."

Okay, so that didn't work. I took a sip of water and waited for another opportunity.

"So, you decided to go dressy, huh?" Mom

noted as she helped herself to more salad.

"Yep." Ashley nodded. "Mary-Kate and I saw a few things in my magazines that would be perfect."

"You know, it's actually almost too bad we don't have guys coming," I chimed in, twirling a few strands of hair around my finger.

"What do you mean?" Ashley asked.

"Wouldn't you love to see them all dressed up?" I asked, appealing to Ashley's cute-boy-loving side. "They never wear anything but jeans and sweats."

Ashley shifted in her seat, staring at me uncertainly. "Yeah, but—"

"And imagine the torture it would be for them, having to wear those fancy suits!" I exclaimed. "It would be worth it just to see some of them squirm."

"Yeah," Ashley said. "But I really think we were right with this all-girls thing. We're going to have a great time. Besides, the guys *would* be squirming the whole time, and if they were miserable, we'd all be miserable."

"Mary-Kate, you've already decided on a girl power theme, and you've got the ball rolling," Mom said. "There's no need to go back on that now."

"I know," I admitted. "I didn't want to *change*

it, I was just saying it would be funny...you know...to see the guys dressed up. That's all."

Mom pushed her chair away from the table. "Good. It's all settled then."

"You two are going to have a great party," Dad put in, picking up a few dishes as he rose from the table.

"Yeah. We definitely are." I tried to sound enthusiastic as I got up to help.

But my whole body felt heavy as I carried a couple of the serving dishes around the table. I couldn't believe Ashley was clinging so hard to the all-girls idea. Convincing her should have been a snap.

Getting her to change her mind was obviously going to be tougher than I'd thought, but I had to do it.

I had to.

After dinner, our parents went up to their room, and I followed Mary-Kate into the living room to start our geometry study session.

"So...ready to study?" I asked.

"Oh! I forgot to tell you," Mary-Kate said, grabbing her bag from the floor by the front door. "Jake's coming over to help me study tonight."

I crossed my arms over my chest. "When did you decide this?" I felt like I'd just been punched in the stomach. She couldn't be serious.

"This afternoon on our way back from the park." Mary-Kate's grin faded a bit. "I told him that I was stressed out about the test, and he offered to tutor me. I figured you'd be happy not to have to work tonight."

I took a deep breath and let it out slowly, trying not to get overly annoyed. "Mary-Kate, I *planned* to help you tonight," I said. "I could have gone over to Lauren's, remember?"

"I'm sorry!" Mary-Kate said as she pulled a couple of books out of her bag. "I wouldn't have said yes if I knew you were going to be mad. I thought you'd be relieved that you didn't have to help me with geometry *again*."

I held Mary-Kate's gaze for a moment longer, but I felt my anger wavering. She probably did think she was doing me a favour by taking Jake up on his offer. It just irritated me that I was being brushed aside for Jake for the second time that day. The third time if you counted the whole Driver's Ed thing.

"I'm sorry, okay?" Mary-Kate said sincerely.

"It's okay," I said with a sigh. "I guess I'll just watch *Spencer Academy* while you guys work."

At that moment the doorbell rang, and Mary-Kate grinned. "That's him!" she cried giddily. "Do I look okay?"

"You look great," I told her.

She bounded across the room and opened the door. Jake was standing on the front step, and his whole face lit up when he saw Mary-Kate. I couldn't help feeling happy for my sister. If Jake was looking at her like that, he definitely had it as bad as she did.

"Hey, Mary-Kate. Hey Ashley." He nodded at me.

"Hi, Jake! Come on in." Mary-Kate led him into the living room.

"So I hear you're relieving me of my tutoring duties," I said to Jake, shoving my hands in the back pockets of my jeans as we all walked into the living room together. "I guess I should thank you."

"No problem," Jake said. He adjusted the strap of his backpack on his shoulder. "I actually kind of liked the class. Don't tell anyone, though."

"He's obviously insane," Mary-Kate joked, prompting a laugh from Jake.

We all turned when we heard somebody on the stairs. "You must be Jake," Dad said as he walked into the room. He didn't seem surprised to see a guy in the living room, so I assumed Mary-Kate had told my parents he was coming over.

"Hi! It's nice to meet you," Jake said, reaching over to shake hands.

"You, too." Dad smiled approvingly at

91

Mary-Kate, obviously happy to find that Jake was so polite.

"Well, I guess we should just get this over with," Mary-Kate said, clearing a few magazines off the coffee table as Jake settled down on the couch.

I felt my shoulders tense up as he opened his bag and pulled out his old notebook. "Wait a minute," I said. "You guys are going to study in here?"

"Yeah… why?" Mary-Kate said.

"I was going to watch *Spencer Academy*," I said, hating the whiny sound of my voice. I cleared my throat and lifted my chin. "I mean, can't you guys study in Mom's office or something so I can have the big-screen T.V.?"

"Ashley." Dad came up behind me and rested his hands on my shoulders. "It's a lot more comfortable for two people in here. You can watch your show up in your room."

My skin grew warm from embarrassment as I stood there, basically being scolded by my father in front of Mary-Kate and her new boyfriend.

"Fine." I threw my hands up and let them slap back down against my jeans.

Before anyone could say anything else to me, I turned and took the steps two at a time. I couldn't believe the way this night had turned out. First I bailed on Lauren and my other friends to help Mary-Kate, who basically tossed me aside. Now I was getting kicked out of my own living room. It was so unfair!

I walked into my bedroom and closed the door behind me. Flopping down on my bed, I grabbed my remote and flicked on my tiny portable T.V. *Spencer Academy* hadn't started yet.

The phone rang, and I reached over to my nightstand to answer it.

"Hello, this is Wilson Miller," a voice said on the other line. I could hear hip-hop music playing in the background. "I'd like to speak to Ashley or Mary-Kate, please."

"Hi, Wilson, it's Ashley," I said. "What's up? Where are you calling from?"

"I'm at a video shoot in Aspen," he explained. "But I wanted to check in with you. How are you party plans coming?"

"Well, I was thinking about getting a karaoke machine and trying to find tapes full of girl power songs," I told him. "What do you think?"

"That's a fabulous idea!" Wilson said. "Really. A great touch, Ashley. I think you have a knack for this stuff."

"Thanks." The compliment from Wilson made me flush happily.

"Now, how about the guest list?" he asked. "I

really need it, Ashley. I thought you'd have e-mailed it to me by now."

I glanced across the room at my purple notebook on my desk and thought about our breakfast guest list conversation. Mary-Kate and I hadn't gotten very far that morning before Jake had called. The list wasn't remotely ready to send out yet.

"We're...working on it," I said slowly.

"We've got to get those invitations out A.S.A.P.," Wilson urged. "The party's less than six weeks away! I need the guest list by the time I get back from Aspen."

Great, I thought. *Like I'm ever going to find more than five minutes alone with Mary-Kate to figure it all out.* But I wasn't going to say that to Wilson.

"No problem," I said breezily.

"Good!" Wilson said. "I'll be back in two days. Talk to you then."

"Okay! Thanks, Wilson!"

I clicked off the phone and sat still for a moment, staring at my desk. Downstairs, Mary-Kate let out a peal of laughter. I sighed. If she kept spending all her time with Jake, we would never get the guest list done. And I, for one, wanted to make sure this party went off with out a hitch.

I got up and grabbed my notebook, a pen, and my address book. Then I climbed back on to my bed, flipped the notebook open to the list of names we'd begun on Saturday, and started looking up addresses.

I never expected to be working on our sweet sixteen alone. But someone had to do it. And it obviously wasn't going to be Mary-Kate. I couldn't help feeling like our sweet sixteen was taking a backseat to Jake.

"Well, if that's the way she wants it, that's fine by me," I said aloud. I heard her laugh again, and I turned up the volume on my little T.V. to drown her out.

Apparently, I was going to have to start making decisions about this party by myself.

chapter eleven

"I've never been this nervous in my life," I told Janine, the red-headed girl from my Driver's Ed class.

We were standing in front of Columbus High on Wednesday afternoon with my mystery guy, Ben Jones, waiting for Ms. Junger to pull the student driver car around.

We watched as a little white car wound through the parking lot and stopped in front of us. There was a huge red sign on the roof that read: "Columbus Driving School – Student Driver!"

"Why doesn't it just say 'Danger! Idiot behind the wheel!'" Ben joked.

Janine and I laughed as Ms. Junger got out of the car. She flashed us her now familiar glare.

"Driving is no laughing matter, people," she said. Then she looked down at her clipboard and held out the keys in front of us. My heart pounded just looking at them. This was really happening! I was really going to learn to drive!

"Let's see...who's going first?" Ms. Junger muttered to herself.

I glanced at Ben and Janine, who both looked as scared as I felt. *Don't pick me*, I thought. *Just don't pick me!*

"Ashley?" Ms. Junger said. "Get behind the wheel."

She slapped the keys into my hand, and my legs instantly turned to Jell-O. Then she walked over to the passenger side door. "Let's get going!"

"You'll be fine," Janine said when she saw me hesitating. "We're all in this together."

Ben opened the door to the back seat and let Janine slide in before him. "Don't worry," he said, his deep brown eyes reassuring. "You're going to do great."

I slipped into the driver's seat and closed the door. Then I glanced at Ms. Junger for direction.

"What's the first thing you do?" she barked.

*First thing, first thing...*How was I supposed to be able to remember our lesson when I was shaking so hard?

"Seat belt and mirrors!" I cried. I pulled the seat belt on and snapped it into the buckle, then adjusted the rearview mirror.

"Okay, now put the key in the ignition and your right foot on the brake pedal," Ms. Junger ordered.

I did as she said, started up the engine, and clasped the steering wheel so hard my knuckles turned white.

"Now, put on your left blinker, check your mirror for traffic, and slowly pull out," Ms. Junger instructed.

Here goes nothing, I thought.

Ever so carefully, I picked my foot up off the brake and pushed down on the gas pedal. Suddenly, we flew forward, and I let out a little squeal. I heard Janine shriek from the back seat, but Ben just laughed.

"Brake!" Ms. Junger yelled.

I slammed on the brake, and we all jerked forward. My seat belt cut into my chest as I gasped for breath, my hair blanketing my face.

"I said, slowly," Ms. Junger growled through her teeth.

"Sorry," I said. "I've never done this before."

Ms Junger took an audible breath in through her nose and let it out slowly. "It's okay. It happens to everyone."

Hey! That was the first nice thing I ever heard the woman say.

"Let's try it again," she prompted.

This time, I pressed gently on the gas pedal, and we moved slowly through the parking lot. By the time I got to the exit, I was calming down a bit. It just took a little while to get a feel for the power of the gas and the brake.

Ms. Junger instructed me to make a right turn. I looked both ways, then turned the wheel. Suddenly, we were driving on the wrong side of the street! Luckily, the school was on a quiet back road, so there were no other cars around. Ms. Junger reached out and gently turned the wheel further to the right.

"There you go," Ms. Junger said. "Now go up to that stop sign – slowly – and try it again."

I jerked the car only a little coming to a stop, then I turned on my blinker.

"Hey! We're turning on to my street," Ben said. "That's my house right on the corner."

I glanced up at the big blue house he was pointing to. Then I hit the gas, cutting the wheel more this time, and before I knew what was happening, we were flying straight for the curb...and a big black mailbox!

"Brake!" Ms. Junger shouted.

I slammed my foot down hard. I let out a shriek as the car jumped the curb and ploughed right over the mailbox. *Ben's* mailbox.

I slowly turned to look at Ms. Junger. "Sorry."

The instructor had her hands braced on the dashboard. Ben clutched his stomach and laughed like a hyena in the back seat and Janine turned white. My foot was still pressed hard into the brake, and I was afraid to move a muscle. I couldn't believe I had an accident on my very first day of driving!

Ms. Junger gritted her teeth. "Just put it in reverse and pull back out."

My eyes filled up with tears as I reached for the gear shift, but I managed to get back out onto the road. I put the car in park, and we all climbed out to assess the damage.

It was pretty bad. Ben's mailbox was lying on its side, all dented. Ms. Junger left the three of us by the car and went up to his house to apologise for the accident.

"Are you okay?" I asked Janine.

"Oh, I'm fine," she answered with a wave of her hand. She was still pale, but she seemed to be handling it well.

"Ben, I am so sorry," I said. "Really. I'll pay for it…somehow."

Ben finally stopped laughing and looked at me, his eyes glimmering. "Geez, Ashley. Ever thought of trying out for the demolition derby?"

"No." I crossed my arms over my chest. "But maybe you should consider calling Bad

Jokes Anonymous."

Ben blinked, obviously taken aback. But then he smirked, impressed. I couldn't believe it myself. Wow! I actually thought of a comeback at the exact moment I needed it instead of two days later! Mary-Kate would have been so proud.

Ms. Junger returned and instructed Ben to get behind the wheel.

By the time we got back to the school, Ben and Janine had both had their turns behind the wheel and had done well. Ms. Junger dropped us off at the school, and we all walked inside, chatting happily.

Ben swung open the door. "Well, that was... interesting."

"And fun," Janine added. "If I had to go through that with someone, I'm glad it was you guys."

"Thanks." I smiled. "I'm glad it was you guys, too."

"Hey! You know what?" Janine said, coming to a stop in front of our classroom. "I'm having this party on my dad's boat on Friday night. You two should come."

I hesitated for a moment. What about Mary-Kate? We always went to parties together. Maybe she would want to come along. Then I realised she probably had plans with Jake for the weekend. So why shouldn't I make some plans of my own?

"I'd love to," I told Janine.

"Me, too." Ben glanced at me. "In fact, I'll pick you up if you want." He shrugged. "I mean, my parents and I will...you know."

"Do you really think they're going to want to drive the girl who levelled their mailbox?" I asked, raising my eyebrows.

"They're very forgiving people," Ben assured me.

"This is great!" Janine exclaimed, clapping her hands. "It's like a date!"

I grinned and stared straight into Ben's deep brown eyes. "Is that what it is?" I asked. "A date?"

Ben rubbed at the back of his neck. "Sure! I mean, yeah. If that's okay with you."

"That is *definitely* okay with me," I told him.

Wednesday evening, Jake was driving me home in his Jeep after a whole afternoon of studying and swimming.

Now we zipped through the streets with the top down, blaring our favourite radio station on the stereo. I had my sunglasses on, the wind was whipping through my hair, and with the cutest guy in school behind the wheel, I'd never felt so cool in my life. Too bad we couldn't drive by the houses of every single person I knew!

"Thanks again for helping me with geometry," I shouted to Jake over the radio. "I really think I'm picking it up."

Jake smiled. "Believe it or not, I had fun."

"Yeah, right," I said.

But I knew he was telling the truth. The past couple of times we'd got together really had been fun, even though we were studying. Jake was constantly making me laugh. And somehow it really helped me remember things.

"Well, you can reward me for all my trouble by dancing with me at your sweet sixteen," Jake said as he turned onto my block.

My stomach dropped. I had to make Ashley change her mind about the party, and fast! The longer I waited to straighten this all out, the more I felt like I was lying to Jake *and* Ashley.

Jake dropped me off. I gave him a quick kiss, then jogged into the house. As I slammed the door behind me, I decided that it was time to take the direct approach. That has always been my style, after all.

Outside Ashley's closed bedroom door, I paused and took a deep breath, planning what I was going to say. Then I knocked and opened the door. Ashley was sitting at her desk doing her homework. Her music was so loud she didn't even hear me walk in.

"Hey, Ashley!" I shouted.

She flinched and put her hand over her heart. "You scared me!" She laughed.

"Sorry!" I crossed the room to turn her music down a bit. "I need to talk to you."

Ashley turned in her chair, resting her arm on the back. "Everything okay?"

"Yeah. Everything's fine." I perched on the edge of her bed and crossed my legs, then uncrossed them and leaned back on my hands. Why was I so fidgety?

"Listen, I've been thinking about this whole girls-only thing," I said, finally sitting up straight. "And I've changed my mind. I think we should invite guys to our party."

There was a long moment of silence, and it hung in the air like a dark cloud. Ashley's face tightened. She looked shocked – *angry* and shocked.

"You *have* to be kidding me!" she shouted, jumping to her feet so fast her chair almost tipped over. She caught it just in time and glared at me. "You haven't been involved with the party planning at all and *now* you're springing this on me?"

"Wait a minute," I protested, standing. "What do you mean I haven't been involved at all?"

"All you've been thinking about for the past week is Jake, Jake, Jake," Ashley complained, tilting her head back and forth each time she said his name. "You spend every second with him, and we've barely had a chance to talk about the party."

My mouth fell open. I was stunned by Ashley's reaction. After all, hadn't we made a guest list together? Hadn't we decided on dresses together? And I knew I had been in on the whole karaoke conversation.

"I'm sorry, Mary-Kate," Ashley said, sitting down again. She picked up her pen and deliberately turned her back on me. "There is no way I'm going to change the party now. Not after all the work I've done."

"Ashley, you don't understand." I tried to stay calm so I could explain. I moved to the side of her chair to try to get her to look at me. "When Jake and I were at the park the other day—"

Ashley interrupted me. "You know what? It doesn't matter anyway. I already finished the guest list, complete with addresses, *on my own*, and sent it to Wilson. And every guest on that list is a girl, so there's no turning back now."

"You *what*?" I blurted. "How could you do that without showing it to me? Or even *telling* me anything about it?"

"Well, I'm sorry," Ashley said sarcastically, slapping her pen down on the desk and finally looking up at me. "But if you hadn't been so busy with Jake I would have asked for your help."

"I know why you're doing this," I said. "You just don't want to change the party because I have a boyfriend and you don't."

Ashley pulled back as if she'd been slapped. Then her eyes narrowed into little slits, and she stood up to face me.

"I can't believe you just said that," Ashley said, her voice cracking. "Can you please just leave?"

I just stood there for a moment, unsure of what to do. She'd never thrown me out of her room before.

"I'm serious, Mary-Kate," she warned, her voice growing louder. "Leave me alone."

"Fine!" I said. I turned on my heel and stormed out of her room, slamming the door behind me.

Two seconds later she turned her music back on, even louder this time. I stood outside her door and listened, my eyes filling with tears. Ashley and I had never had a fight this big before. And I don't think either one of us had ever said such hurtful things to the other.

I wiped my eyes and walked back to my room, wondering if things were ever going to be the same between Ashley and me again.

chapter twelve

That night at dinner I couldn't even look at Mary-Kate, let alone talk to her. The silence was definitely driving my parents insane.

"So, Ashley," Mom said to me, fiddling with her earring. "Didn't you have your first turn behind the wheel today?"

I sighed loudly, pushing my rice around on my plate. "Yep."

I glanced at Mary-Kate. There was so much I wanted to tell her about – my driving lesson, the comeback I'd flung at Ben, and my new friend Janine and her party. And about the fact that I had a date, an actual *date* with the amazingly cute mystery guy from Todd Malone's party.

But that obviously wasn't going to happen.

"What about you, Mary-Kate?" Mom prompted, turning towards my sister. "How was your afternoon?"

"Well, I'd tell you, Mom, but I don't think some people at the table want to hear about Jake any more."

"Ooookay." Dad took a long sip of water and studied each of us, running his hand over his slightly shaggy brown hair.

"What about your party?" he asked. "How's the planning going?"

"I don't want to talk about it," Mary-Kate and I said at the exact same time, in the same annoyed tone.

I scowled at her and she scowled right back. I looked down at the table and felt like crying. At that moment I couldn't even imagine celebrating our birthday together.

"Can I be excused?" I asked, pulling my napkin off my lap.

"Ashley, you've barely touched your dinner," Mom said.

I knew she hated it when Mary-Kate and I were upset with each other. "Maybe I'll eat it later," I said.

"Well...okay, sweetie," she said. "You can go."

I stood up slowly and walked out of the dining room. And even though I could feel Mary-Kate watching me, I didn't look back.

"Okay, Mary-Kate, you're doing fine," Ms. Junger

said. "Please pull to the next stop sign and make a right."

It was Thursday afternoon, and I was taking my first turn behind the wheel. Ashley was right – Ms. Junger was definitely strict. I gripped the wheel tightly and followed Ms. Junger's instructions. Two girls I didn't know chattered away in the back seat.

I drove to the stop sign, and carefully looked left and right. I turned the wheel while lightly pressing down on the gas when I saw that no one was coming.

"Just continue down this road," Mrs. Junger requested.

My shoulders relaxed a bit. Driving in a straight line? I could handle that. I steered the car and kept a slow but constant speed.

As I stared at the road ahead, I found myself thinking about Ashley's accusation – that I had been spending all my time with Jake and not helping her with the party.

It's true, I realized as I remembered all the hours I had spent with Jake this week. *Ashley is right. I haven't been helping with the party at all.*

"Stop sign, Mary-Kate! Stop sign!"

"What?" I stomped down on the brake. Too late!

The car's tyres squealed on the pavement. The girls in the back seat screamed as we drove right past the bright red sign and through a four-way intersection.

The car skidded to the other side of the intersection and stopped. I struggled to catch my breath. "Is everyone okay?" I asked.

Luckily, I hadn't done any serious damage.

I turned to Ms. Junger. Her eyes were squeezed shut, and I swear I heard her mutter, "Just like her sister."

"Pull over, Mary-Kate," she said. "I think it's Monica's turn to drive now."

I felt like a total moron. My legs shook as I got out of the car and switched places with Monica. But as soon as I settled into the back seat, I started thinking about Ashley again, trying to see things from her point of view. I *had* been spending a lot of time with Jake lately. And the other day, when we were making up the guest list, I *had* ditched her to talk on the phone with him. Plus I did bail on her at lunch when we were talking about dresses.

I swallowed hard and looked out the window as Monica lurched the car around a corner. A wave of guilt washed over me. I hugged myself and sighed.

I'm going to have to un-invite Jake, I realised. It

was the only way Ashley and I were ever going to be friends again.

"Hey, Mary-Kate!" Jake called as I weaved my way through the crowded school hallway the next afternoon.

"Hey!" I said brightly.

Jake's eyes narrowed and he put his hands in the pockets of his varsity jacket. "Everything okay?"

"Funny you should ask," I replied. One of the benches by the wall was empty and I gestured towards it. "Want to sit?"

"Uh-oh." Jake gave a little nervous laugh. "This does not sound good."

I put my hand on his arm. I realized it must have sounded like I was going to dump him or something.

"It's about my party," I explained, taking a seat.

I paused to take a deep breath and told myself to just do it. Quick and painless, like ripping off a Band-Aid. Although, whatever people told you, that band aid thing usually hurt.

"I don't know how to say this, so I'm just gonna say it," I began. "I'm sorry but I can't invite you to my sweet sixteen."

"Oh," he said, obviously confused. "That's...ummm...why not?"

"Ashley and I had decided to have an all-girl party, but I really wanted to invite you, so I did. I figured I'd be able to change her mind—"

"But you couldn't," Jake finished.

"Right," I said, scrunching my nose. "We had a big fight, actually. I would keep trying to convince her, but I think I need to let it go, you know? It's the only way we're going to make up."

"That's okay," Jake said. "I understand. But I want to take you out for your birthday, if that's okay. You know, on another night."

I reached out to hold his hand. "I'd love that."

Then, before I even knew what was happening, Jake was leaning in to kiss me. My whole body tingled with nervousness, but I managed to tilt my head and close my eyes just in time.

Our lips met, and it was as though everything around us disappeared. The kiss was long and slow and totally amazing – I wanted it to go on forever. Now I knew what people meant when they talked about a *real* kiss!

That night when Jake dropped me off, I ran right into the house and bounded up the steps to Ashley's room. I couldn't wait to talk to her and get everything straightened out. I knocked and walked in, but she wasn't there.

Disappointed, I went back downstairs and

found my parents snuggled together on the couch in the living room, watching the evening news.

"Where's Ashley?" I asked, resting on the arm of the comfy chair.

"She went out to a party," Mom told me.

"A party?" I repeated, stunned.

I felt all the blood rush out of my face as I tried to process what Mom was saying. What? Ashley went to a party and she didn't even tell me about it?

"Yes." Mom pulled away from Dad slightly so she could see me better. "I'm surprised you didn't know. She's been talking about it for the last two days."

"Whose party was it?" I asked, slowly sliding off the arm of the chair and into the seat. I hadn't heard about any parties at school. Usually, if one of us is invited to something, the other one is, too.

"It's at her friend Janine's house," Mom answered. "She really didn't tell you?"

"No," I replied with a shrug. I didn't even know Ashley had a friend named Janine.

"Did you guys drop her off?" I asked, wondering if maybe this Janine girl was from another town or something.

"No, actually," Dad said, stretching his arms out and yawning. "A boy came by with his parents to pick her up. Ben was his name. Nice kid."

"Excuse me?" I blurted. "She had a *date*?" My

brain was reeling. Ashley had friends I'd never heard of. She had a date she'd never even said a word to me about!

"Um, Mom?" I said, toying with the hem on my sweater. "Do you happen to know where Ashley met Ben?"

"He's a friend of hers from her Driver's Ed class," Mom answered. "She said something about bumping into him at Todd's party and then he ended up being in her class. That's where she met Janine, too."

"Oh," I said.

Driver's Ed. That made sense.

"I knew you girls were fighting on Wednesday, but I was hoping you'd made up by now," Mom said.

"Don't worry about it, Mom." I didn't want to worry her. "It's no big deal."

But it was a big deal. It was a *tremendous* deal. Ashley had new friends and a new guy to date and a party to go to in some totally different town with different people. And I wasn't a part of it. I didn't even know anything about it.

A feeling of dread seeped into my chest. Ashley was right. I *had* been neglecting her in favour of Jake. Not just the party, but *her*. My sister. My best friend in the whole world.

chapter thirteen

"Watch your step, Ashley," Ben teased, his dark eyes shining. "And whatever you do, don't knock me over."

"Look out," I joked. "I'm a one-woman safety hazard."

Ben smiled. He held out his hand to help me from the pier to Janine's father's sleek white boat. "This place is so beautiful," I gushed.

"Definitely cool," Ben agreed.

He held on to my hand after I'd safely made it to the deck. I didn't want him to let go. I was so attracted to this guy. I couldn't believe I was finally on a date with him!

"Hey, guys!" Janine called. "I'm so glad you came."

Janine had set up tables of snacks and drinks on the deck of the boat, but most of the party was actually taking place on the pier itself. Little white lights were strung from the lampposts that lined either side of the long wooden pier. A sound system on the bow blasted one of the local pop stations.

There were dozens of people milling around, talking and laughing.

She poured two Cokes and handed them to us.

"Thanks for inviting us," I said.

"Well, just make yourselves at home. The pier is all ours tonight."

"Janine! Come here! I can't find the plates!" one of her friends shouted from down below.

"Sorry, I'll catch up with you later," Janine said with an apologetic smile.

"So – do you want to walk down to the end of the pier and check out the view?" Ben asked.

I took a sip of my soda. "Don't you want to mingle?"

"Nah. I'm totally antisocial."

We climbed off the boat, then moved together through the crowd. We walked out to the end of the pier, where we were entirely alone. I leaned against the railing and gazed out across the ocean to the moonlit spot where the water met the sky. I sighed. It didn't get better than this. Beautiful night. Great party. Gorgeous boy...

"I'm really glad you came to the party with me tonight," Ben whispered.

"Me, too," I said, my heart pounding.

All I wanted at that moment was for him to kiss me.

Then he leaned in. I closed my eyes...

When our lips met, it felt as if the pier was moving below my feet. I couldn't have imagined a more amazing kiss. When we parted, Ben's eyes were still closed, and I smiled. Apparently he'd thought it was amazing, too.

"Wow," he said.

"Yeah," I said, biting my bottom lip. "Wow."

We moved over and sat down on the bench, which was good because my knees were so weak I probably couldn't have stood for much longer.

Now I understood how Mary-Kate felt about Jake – and why she tried to change our sweet sixteen plans. She didn't want to spend her birthday without him.

"What are you thinking about?" Ben asked.

"I'm thinking I'd like to invite you to my sweet sixteen." I smiled. "Want to be my date?"

Ben flashed his lopsided grin. "I'd love to," he said. "As long as there are no party hats involved because, you know, I have a rep to protect."

"No party hats," I laughed. "I swear."

"Then I'm in," Ben said. He reached out and took my hand again, lacing my fingers through his. "Thanks for asking."

"Thanks for saying yes," I answered.

I was so ridiculously happy at that moment, part of me wished the night would never end. But another part – a big part – couldn't wait to get home to tell Mary-Kate the good news. The boy-girl party was back on, and now we *both* had dates!

"Mary-Kate, are you awake?" Ashley whispered late on Friday night. I heard her come in after her party and was hoping she'd stop by my room! It was way past time to apologise.

"Come on in," I said, sitting up.

Ashley flicked on my bedside lamp as she sat down on the edge of my mattress.

"I'm sorry!" we both said at the exact same time.

"You're sorry?" we both said again.

Then we both laughed. It felt as if a huge weight was being lifted off my shoulders.

"I'm really sorry for being such a jerk about the party," I said, leaning back against my headboard. "I mean, for not helping and all that stuff. I realised that you were right. I have been spending a lot of time with Jake, and I haven't been paying much attention to...you know...to you."

"It's okay," Ashley said. "I understand that Jake is really important to you right now. I didn't mean to be so critical." She sighed and shifted her position, crossing her legs and bringing her knees up under her chin. "I'm really happy for you, Mary-Kate."

"Can we just never fight again?" I smiled.

Ashley broke into a wide grin. "Sounds good to me."

She reached out and wrapped her arms around me, and I hugged her back, hard. It felt so good to have all of that dread and guilt and misery hugged away!

"So?" I said. "Tell me about your date!"

Ashley glanced down at her hands. "Mom and Dad told you about that, huh?"

"Well, of course they did!" I answered. "It was totally weird. They kinda had to fill me in."

"Remember that mystery guy from Todd's party? His name is Ben Jones," Ashley explained. "He's in my Driver's Ed class and he's soooo cute. Mary-Kate, you'd really like him. He has this amazing sense of humour, and…"

She trailed off and stared at some far point over my head, all dreamy-eyed.

"And what?" I asked. "What?"

"And he's the best kisser ever," Ashley sighed.

"He *kissed* you?" I blurted.

"Yeah." She nodded absently.

For a second there I thought she was going to

float off into the clouds.

"Wow," I said. "This is pretty serious."

"I guess so," Ashley agreed. She shrugged and leaned back beside me, her head propped up on a couple of my throw pillows.

"I'm really comfortable with him," she told me. "He's a great guy."

I scooted down so that I was closer to her. "I'm really happy for you, Ashley," I said. "I can't believe we both met such amazing guys at practically the same time. It's almost as if it was meant to be or something."

"Yeah, it is," Ashley said.

"So?" I patted her arm in the silly, excited way Mom always did when she wanted news from us. "When do I get to meet him?"

Ashley turned onto her side and propped her head up on her hand. "That's something I wanted to talk to you about," she said. "How would you feel about having a boy-girl party after all?"

If I could have screamed without waking up my parents, I would have. Instead, I jumped out of bed – and almost tripped doing it.

"Are you kidding me?" I glared at Ashley.

"What?" Ashley asked, sitting up straight. "I thought you'd be happy. Isn't that what you wanted?"

I felt like I was going to explode from frustration. "Yes! That was what I *wanted*!" I pushed my hands into my hair and held it back from my face. "But, Ashley, after our fight I un-invited Jake."

"Well then, all you have to do is re-invite him the next time you see him," Ashley said. "He'll be psyched and we'll get to have a guy-girl party. See? Everyone wins!"

I sighed and closed my eyes, telling myself to breathe. Then I sat down on my bed again and stared up at the ceiling.

"You're right," I answered slowly. "I'll just re-invite him and everything will be fine – once Jake gets over the fact that I'm a total nutball."

Ashley was quiet for a couple of moments. Then she sighed. "Remember the other day when we were talking about what it was going to be like to be sixteen?"

"Yeah. Parties...driving...clothes...boys," I said.

"Well, I'm starting to think it's not going to be that simple," Ashley said. "I always figured we'd be doing all that stuff together."

"But we're not," I finished. "We're not driving together or going to parties together...and the guys we like even go to completely different schools."

"Exactly." Ashley's eyes narrowed with concern. "What if turning sixteen means we're going to grow apart?"

My stomach tightened. "Well, we won't let it," I said, determined.

"How can we not?" Ashley asked.

"We'll make a pact," I said. Ashley laughed and rolled her eyes, but I was dead serious. "I mean it! We'll say we both understand that we might be doing a lot of things without each other, but no matter what, we'll always be there for each other and we'll always be best friends."

"Sounds good to me," Ashley smiled.

After not talking to Ashley for two days, this conversation was like heaven. Everything was going to be fine between Ashley and me. And I would talk to Jake and make him understand. We'd invite the guys and we'd have the most amazing sweet sixteen party ever.

Everything's going to be fine now, I thought. *Absolutely, totally fine.*

chapter fourteen

Monday afternoon I walked into the cafeteria and spotted Jake at the front of the lunch line, digging in his pocket for his wallet as he balanced his tray with his free hand.

"It's now or never," I coached myself.

I rolled my shoulders back, ignoring the nervous knots in my stomach, and weaved my way through the crowd.

"Jake!" I called.

He looked up, and his face turned grim. Then he walked off in the other direction, heading for the window wall. My stomach tightened as he slid his way along the windows to get to his table. There was almost no space over there, so he was basically taking the most difficult route to his table. Was it just to get away from me?

I intercepted Jake before he could get to his friends. He stopped short, sighing impatiently.

"Jake, what's wrong?" I asked. "I tried to call you all weekend."

"Yeah, well, I was busy," he mumbled.

"I...uh...I need to talk to you." I started to play with the rings on my right hand, twisting them around and around my fingers.

"Sorry. I have to go," Jake said.

He took a step forward, forcing me out of his way, and walked off toward his table without looking back.

My heart was pounding like crazy as I watched him go. What happened? Jake and I had a great time last week. Why was he suddenly treating me like he didn't care about me?

Hot tears pricked at the corners of my eyes. I hurried to the bathroom so no one would see me cry.

"Oh my gosh, Mary-Kate! Are you okay?" Lauren blurted when she saw me. She and Brittany had found me in the library after lunch.

"You're all puffy!" Brittany whispered, handing me a couple of tissues from her bag. "What happened? Where were you at lunch?"

"In the bathroom," I told her, wiping my eyes. "I tried to talk to Jake, but he wouldn't even *look* at me." My heart sank all over again. "He just...*dismissed* me."

"Why?" Lauren asked, her forehead wrinkling. "Did you have a fight?"

"No!" I said, loudly enough to earn a "Shhh!" from the librarian at the front of the room. "That's the thing. Everything was fine on Friday."

"What a jerk!" Brittany slumped back in her chair. "You don't need a guy who's going to treat you like that, Mary-Kate."

I sighed miserably. Jake wasn't a jerk. At least, he never had been before. I wished I could figure out what had set him off.

"Are you sure you didn't do *anything*?" Lauren asked.

"The only thing I can think of is the conversation we had on Friday about the party." I pulled my bookbag towards me and rested my chin on it.

"Oh, so you did un-invite him?" Lauren asked.

"Yeah, but he was totally cool about it. He said he understood," I explained. "Now he won't even talk to me!"

The second bell rang, and Todd Malone slipped through the library door. I felt a quick surge of hope. Todd was friends with Jake. Maybe he'd know what was going on.

"Todd!" I whispered as he started towards the periodical section. I waved him over to our table.

"Hi, guys," he said. "I guess you want to talk about Jake, huh?"

"Do you know what's going on?" I asked.

"Yep," Todd said. I could tell by the strained look on his face that he didn't want to be in the middle of this, but I didn't know where else to turn. He lowered himself into the free chair at our table. "I was there when it happened."

"What are you talking about?" I demanded.

"Here's the deal," Todd said. "The other day I went to the park with John Lee and my friend Ben, from Harrison. Jake was already there shooting hoops, so we decided to play two on two."

"Okay," I said.

"So we're playing and Jake and Ben get to talking and pretty soon they both realised that they were dating twin sisters," Todd explained.

"Wait – Ben from Harrison is Ashley's Ben?" Brittany asked.

"Right," Todd said. "So then Ben asks Jake if he's going to your sweet sixteen and Jake says 'No, it's an all-girl party' and Ben gets all confused because Ashley had just invited him the night before and then—"

"And then Jake went ballistic." My stomach flipped over.

"Well, Jake doesn't ever really go ballistic," Todd said. "But he did get quiet, and he left pretty soon after that."

I felt sick. This couldn't be happening.

"I still don't get it," Lauren whispered. "Why is Jake mad at you?"

"Because he thinks I lied," I said flatly. "When he found out Ben was invited to the sweet sixteen, he figured I lied when I told him it was an all-girl party. He probably thinks I just didn't want him to come so I made up the all-girl thing as an excuse."

"Wow," Brittany said. "No wonder he's mad."

"Well, you're just going to have to explain it to him," Lauren declared. "Tell him what really happened."

"Right," I replied. "If he'll ever talk to me again."

"This is a nightmare," Mary-Kate said after she explained what had happened with Jake. She flopped back on my bed and stared up at the ceiling.

"Listen, we can fix this," I said, clicking into organisation mode. "You'll talk to Jake in the next few days. He's hurt right now, but he has to listen to you eventually. You'll explain everything, and he'll be fine."

"Do you really think so?" Mary-Kate asked hopefully.

"Yes," I told her. "Then, all we have to do is call Wilson, and tell him not to send out any of the invitations. We'll cut half the girls from our list, add a few boys, and – ta-da! – problem solved!"

Just having a plan made me feel better. I grabbed the phone to dial Wilson's number, but it rang in my hand. I jumped at the sound, then answered.

"Ashley? Hi, it's Wilson!" the voice on the line said.

"Wilson! I was just about to call you. There are some things about the party that Mary-Kate and I need to discuss with you."

"Great!" Wilson said. "But before you get into that, I have good news. I flew back from Aspen a day early so I got your invitations out in the mail today!"

Uh-oh. A lump formed in my throat.

"Ashley? What's wrong?" Mary-Kate asked when she noticed my expression.

I told Wilson I'd call him back, and hung up the phone.

"Mary-Kate, we've got trouble," I told my sister. "Wilson's already sent out the invitations!"

My sister looked ill. "You mean, we're stuck having an all-girl party?"

"Not if we act fast." I grabbed a jacket from my closet. "Come on, Mary-Kate. We have to find a way to get those invitations back!"

*The countdown to the biggest party
of the year continues!
Find out what happens next in*

Sweet 16

Book 2:

WISHES AND DREAMS

Ashley and I were walking down the hallway at the end of lunch period when we ran into Melanie Han and Tashema Mitchell.

"Hey, you guys! We're *so* excited about your party!" Melanie said.

"Sending updates about your sweet sixteen by e-mail is so cool. How'd you come up with that idea?" Tashema asked.

"Oh, it just, um – came to us," I said.

My sister and I exchanged a look. No one knew that the location of our sweet sixteen was a secret – because *we* didn't even know where we were having it! There were fourteen days and counting until our big party and we still hadn't found the perfect party place!

But that was okay. I knew that Ashley and I would come up with something awesome – even if we did it with seconds to spare.

"So when's the next update?" Melanie asked.

"Soon," Ashley teased. "But we can't tell you when, because that would ruin the surprise."

"Can't you give us a clue? A teensy tiny clue?" Melanie begged.

"Not even one," I told her. "Just keep checking your e-mail."

"Okay, but the suspense is killing me," Tashema said before she and Melanie walked off.

I nudged Ashley with my elbow. "Sounds like our plan is working great!"

Ashley smiled. "You're right. No one suspects a thing!"

We turned the corner at the end of the hall – and nearly crashed into Rachel Adams.

"Hey, Mary-Kate. Hi, Ashley. I got your e-mail invitation – thanks!" she said.

"You're welcome," I told her with a smile. "Do you think you can make it to our party?"

"I'll be there for sure – and I *love* that the girls are inviting the guys. I'm asking tons of boys, so we should have enough to dance with and—"

I turned and looked at Ashley, whose face had gone completely pale. "Um, did you just say you're inviting *tons* of boys?" I asked Rachel. "You were only supposed to invite one."

Rachel looked at me with a confused expression. "Well, your e-mail said to invite *guys*. Plural," she explained. "So I thought I'd invite the guys' basketball team. Then I asked my older brother if he'd come along and bring a couple of his friends, because some of them are really cute."

"Yeah, um, that sounds great!" Ashley said. She started pulling me away. "I'm sorry, Rachel, but we have to run now. See you later!"

Ashley and I raced down the hall. I knew

where we were headed. We had to get to the computer lab to check out the e-mail we sent.

"We didn't," I said as we ran.

"We couldn't have," Ashley agreed. We raced into the lab and grabbed a seat at one of the terminals. Ashley signed on to our e-mail account in record time. She pulled up our "Sent Mail".

Suddenly, there it was on the screen: our latest e-mail update about our sweet sixteen party. Ashley ran her finger along the message until she got to the important line:

"Please invite the guys of your choice," she read.

"Rachel was right! It's *guys* – plural!" I wailed.

Several heads popped up from behind computer monitors as people strained to see what was going on.

"Mary-Kate," Ashley whispered, "the entire school is going to come to our party now. The entire city! We can't have a party for all those people. What are we going to do?

mary-kateandashley

Sweet 16
WISHES AND DREAMS

Kathy Clark

HarperCollins*Entertainment*
An Imprint of HarperCollins*Publishers*

A PARACHUTE PRESS BOOK

chapter one

"Calm down, Mary-Kate." I opened my purple notebook to my "Sweet Sixteen Party – To-Do" list. "Here's what we have to do. If we just follow this list, everything will be all right."

Together we read the list.

(1) Go to post office – get invitations back.

(2) Call Wilson!

(3) Redo the guest list to include boys.

(4) Mail out new invitations.

Mary-Kate pointed to the first item on the list. "See, we already have a problem," she complained. "How are we going to get the invitations back? They're sitting in the post office right now!

"The city bus lurched to a stop at a red light. It was Friday afternoon, and Mary-Kate and I were rushing to the post office.

Our party planner, Wilson Miller, mailed our

party invitations that afternoon. Wilson was planning our sweet sixteen as a favour to Dad. You would think that throwing a party would be easy with the help of a professional planner. But somehow Mary-Kate and I made it very complicated.

At first we wanted to have an all-girl sweet sixteen – so we invited fifty girls. The invitations addressed to those fifty girls were sitting in the post office, ready to be delivered.

But then Mary-Kate and I changed our minds. She wanted to invite her boyfriend, Jake Impenna – and I wanted to invite my new boyfriend, Ben. How could we celebrate our sweet sixteen without them? So we wanted to uninvite half the girls and invite twenty-five boys.

The problem was, we didn't tell Wilson in time. And once the girls received their invitations, there would be no way we could uninvite them. That would be mortifying!

The bus stopped in front of the post office. Mary-Kate looked determined. "Operation Rescue-the-Invites begins," she announced.

"Next?" a mail clerk behind the counter called.

Ashley and I sprinted up to the counter. As we approached the clerk, I noticed that she was wearing a yellow smiley-face button on her cardigan sweater. She had another pin next to it that said SERVICE WITH A SMILE – GUARANTEED. I hoped she was as friendly and cheerful as her sweater said she was.

"May I help you?" the clerk asked.

"Yes, thank you – Nancy," I said, sneaking a peek at her name tag. "We have a problem. We're having a sweet sixteen party in a few weeks, and someone just dropped off the invitations here – to be mailed. But there's a *huge* mistake on them, so we've got to get them back."

"Hey! I think I see the invitations right over there!" Ashley pointed to a white box sitting on a metal cart behind the clerks' stations. "Those square envelopes that look like CD covers – that's them!"

I squinted at the cart and gasped. "That *is* them! Could we have them back, please?"

"Hold on, girls. We're not even sure those are the correct items," Nancy said. "And even if they were, I'm not allowed to—"

"Look!" Ashley grabbed my sleeve. "That's Wilson's logo on the side of the box. Those are *definitely* our invitations."

"Excellent! We can just take them back before anyone sees them," I said.

I smiled. This was all working out so easily!

Nancy shook her head. "No, girls, I'm afraid I can't help you. We're not allowed to return mail once it's been given to us."

"*What?*" I slumped against the counter.

I couldn't believe that Nancy wouldn't help us. Maybe I should tell her the whole story.

"My boyfriend broke up with me because of this mix-up. . . ." I said. I felt tears prickling the backs of my eyelids. "I told Jake the party was for girls only – but then Ashley invited her boyfriend, Ben, and Jake heard about it. Jake thought I lied to him! And now he isn't speaking to me!"

Nancy reached over and patted my arm. "That's terrible! You poor thing. My daughter went through a terrible break-up last month, too."

"So . . . you understand?" I looked at her and blinked away a tear. "You'll make an exception and give those envelopes back to us?"

"What? Oh, no." Nancy shook her head. "I'm sorry, girls, but there's nothing I can do."

I watched as one of the postal workers approached the metal cart. He pushed it around the counter and out into the hallway. I gulped. In a second, our invitations would be in a truck and on their way to fifty girls!

"Please," I begged. "My relationship is at stake here!"

"Not to mention our social lives!" Ashley added. "We will *not* be popular if we have to uninvite twenty-five girls from our party!"

"No one will ever talk to us again," I said. I leaned on the counter, did an extreme slump and tried to look as pathetic as I could. "We'll be complete outcasts." I paused. "Let's face it, Ashley. Our social life is now officially over."

Nancy's expression didn't change. She looked over our heads to the line that had formed behind us. "Next!" she called.

We shuffled down the counter, away from Nancy's window. I glanced over at the metal cart, where our invitations still sat. The postal worker had stopped in the hallway. The cart itself was within easy reach.

"Wait a second!" I whispered to Ashley. "We're not going anywhere yet. I have a plan."

"What is it?" Ashley asked in a soft voice.

"We have to cause a distraction," I whispered.

"Why?" Ashley wanted to know.

"Just do it!" I said.

Ashley walked towards the exit and then pitched forward to the floor, throwing her arms into the air with dramatic flair. "Yikes!" she cried as she tumbled forward on to the slick linoleum floor.

"Perfect," I said under my breath.

"Oh, dear. Are you all right?" the worker pushing the cart asked. He rushed over to check on Ashley, leaving the cart completely and totally unguarded.

Two more people – including Nancy – followed right behind.

"Don't move, Ashley!" I cried. "I'll call a doctor."

Ashley had just enough time to glance up at me with a confused look before the entire staff of clerks and customers crowded around her. "Honey, let me have a look at that ankle," Nancy said.

I ran towards the hallway where our invitations were abandoned. Excellent! No one had seen me. I tiptoed over to the metal cart. I grabbed the box of invitations.

I checked the return address on the envelopes to make sure I had the right box. Yes! They *were* our invitations! Now all I had to do was get them out of the post office!

With the box under my arm, I sneaked towards the front door.

"What do you think you're doing?" a man's deep voice bellowed.

I looked up, and came face to face with a stern-looking man in a brown suit.

"Exactly where do you think you're going with that box, young lady?" the man asked.

"Um . . . isn't this the mail drop?" I asked.

chapter two

"Look on the bright side, Mary-Kate. We may not have got the invitations back, but at least the postmaster didn't call our parents."

My sister and I were lying on my bed, trying not to get too upset about the invitation fiasco.

"I mean, who would have thought that taking mail back from the post office is a federal offence?" I asked.

"Whoop-de-doo," Mary-Kate mumbled. She was lying on her stomach with her face pressed into the duvet. I could barely hear her muffled voice. "I'm so thrilled."

"Hey, we're lucky they let us go," I reminded her.

Mary-Kate turned over on to her back. "Yeah. Lucky. I just feel so *lucky* right now," she said.

I whomped her with one of my pillows.

I knew she was upset about Jake – and I

totally understood. Mary-Kate was crazy about him, and he wouldn't talk to her! But I wasn't going to let her wallow in misery.

I moved over to my desk and flipped on my computer. I signed on to my e-mail account. "Plan A failed. So *now* we come up with Plan B."

Mary-Kate stared at the ceiling. She tossed a pillow up and down, thinking. "Maybe there's some way we can stop all the invitations from being put in people's mailboxes," she suggested.

"Could we slip the mailed invites out of everyone's mailboxes before they read them?" I asked.

Mary-Kate cleared her throat. "Ashley, I know you're organised and all. But I don't see how we can be *fifty* places at once when the mail is delivered."

"Okay, bad idea," I laughed. "Forget that."

I opened up a 'send mail' window on my computer. "I'm going to e-mail Brittany and Lauren," I said. "Maybe they can help us."

"Good idea," Mary-Kate said.

Brittany and Lauren were our best friends. They had the best ideas for salvaging any bad situation. We knew we could count on them to help us.

I had just entered Brittany's e-mail address, when an Instant Message flashed on the right side of my screen. It was from Ben! A smile spread across my face as I read:

Hey, Ashley – I saw that you were online so I

wanted to ask – how about going to the Eastside mall with me on Monday after the drivers' ed class?

"Who's it from?" Mary-Kate asked as she sat up on the bed.

"Ben," I told her excitedly.

Mary-Kate climbed off the bed. She grabbed my extra chair to sit beside me at the desk. "What did he say?"

"He wants me to go to the mall," I told her.

"So are you going?" Mary-Kate asked.

"Of course!" I said. I typed in my answer. Ben and I went to different schools, so for a boyfriend and girlfriend we didn't see each other often – except in drivers' ed on Mondays and Wednesdays.

I glanced at my calendar: I had only four more lessons of so-called behind-the-wheel instruction before our drivers' tests.

Mary-Kate sighed. "I wish Jake would ask me to meet *him* at the mall. Of course, he'd have to stop being mad at me before that would ever happen."

"Don't worry – you guys will get back together," I said.

"How can you be so sure?" Mary-Kate asked. "I'm not." She picked up the Magic 8-ball on my desk. "Will Jake and I get back together?" She swirled the ball around and looked at the cube floating inside for an answer.

"Reply hazy – try again later?" Mary-Kate groaned. "That's not what I wanted to see."

"You can't go by *that*," I said. Another IM blinked on to my screen. Ben again. *Okay – talk to you tonight*. We IM'd each other goodbye. Then I wrote to Brittany and Lauren, begging for our best friends' help.

After we sent the message, Mary-Kate leaned back in her chair. "Okay, so what else can we do?"

"Hold on, let me check." I grabbed my purple notebook and scanned the list I'd written on the bus. "We've got to call Wilson," I said.

"Of course!" Mary-Kate said.

I looked for his phone number in my address book. "Where do you think he'll be this time?" I asked.

Wilson, our party planner, has a totally cool life. We met him because of our dad, who's in the music business.

Wilson is a major jet-setter type. He plans parties for celebrities and travels all over the world to do it. But he never stays in one place long. He could be in his L.A. home office one day, skiing in the Alps the next, and backstage at a concert in New York City after that! We can usually reach him on his mobile, but we never know where it's going to ring!

Mary-Kate ran downstairs to grab another phone, so we could be on the line at the same time. Wilson's number rang four times. I had almost given up hope, when there was a click. "This is Wilson."

"Hey, Wilson!" I said. "This is Ashley."

"And this is Mary-Kate. Wilson, we have a complete disaster on our hands!" she said.

"What? Hold on a second; let me find a quiet place where I can talk," Wilson said. In the background, I could hear loud music playing, and then people shouting to each other and applause. Then there was a click, as if Wilson had gone into a separate area and closed a door. "Now. What did you say about a disaster? Tell me the problem and I'll help."

"Okay, great." Mary-Kate quickly told Wilson about us changing our minds *after* he sent out fifty invitations. "So we either have to uninvite twenty-five girls – which we don't want to do, because that's rude and everyone will hate us. Or we have to invite fifty guys now, in order to have an equal number of girls and guys. That means we'll have to have one hundred guests, which is one *insanely huge* party!"

"Well, you're right, you can't *un*invite people," Wilson said. "So if you want to add guys, we have two problems. First, we need to clear this with your mom and dad. Second, we'll need to find a new place for the party."

"And we need to let everyone know that the

invitation they're about to get is totally *wrong*," I pointed out. "But how do we do that?"

"Hmm. Hold on a sec." Wilson was humming and tapping something against his phone. He didn't say anything for a minute, and I started to worry.

In the meantime, an IM from Brittany popped up on my computer screen.

That's when it hit me – the perfect solution!

"I know!" I yelled. "I've got it!"

Wilson laughed. "That was totally loud, so this better be good," he teased.

"It is," I said. "We can use e-mail! We can send an e-mail to all the people on our list – telling them that the invitation they're about to get in the mail doesn't tell the whole story – that there's new information!"

"Hey! That's perfect," Mary-Kate said. "We can tell them something like . . . our party has just become new and improved! Maybe that's what we can call it – Mary-Kate and Ashley's New and Improved Sweet Sixteen!"

Wilson laughed. "Excellent! An e-mail will create tons of buzz about your party. I don't even know why you guys called me – you've got this all figured out on your own."

"Not exactly!" I objected. "I mean, what do we *write* in this e-mail, since we don't know where the party is or *anything*?"

"Well, we can keep it vague for a while yet,"

Wilson said. "We've got a month until the party. So why don't you hint that people will have to stay tuned for the latest updates – that they'll need to check their e-mail daily for news on the big event. That'll build lots of hype."

"Okay, that sounds good," I agreed.

"And I'll start thinking of places we can have this new, bigger party," Wilson continued. "If we can stall people for a little while, that'll give us time to find a new location."

"Okay. When you say bigger . . . how much bigger?" I asked. I was worried about whether Mom and Dad would go for this!

"Well, it's like Mary-Kate said. Since you already invited fifty girls – and you can't take those invitations back – you should probably think about inviting fifty guys," Wilson said.

"Which means we have to ask Mom and Dad if we can have a hundred guests instead of fifty," Mary-Kate added. She looked at me and grimaced. Suddenly this didn't sound so easy any more.

"Guys, you're going to have to act fast. I'll work up a list of new locations – you talk to your parents, okay? As soon as possible." He covered the phone briefly and yelled, "Be right there." Then he came back on the line. "I hate to run, girls, but I'm in charge of a backstage party that starts in five minutes," Wilson said. "So – you'll talk to your parents about this tonight and don't send out the e-mail until we talk again – I'll be in the office in a few days and we'll meet then, okay?"

Mary-Kate and I said goodbye, then hung up our phones.

I looked at Mary-Kate. "So. Are you going to ask Mom if we can add fifty guests and have the party somewhere else, or am I?"

"We'll both do it. At dinner tonight," Mary-Kate said.

"Are you sure *you* don't want to do the talking?" I asked with a pleading look.

"All right, I'll do it," Mary-Kate said. "But you owe me."

"Deal," I agreed.

"And how was your day, Mom?" I smiled brightly at her as I stirred my bowl of pasta that night at dinner. "Everything okay at work today?"

Mom works at the Sunshine Day Care Centre. All the little kids there totally love her.

"I had a great day," she said. "Everything went exactly the way it was supposed to. Thanks for asking!"

"Oh, no problem," I said. "Boy, this pasta is good. It's *amazing*, actually."

"Thank you, Mary-Kate, but it's just my regular recipe. You must be hungry." Mom laughed. "So, what did you girls do after school today?"

Not much, I thought. *Just nearly got arrested for stealing some mail*. I smiled nervously. "Oh, nothing interesting," I said. "Very ordinary stuff. Homework. You know."

Under the table, Ashley nudged my foot with hers. I knew she wanted me to ask Mom about the new party plan, but I couldn't – not yet. I was working my way up to it.

"So I was thinking about your girl power theme this afternoon, after work," Mom announced. "I did some surfing online for decorating ideas. I want this place to look *really* cool for your party."

I gulped. We had to tell Mom we couldn't have the party here – and she was looking forward to it so much.

"So what did you come up with?" Dad asked as he passed the basket of garlic bread to Mom.

"Well, we can have Wilson get some stand-up cutouts of female superheroes," Mom said. "Like Wonder Woman, Super Girl. Maybe we could place them at the entrance to different rooms. I don't want the cartoon thing to seem young, though – so we'll contrast with photos of famous women – music celebrities, actresses, writers, politicians – a giant collage, maybe." She passed the bread to Ashley and smiled.

"Umm . . . great," Ashley mumbled. She set

down the basket without taking a piece of garlic bread.

"There's just so much to do. It's got to look perfect. We'll have to clear out some furniture to make room for dancing and mingling," she went on. "Right?"

"Of course," I murmured.

Ashley nudged me under the table again. I looked at her and shrugged. Mom seemed so happy. What was I supposed to do – tell her to just forget about her plans?

"What do you girls say?" Dad asked. "Mom's ideas sound good to me." He glanced from me to Ashley and back again.

"Yeah, they're, um, great," I said. *Do it, Mary-Kate!* I told myself. *Just tell them – you goofed and now you need to invite a hundred people to the party!* But I couldn't. I had to change the subject – and fast.

"So, speaking of our birthday. Is it time for us to begin the yearly present hunt?" I asked, stalling for time.

Every year since we were little, we've had this game with our parents. They always hide our birthday presents, and we always try to find them. "I was thinking you got us something like electronic organisers for our birthday. We'd probably never be able to find those, they're so small."

My mother shook her head. "Nope."

16

"Okay . . . let's see. How about clothes? Always possible. Or a trip somewhere? Wait – I know. New mountain bikes! Those are pretty hard to hide, though." I looked at Dad. "Well? No hints at all?"

He shrugged and took a sip of water. His face started to turn red. "We don't have any hints, because, uh, we didn't buy you guys a present this year."

I started laughing. Dad is the world's worst liar – he always blushes when he tries to, and he can barely get the words out without stammering a little. "Oh, sure, Dad," I teased him. "Right."

"What? I'm . . . I'm serious," he said, his face getting even redder.

"I know!" Ashley snapped her fingers. "You probably got us tickets to your music festival."

Dad shook his head. "Oh, no. No. Nope."

"Actually, Dad and I thought the sweet sixteen party would be your gift this year," Mom said, coming to his rescue.

I glanced at Ashley. We cared about the party a hundred times more than any present. And Mom and Dad were being so generous with us about it. How could we ask them to do anything more?

But we had to find a new place to hold the party right away – or there wouldn't be a party at all!

I could read the panic in Ashley's eyes. She had the same question burning in her mind – *What are we going to do?*

17

chapter three

"You know what I think?" I asked.

"That I look awful in green?" Mary-Kate turned around in front of the three-way mirror to check the fit of the shiny green strapless dress she had tried on. "Because this colour is terrible on me. Totally."

"Actually, I was thinking that I look like a football player." I frowned at the short puffy sleeves of the blue dress I had tried on.

"You do not," Mary-Kate said. "A hockey player, maybe."

We both laughed, and each grabbed another dress to try on from the rack outside the dressing room. "Finding the perfect party dress – take six!"

I said as we ducked into our separate room to change.

We were with Mom on Saturday at a cool boutique called Kick, shopping for our sweet

18

sixteen dresses. So far we'd tried on five apiece, and hadn't liked any of them. I stepped back and looked at the pale yellow sleeveless linen dress I had tried on. It wasn't me, and it definitely wasn't Mary-Kate.

I walked out of the dressing room just as Mary-Kate came out in a sparkling black dress. "I think this would be good – *if* we were ten years older," Mary-Kate said, turning in front of the mirror.

"Same with this one," I said. "Golf, anyone?"

Mom came over to us, carrying two identical dresses. "Hey, look what I found. This is perfect," she said. She showed us a royal blue backless dress with a halter neck and a long, flowing blue skirt. The fabric was silk, and patterned with tiny white stars. "Any interest at all?"

"I don't know. It's kind of long, isn't it?" Mary-Kate asked. She glanced at me.

"It's pretty, though," I said as Mom handed one of the dresses to me. The tiny white stars on the dress sparkled in the light.

"I brought one for each of you, so you could try them on at the same time," Mom said. "I really think this dress would be so beautiful on both of you."

"I don't know . . ." Mary-Kate frowned and held the dress up against her.

"Just try it!" Mom laughed. She gently pushed Mary-Kate towards her dressing room door.

"Okay, okay," Mary-Kate said.

I closed my dressing-room door and changed

out of the yellow dress. Then I took the dark-blue one off its hanger. As soon as I slipped it over my shoulders and fastened the halter tie behind my neck, I knew it was the dress for me. I gazed at my reflection in the narrow full-length mirror. I could just imagine Mary-Kate and me making a grand entrance at the party in these dresses. And then I'd be dancing with Ben. . . .

With every step I took, the silk fabric flowed around my body. I felt totally glamorous – like a movie star walking onstage to accept an Oscar.

"Wow!" Mom said as I came out of the dressing room. "You look gorgeous." Mary-Kate walked out a second later and twirled around. "You look gorgeous, too!" Mom said.

Mary-Kate and I looked at each other. "Well?" I asked excitedly. "What do you think?"

"I can't believe it. This dress is amazing!" Mary-Kate said. "I definitely love it. How about you?"

"I love it, too," I said.

"That could be a problem," Mom worried.

"Maybe not," I said. "I mean . . . we haven't done this in a really, really long time. And you might think it's silly and babyish . . . but I think we should both wear this dress to the party."

"You do, Ashley?" Mom asked.

I nodded. "It makes sense for our sweet sixteen. Because if we wear the same dress, neither one of us will look more important or more special or—"

"More anything than the other?" Mary-Kate finished.

"Yeah. We'll just be who we are, which happens to be nearly identical – and it'll sort of call attention to our bond as sisters. Not to mention that these dresses look really cool. But if you hate the idea, then forget I ever mentioned it."

Mary-Kate grinned. "I think it's a great idea. And it's going to make it way easier for us to pick out our jewellery and shoes, because we can just get two of everything."

Mom dabbed at her eyes with a tissue. "I think it's a very sweet idea. And I don't think you'll regret it for one second." She gave a little sniffle. "I can't wait to see you walk into your party in those!"

Mom pulled the back of my dress a little tighter. "You might need a few little alterations to make these fit perfectly – I'll get the saleswoman. But you know, once the alterations are done . . . and all the *house* alterations are done . . . this is going to be one amazing night."

I glanced at Mary-Kate, feeling a little uneasy. We still needed to ask Mom if we could add fifty guests to our party – *and* find a new place to have it!

"We have to tell her," I said.

"Okay, but you go first this time," Mary-Kate said.

"What do you mean, *this* time?" I said. "You never said anything to her last night at dinner."

"Oh. Well, you go first anyway," Mary-Kate insisted.

"No way! *You* go first," I said.

"Girls! I'm right here," Mom interrupted. "What do you need to say to me?"

I smiled nervously. "Can we wait until we get home so we can talk about it with Dad, too?"

Maybe, if I stalled a little longer, I could think of a better way to explain the reason we'd goofed.

"So what we'd like to do, if it's okay with you guys, is invite an equal number of boys to our party," I explained to Mom and Dad on Saturday afternoon. "But we already invited fifty girls, so that would mean we'd have a hundred guests. Which I know is a really big number—"

"A *hundred* guests?" Dad's eyes widened. "Are you serious?"

"Yes," Mary-Kate admitted. "We're sorry – we messed up because we got our signals crossed. And the thing is that we already invited fifty girls, so we have to stick to that."

Mom nodded. "Yes, you do. And if you want an equal number of boys . . . Well, what do you think?" she asked Dad.

He didn't say anything for a minute, and I held my breath.

"I guess it's all right with me," he finally

agreed. "But doesn't that mean we need to have the party somewhere else?"

"Yes, I think so," Mom said. "Because the idea of a hundred sixteen-year-olds in this house is a little much."

"I know. We're really sorry, Mom," Mary-Kate said. "We didn't mean to make you do all that work for nothing."

Mom waved this away. "I didn't do that much – don't worry about it."

"I'm sure Wilson can help you locate another venue," Dad said. "There is one thing to keep in mind, though."

"What's that?" Mary-Kate asked.

"Well, the party was originally planned for fifty guests," Dad began. "And you can invite as many boys as you like. But you'll have to stick to the original budget we made. That won't be easy if you have twice as many guests as you'd planned for."

I got a sinking feeling, but Mary-Kate took the news in her stride. "No problem," she said. "We can do it. Right, Ashley?"

"Sure," I agreed, trying to think of ways we could cut corners to make our money stretch. "It won't be easy, but—"

"Wilson's an expert on this," Dad said. "You three will have to work together to figure this out."

Mary-Kate nodded. "Okay. Sounds like a plan."

"Good." Dad looked pleased. "By the way, girls, I've been meaning to ask you . . . how are your driving lessons going?"

"Great!" Mary-Kate replied. "Our classroom work is done. We only have three more driving lessons before the big test, but I'm not worried. I *love* driving."

Three more lessons, I thought. Mary-Kate sounded so ready. *Why do I feel like I need* thirty *more lessons?*

"My two little girls – driving!" Mom sighed. "I can't believe it."

"Better get used to it, Mom," Mary-Kate joked. "I'm going to be entering NASCAR races soon."

Mom rolled her eyes, laughed, and turned to me. "How about you? Do you love driving, too?"

"Not exactly. But I definitely like it," I said. I thought about a couple of the disastrous things that had happened during my lessons. First I'd pulled on to the wrong side of the street. Then I'd knocked over Ben's mailbox. The lessons had gone better since then, but I still didn't feel confident about passing the test.

"So you'll both be ready for your driving tests?" Dad asked.

Mary-Kate nodded. "I can't *wait* to get my licence. There's just one thing I'm worried about, though."

"What's that?" Mom asked, concerned.

"That my licence photo will come out as badly as Dad's did," Mary-Kate teased.

Mom and Dad started laughing. I laughed, too, but I was thinking, *Is that really all she's worried about – a bad I.D. photo? Because what I'm worried about is passing the test!*

I tossed and turned in bed that night, visions of our sweet sixteen flashing before my eyes. Ashley and I appeared in our beautiful dresses, floating down a long staircase. Ben stood at the foot of the stairs and reached for Ashley's hand. I reached out my hand, but no one was there to take it. Ben and Ashley danced away, leaving me standing there alone.

I flicked on my nightstand light. Sometimes I felt a little restless on Sunday nights, but this was ridiculous. I'd been lying in bed for an hour and I hadn't even closed my eyes yet.

I couldn't stop thinking about Jake. I knew I'd see him the next day at school, and I was dying to talk to him – if only he'd let me! I really missed him. I knew he was hurt, and I felt terrible about it. But if he'd only let me explain, he wouldn't be hurt any more!

I flopped back against my pillow, groaning with frustration.

Maybe I shouldn't wait until school tomorrow,

I suddenly thought. What if I wrote him an e-mail *now*? That would be a lot less nerve-racking than trying to talk to him.

I got out of bed and turned on my computer. I pulled my robe around my shoulders and started to type:

Dear Jake—

Please don't delete this!

I know you're really angry and hurt because you think I don't want you at our party – but you're so wrong! I want you there more than anyone else. It was just a big misunderstanding between Ashley and me.

I told you that we'd decided not to invite any guys because I thought that was what she wanted. I didn't know that at the very same time she'd changed her mind and invited Ben.

My shoulders slumped as I reread what I'd written. I could just see Jake signing on to his e-mail, seeing a message from me, and hitting the Delete key.

Who was I kidding? An e-mail wasn't going to make it up to Jake. I needed to see him in person, meet him face to face.

I'll find Jake at school tomorrow, I told myself. *And no matter what, we're going to talk!*

chapter four

"Okay, Mary-Kate. Let's start with the facts. Your party is two weeks from Thursday and you don't know where you're having it yet?" Brittany raised her perfectly shaped eyebrows.

It was Monday afternoon, and school was over for the day. Brittany and I settled on a picnic table outside. She's African-American, with dark brown eyes, tight, short curls, and a no-nonsense attitude.

"At least it's okay with Mom and Dad," I told her. "Wilson's giving us a list of party places tomorrow." I tapped my feet nervously against the bench. A bunch of boys were playing basketball on a court nearby. One of them was Jake.

As soon as the game's over, I'm going to talk to him, I told myself. But every time I even *thought* about talking to him, I got so nervous my palms started sweating.

"Well," Brittany said. "You better hope this Wilson guy comes up with something good." She zipped up her orange hooded sweater.

"He will," I said. "I just hope the best places aren't already booked." I watched Jake dribble the ball towards the basket. He looked totally cute, wearing a black T-shirt, faded jeans and sneakers.

If we could just spend five minutes together, I knew I could clear up this whole misunderstanding. "Five minutes – is that so much to ask?" I muttered out loud.

"Five minutes for what?" Brittany looked puzzled.

"Sorry," I said. "Just thinking about talking to Jake."

"You're losing it, Mary-Kate," Brittany teased me. "Don't worry – you'll get to talk to him."

"I know – I'm just nervous."

Jake made a perfect lay-up. There was a loud cheer. The game was over. The guys picked up their jackets and backpacks and headed off in different directions.

"Here goes nothing," I told Brittany as I hopped off the picnic table.

"Good luck!" Brittany said.

I walked over to Jake, who was busily repacking something in his backpack. My stomach was doing flips. "Hey, Jake," I called, trying to sound casual. "Good game – that last lay-up was great!"

28

He stood and stared at me. His grey eyes didn't light up at all, the way they did before all this happened. "Thanks," he said.

"Um-um – I was wondering if you wanted to do something. Together," I stammered. "Like grab a slice of pizza, maybe. Do you have time?"

"I can't," he said. "I have to get home and watch Tristan and Caitlin now."

"Oh." I'd met his little brother and sister once before. They were really cute. "Well, maybe tonight? Or maybe I could go with you," I said. "I think we really need to talk."

"Yeah. Well, I really have to get home. I'm kind of late," Jake said quickly. He brushed past me and took off down the sidewalk towards his red Jeep.

I stared after him, my pulse drumming in my head. Why wouldn't he give me a chance?

I wanted to run after him, to make him listen to me. But I stopped myself. There was no point in chasing after him. Jake still didn't want to talk to me – and there was no way I could change his mind.

Brittany crossed the grass to where I stood frozen in place. "Tell me that wasn't as bad as it looked," she said.

I faced her, blinking back tears. "He totally blew me off," I told her. "A week ago we were so happy together, and now—"

Brittany threw an arm around my shoulders. "This is not right," she said. "Maybe Jake's not the guy you thought he was. Maybe you should move on."

But I didn't want to move on. I still wanted to get back together with Jake. And I wasn't going to give up on us – not yet!

"So what's happening with the party of the year?" Ben asked as we walked out of the CD store in the mall on Monday afternoon. Right after our driving lesson we'd caught the bus over. Ben switched his bag of CDs from his right hand to his left, and then reached for my hand.

"We still have a few things to figure out," I admitted. "Like where to have the party! We've got seventeen days. But who's counting?"

"Wait – isn't it at your house?" Ben asked.

"It was going to be," I said. "But now it isn't."

"Well, where are you thinking of having it?" Ben asked.

"We don't even know!" I confessed. "But don't tell anyone. We want people to think the party location is a big secret. Promise?"

"I won't tell anyone," Ben swore.

"We're meeting with Wilson tomorrow – he's going to give us some ideas." We rounded the corner to the food court. "Hey!" I cried as I spotted Lauren. She was sitting in a chair, sipping a soda, a shopping bag at her feet. Her long, wavy brown hair was wrapped up into a bun, held together with a pencil.

"Hey, guys!" Lauren said. "What are you up to?"

"About twenty-eight dollars so far." Ben gestured to the bag with CDs he was holding. "Plus tax."

Lauren and I both laughed. "We were thinking about getting some frozen yogurt," I told Lauren. "Do you want us to get you anything?"

"You guys hang out," Ben offered. "I'll get the frozen yogurt. Do you want something, Lauren?"

"Just water, if that's okay," she said.

"Gee, I don't know if I can afford that." Ben grinned. He went to the yogurt counter and waited in line. I took a seat across from Lauren.

"You know what?" Lauren leaned back in her chair. "Ben is the nicest guy."

"Yeah, he is," I agreed.

I gazed at Ben as he stood in line. "And he's definitely cute," I said.

"You're so lucky you ended up in that drivers' ed class together," Lauren said. "It's like . . . fate."

I thought about it for a second. "Fate." That was a word people used when they were talking about finding the love of their lives. Was Ben the love of my life? We'd been dating for about a month, but I wasn't sure.

"And it's so perfect how Mary-Kate found Jake, and then right afterwards, you found Ben – you know?" Lauren asked.

I nodded in agreement.

"Speaking of Mary-Kate and Jake . . . are they talking yet?" Lauren asked.

"No, and it's awful," I said. "She's so miserable. I mean, she thinks about him *all* the time. Have you seen her notebooks? They're covered with Jake's name!"

"She's totally crazy about him." Lauren sighed. "Just like you and Ben. It's so romantic."

I glanced up as Ben walked back towards our table. *He's great, but I don't think about him day and night*, I realised. My notebooks were full of class notes and to-do lists, not Ben's name surrounded by hearts. I didn't e-mail him twenty times a day the way Mary-Kate and Jake did before their fight. Mary-Kate said her heart did flip-flops every time she saw Jake. When I saw Ben, I felt fine – but no flip-flops. No nothing.

Mary-Kate and I aren't exactly alike, I told myself. *So maybe we don't act the same about boyfriends. We're different, that's all.*

But a little alarm went off in the back of my mind: *What if I'm trying to convince myself that I'm crazy about Ben – but I'm really not?*

What if he's not the guy for me after all?

chapter five

"It's great to see you guys again," Wilson said. "Even if it is kind of an emergency."

Ashley and I sat down across from Wilson's big oak desk on Tuesday afternoon. Dad had picked us up after I got home from my driving lesson. He waited outside Wilson's office, doing business on his mobile. Wilson's office was in his house – a gorgeous Spanish-style ranch house.

Wilson himself was totally hip – in a post-college-guy sort of way. He was dressed in baggy cargos, a maroon T-shirt and a well-worn cream-coloured baseball cap.

"Let's get right down to it." Wilson pulled a sheet of paper out of a folder. "You have two weeks and two days until your party. I've made up a list of party locations that fit a hundred people *and* your budget *and* should be available on short notice."

He handed the sheet to me, and I promptly handed it to Ashley. After all, she's the organised one.

"This is so awesome!" I said. "Thanks."

"Do you think we can find a place in such a short amount of time?" Ashley asked.

"Definitely. Just remember – you have a limited budget. So if some of these places don't seem perfect, don't focus on their flaws – think about their potential. With some window-dressing and the right lighting, any place can look amazing," Wilson said. He poured himself a glass of orange juice from the pitcher on his desk. "So, what information do you want to put on your new e-mail invitations?"

Ashley tapped her pen against her glittery purple notebook. "Well, we have a really good start." She opened the notebook and read out loud: "'Mary-Kate and Ashley's New and Improved Sweet Sixteen.'"

Wilson raised his eyebrows, as if he were waiting for more. "Go on," he said.

"We can't," I said. "That's all we have."

Wilson laughed. "I like it." He took off his cap and ran his hand through his long blond hair. "But it doesn't say much, because we don't have much to say. Not until you know where the party will be, right?"

"Right," I agreed. "That's the problem. So we

need to say something that *sounds* exciting. Something that sounds as if we know exactly what we're doing—"

"—but not actually say anything at all!" Ashley finished.

"Ah, the fine art of publicity," Wilson said.

"How about 'Mary-Kate and Ashley's New and Improved Sweet Sixteen. Hot new location!'" I began, thinking hard. "'Hot new guests! Watch your e-mail for more details.'"

"That's great!" Ashley said.

"Excellent," Wilson agreed. "So we have new invitations. You're working on finding a new place for the party. There's just one more problem."

"There is?" Ashley said.

"Have you made up a list of the boys you're going to invite?" Wilson asked.

Ashley glanced at the to-do list in her notebook. "I have that written down here. Really."

"Why don't you tackle it tonight?" Wilson suggested. "You'll want to invite the guys as soon as possible, so they can set aside the date."

"Right!" Ashley put a star next to that item in her notebook.

I smiled nervously. There was only one boy I wanted on the guest list: Jake. If you subtracted Ben, that left forty-eight boys we needed to invite. Did we even *know* forty-eight boys?

• • •

"What about Brandon – that guy two houses down?" I asked. "I mean, he's always been nice to us.

How many would that make?" Mary-Kate asked me.

We were in my bedroom on Wednesday night. I was sitting at the computer, entering the names as we thought of them. "That makes twenty-three," I told her.

"Okay. So there's Mark from the drama club," Mary-Kate said.

"Mark?" I asked.

"Yeah. The one we met when we were acting in the play last year. He was the . . . um . . . assistant director or something," Mary-Kate said. "Remember how funny he was? He'd be great at a party."

"I think you mean Mike. He was the stage manager," I reminded her. "And he moved. He doesn't go to our school any more."

"Oh. So that's why I haven't seen him around." Mary-Kate frowned. "All right. Let me think. There's always Melvin."

"Melvin? You mean our third cousin Melvin, whose idea of fun is playing video games for seven hours straight?" I asked in horror. "No way! We're not *that* desperate."

"We're not?" Mary-Kate asked. "Because it kind of seemed like we were. I mean, *I* can't think of anyone else. Unless we invite everyone in school, which seems very second-grade to me, like when we gave our whole class valentines."

"Tacky," I agreed.

"Exactly," Mary-Kate said.

"We don't know enough boys – you're right," I admitted. "But if we asked our friends about boys *they* know, I bet we'd come up with more than enough." Then it hit me – that was the perfect thing to do. Ask for assistance – in our new invitations!

I jumped out of my chair. "Brainstorm!" I yelled. I leaped on to my bed and started jumping up and down on it.

"What?" Mary-Kate stared at me as if I'd just sprouted another head. "What is it?"

"We can make it a Sadie Hawkins party!" I said. "Our theme is girl power, right? Well, it's a girl power thing to ask a guy out instead of waiting for him to ask you, isn't it?"

Mary-Kate shrugged. "Sure."

"So this is just like another twist on the theme. And if everyone we already invited brings a date, or a friend, then there will be a totally equal number of boys and girls at our party," I explained, "just like we want there to be."

"Hey – that's a *brilliant* idea!" Mary-Kate cried. She climbed on to the bed and started to jump beside me.

Yikes! The bed groaned, then lurched a little to one side, as if it were about to collapse.

I laughed. "Maybe we're getting too old for this." We both got off the bed and sat back down at my desk.

"First things first," I said. I deleted our list of boys to invite. Then I opened a new e-mail and typed in the announcement about our party and its secret location. We told everyone to watch her e-mail for further announcements. Then we said that in keeping with our girl power theme, everyone should invite the guy of her choice to the party, whether as a date or as a friend.

"Done!" I quickly read the message over for typos and pressed the Send button.

"Great. Now we just have to find a place to *put* everyone." I heard a flicker of anxiety in Mary-Kate's voice. "Or there won't *be* any party!"

"We've got to work fast," I agreed. "I'll start on Wilson's list tomorrow afternoon while you're at your driving lesson. Mom promised to drive me around to check out a few of the places. She said she wants to help out as much as she can, since the party will be our only present this year."

"Yeah – right." Mary-Kate laughed. "I don't believe that for a second. The more she says that, the more sure I am that it isn't true."

"I don't know," I protested. "They seem pretty serious about it."

"Ashley, did you *see* Dad's face when I asked about it? He was redder than a tomato," Mary-Kate said. "Mom and Dad love playing this game with us every year. I think they're just trying to throw us off the trail."

"Well, in that case . . . where should we look first?" I asked.

Mary-Kate grinned. "Mom and Dad aren't home," she said. "It's a perfect chance to check the birthday closet."

There was a closet in the basement that Mom and Dad had used before to hide our birthday gifts. They locked the door, of course, but we knew where they hid the key – on top of the water heater. They just didn't know that we knew.

We sneaked downstairs, even though no one was home to catch us. I shoved Dad's big toolbox across the floor to the water heater. Then I stepped on it and felt around for the key.

"Got it!" I whispered, handing the key to Mary-Kate.

"We probably shouldn't be doing this." Mary-Kate slipped the key into the lock and slowly pushed the door open. "But it's a tradition, right?"

"Right." I flicked on the light switch. "Uh-oh."

The closet was completely empty – except for a large neon-pink piece of poster board with the words NICE TRY! written on it in black marker.

"They're on to us!" I cried. "They know we've looked here before!"

"Yeah, but this means they *are* giving us a present," Mary-Kate said. "Come on. That's enough snooping for one day."

We trooped back upstairs. Mary-Kate stopped in the kitchen for a snack. I went to my room. Wilson's list of party places lay on my desk, glowing in the light from my computer screen.

We'd better find something tomorrow, I thought, staring at the list. *Or we'll have one hundred party guests all dressed up with nowhere to go!*

chapter six

"Is this it, Ashley?" Mom asked. She pulled the car into a big crowded parking lot on Thursday afternoon.

I reread the address on the piece of paper in my lap. "This is it," I told her. "The last place on Wilson's list. Pizza Pals."

I glanced through the windshield, and my heart sank. A huge statue of a green dinosaur stood guard outside the restaurant. The words PREHISTORIC PIZZA PAL were painted on its belly. A Pals Playground with seesaws and a slide stood on the right side of the restaurant.

"What do you think, honey?" Mom asked.

"This isn't exactly the image we were going for," I complained. "It's a kiddie restaurant!"

The last two places hadn't been much better – we'd seen a sports and recreation centre that smelled like chlorine, and an old warehouse space that was cool-looking but a little too grungy for Mom's taste.

Before that, Mom and I had visited three other restaurants, a bowling alley and a botanical garden. The garden was beautiful, but there were several restrictions on what we could do if we had our party there. The biggest problem was that dancing wasn't allowed. I couldn't see having our sweet sixteen without dancing to celebrate!

Then again, maybe I can live without dancing, I thought as the Pizza Pals dinosaur loomed above me.

"Uh, Mom?" I said as we got out of the car. "I'm not sure if we need to go inside. I mean, this pretty much says it all." I tapped the dinosaur with my fingers.

"Well, it might be a little young, but remember – Wilson can transform a place," Mom said. "He wouldn't have put it on the list if he didn't think it was appropriate."

"Appropriate for what?" I muttered under my breath as we walked through the front door. "A kindergarten graduation?"

"Welcome to Pizza Pals!" A teenage girl wearing overalls and a striped T-shirt greeted us.

"Uh, thanks," I said, smiling at her.

"Hi, we'd like to talk to someone about renting your banquet room," Mom said with a polite smile. "Is the manager available?"

"You betcha!" she said. "Be right back." She zipped away on rollerskates.

"Mom, maybe we should think this over," I said. "Are you sure we can't fit a hundred people into our house?"

"Ashley, you've got to consider all your options." Mom looked around at all the families in the dining room. "You know, it sure is popular here!"

"With little kids," I said. I glanced at a clown entertaining a table of small children at a birthday party. Half of them were yelling, and the other half were crying. *Please let the banquet room be booked on June 13,* I thought. *I'll die if I have to have my party here!*

A minute or so later, the clown came over to me and Mom. "Hello, I'm Rick, the manager. I understand you're interested in renting the Pals Party Room?"

"Yes. This is for my daughters' sweet sixteen party," Mom said. "Would the room be available on June thirteenth?"

"Let me check." Rick went behind the host stand and flipped through a calendar.

I crossed my fingers. *Please say no. Please say no.*

"You're in luck!" Rick told us. "It's available."

"Great," I said. So much for crossing fingers.

"Let me show you the Pals Party Room, and if

you like it, you can put down a deposit to hold the room."

The only way we'll have our party here is if the restaurant is completely closed for the night, I thought as I tripped over a balloon. *And the clown called in sick.* But deep down I knew that this place was our last hope.

The banquet room wasn't as bad as I'd expected. It didn't have any personality at all, but that was okay – we could add all the decorations and flavour ourselves. There were several round tables, and a large open space that could be used for dancing.

"We have another entrance at the back here, so it's completely separate from the restaurant. And you can bring your own flowers, candles, et cetera. You can have it catered, or we can provide all the pizza you can eat," Rick explained. "And there's plenty of atmosphere if you plan on dancing." He pointed to the ceiling, where a sad and lonely-looking silver disco ball hung without moving. "You young kids love to dance, right?"

"Right," I said slowly. This place *could* work – in the sense that we could completely change it around to make it what we want. But . . .

"What do you think, Ashley?" Mom asked.

A vision flashed before my eyes – the elegant sweet sixteen I had always dreamed of. Girls in ball gowns,

44

boys in tuxedos, flowers and candles everywhere . . .

Then I faced the reality. A bare room in a pizza place.

I didn't want to admit it, but it was the best place we'd seen so far. If you could forget about the rollerskating waitresses and the giant dinosaur.

But then, everyone would be pulling into the Pizza Pals parking lot . . .

"I guess it might be okay." I groaned, not believing the words coming out of my mouth.

"I think so, too," Mom said. "I mean, it's not perfect, but it will fit your budget. And you really need to reserve a place now."

I pulled Mom aside. "Mom, I've been dreaming about my sweet sixteen since I was twelve," I whispered. "And this place . . . well, it doesn't fit in with my dream!"

Mom frowned. "I'm sorry, Ashley, but the party is two weeks away! The caterer needs to know where the party will be, not to mention your guests—"

"I'll make a deal with you," I offered. "If I can find a better place, we'll switch. But if I can't find something else in time, we'll have the party here. Okay?"

Mom thought it over. "On one condition," she said. She turned to the clown. "Excuse me, Rick. Is the deposit refundable?"

"Yes, of course," he said. "We just need three days' advance notice."

Mom turned back to me. "All right. We've got a deal. We'll reserve this now. If you can't find something else, the party will be here."

I bit my lip. *We are not having the party here,* I vowed. *I'll do everything I can to make sure of that!*

"Okay, Mary-Kate, you'll want to take a right at the next street," Ms. Junger instructed.

I flicked on the indicator and pulled the wheel to the right.

"Nicely done," Ms. Junger said. "We'll stay on this street for a few blocks."

"Okay – no problem." I kept driving along, enjoying being behind the wheel. But I couldn't help wondering how Ashley and Mom were doing. How many places had they seen so far? Had Ashley chosen one yet?

Hey, we could have a primo party spot already! I thought, my excitement rising. *Ashley could be standing in the perfect place at this very moment!*

"Take a right here," Ms. Junger instructed after we had been driving for a few minutes.

I signalled my turn and followed her instruction.

I had to pay close attention to the street signs

because I wasn't familiar with this section of town. I didn't know anyone who lived over here – not that I could think of, anyway. It was pretty, though, with lots of tall palm trees and winding streets.

"And turn left here," Ms. Junger said. I put on the indicator and glanced to the left. There, striding down the sidewalk, was a guy who looked exactly like Jake.

I gasped. *Hold on a second*, I thought as I peered out of the window. *That* is *Jake!*

"Left, Mary-Kate," Ms. Junger said. "Turn left here."

What was Jake doing *here*? I wondered. He didn't have any friends who lived in this neighbourhood.

"Mary-Kate, you missed that turn, so take the *next* left," Ms. Junger said.

I nodded at Ms. Junger's words, but I didn't actually hear them. My mind kept racing. If Jake didn't have any friends in this area, maybe he was here for another reason – and there was only one I could think of. Maybe he was here to see a new girlfriend—

"Stop here. Mary-Kate are you listening? Mary-Kate, stop. *Stop!*" Ms. Junger ordered me.

The car screeched to a halt. I broke out of my trance and stared at Ms. Junger. I winced, realising that she had stepped on the dual brake.

"Pull over here and we'll switch drivers," Ms. Junger said. "I told you to turn left twice and you didn't. You're not paying attention at all!"

Jerry, my classmate in the back seat, muttered, "Uh-oh," under his breath.

"I – I *was*," I said, "but just then I saw something, um, bizarre, and so . . ."

I pulled towards the curb. Ms. Junger told Jerry and me to trade places.

I got out of the car and glanced around. Jake was gone.

I climbed into the back seat and stared out of the window, watching for him.

We were nowhere near his neighbourhood. I racked my brain, trying to come up with some reason why Jake would be here. But my mind kept going back to the same thing. There was only one explanation that made sense.

He must be seeing another girl, I thought. *That's why he doesn't want to talk to me! Here I am, completely miserable over him, and he's already dating someone else!*

Tears pricked the backs of my eyelids. *That's crazy,* I told myself. *How could he have found someone else so soon?*

But what if my crazy thought was true? What if Jake really did have a new girlfriend?

chapter seven

I dropped my tray on to the cafeteria table Friday at lunchtime. "Have either of you guys heard that Jake has a new girlfriend?" Brittany, Lauren and Ashley stared up at me.

"Mary-Kate, what are you talking about?" Brittany asked. "Jake with a new girlfriend? Since when?"

"No way." Lauren shook her head. "He wouldn't. He couldn't."

"And what makes you think he *does*?" Brittany asked.

"Okay. Ashley's already heard this, but when I was taking my driving lesson yesterday, I *saw* Jake." I explained how I'd completely missed Ms. Junger's instructions because I was so busy watching Jake walk down the sidewalk. "He doesn't live anywhere near that neighbourhood," I said. "Why else would he be there?"

"Mary-Kate, come on," Brittany said. "He could have been out for a walk. Or visiting his grandmother. Or selling magazine subscriptions door to door. I mean, there are a dozen explanations that *don't* involve him having a new girlfriend."

"That's what *I* tried to tell her." Ashley sighed.

"I haven't heard anything around school, either," Lauren said. "But I guess you could always ask Todd Malone if you wanted to find out. He and Jake are good friends."

I wished I could ask Todd – I was dying to find out the truth. But Todd might tell Jake that I'd asked. "No way!" I groaned. "Then I'd look even more pathetic."

"Look, Jake does *not* have a new girlfriend," Brittany declared. "You guys are going to get back together. Just wait."

"I *hate* waiting," I wailed.

"We know," Brittany, Lauren and Ashley all chirped at the same time.

I laughed for the first time that day. Okay, so I can be a little impatient sometimes. Anybody would be in my place if she thought her boyfriend was seeing another girl. Especially if she liked him as much as I liked Jake. I couldn't relax until I found out the truth.

Lauren leaned across the table and whispered, "Have you guys decided where you're having the party yet?"

Ashley glanced around to make sure no one was eavesdropping. "I saw a bunch of places yesterday," she whispered. "But nothing was really *right*."

"Something had better be right soon," Brittany said. "You guys, there are less than two weeks until your party!"

"I know," I groaned. "We have to choose a place *now*."

"Mom put down a deposit at this place called Pizza Pals, but we're not having the party there unless we absolutely have to," Ashley said.

"Pizza Pals? Is that the place with the giant dinosaur out front and the skating waiters?" Lauren asked.

I held up my hand. "Please. Don't remind me."

"At least we have appointments to get our hair and nails done on our birthday," Ashley said. "And our dresses are ready – all the alterations are done!"

"Oh, yeah. That's great. Except you won't have a place to *wear* them unless you get moving," Brittany commented.

"Stop!" I tossed a french fry on to her tray. "We will have a place. Soon." I looked at Ashley and smiled. "Right?"

"Right. Sure." She smiled back at me. "And we'll pass our driving tests. And then we'll, you know . . . create world peace. In our spare time."

• • •

Ashley and I were walking down the hallway towards our lockers at the end of lunch period, when we ran into Melanie Han and Tashema Mitchell.

"Hey you guys, we're *so* excited about your party!" Melanie said.

"Getting updates by e-mail is so cool. How'd you come up with that idea?" Tashema asked.

"Oh, it just, um . . . came to us," I said.

"It's awesome. When's the next update?" Melanie asked.

"Soon." Ashley nudged me with her elbow. "But we can't tell you when, because that would ruin the surprise."

"I can't wait to find out where this party is," Tashema said.

I covered my mouth to stifle a laugh. *Neither can we!* I thought.

"Can't you give us a clue? A teensy tiny clue?" Tashema begged. "I want to pick out what I'm going to wear, and I need to make sure it's right."

"We'll be sending out another update in the next couple of days – so just keep checking your e-mail," Ashley said. "We'll give you plenty of advance notice, don't worry."

"Okay, cool." Melanie waved to us.

"I'm going to check it every hour, on the hour," Tashema said before she and Melanie walked off.

"Sounds like our plan is working great!" I said to Ashley. "No one suspects a thing!" We turned the corner at the end of the hall and nearly crashed right into Rachel Adams, who was walking towards us.

"Hey, Mary-Kate and Ashley. I got your invitation – thanks!" she said.

"You're welcome," I replied. Rachel was a good friend of mine from when I played on the basketball team. "Can you come?"

"I'll be there for sure – and I *love* your Sadie Hawkins idea. I'm inviting tons of boys, so we should have enough guys to dance with and . . ."

I turned and looked at Ashley, whose face had gone completely pale. "Um, did you just say you're inviting tons of boys?" I asked Rachel. "You were supposed to invite only one."

Rachel looked confused. "But your e-mail invite. It said to invite *guys*. Plural. So I thought I'd invite the guys' basketball team for a start. Then I thought of asking my older brother if he'd come and bring a couple of his friends, because some of them are really cute."

"Yeah, um, that sounds great!" Ashley said as she pulled me away. "I'm sorry, Rachel, but we have to run now. See you later!"

Ashley and I hurried down the hall. "We *didn't*," I groaned as we broke into a run.

"We *couldn't* have," Ashley said. We raced into

the computer lab and grabbed a seat at one of the terminals. Ashley signed on to her e-mail account in record time. She pulled up her 'sent mail'. Suddenly, there it was on the screen: our latest e-mail invitation. Ashley ran her finger along the invitation's text until she got to the important line:

"Please invite the guys of your choice."

"*Guys* – plural!" Ashley wailed.

Several heads popped up from behind computer monitors as people strained to see what was going on.

"Shh," a couple of people said.

"Oh no. The entire school is going to come to our party now. The entire city. The entire *world*!" Ashley whispered. "What are we going to do?"

chapter eight

"Mary-Kate, we should be out looking for party places," I complained later that afternoon. "Or we'll be stuck with Pizza Pals!"

The two of us stopped in front of a storefront window with MENU BY MARGO printed on the glass. Wilson had hired Margo to cater our party.

"This is important, too," Mary-Kate insisted, opening the door. "No matter where the party is, we're having at least a hundred guests. And Margo thinks we're having only fifty. We've got to let her know what's going on."

"Good afternoon, may I help you?" Margo asked, coming out of the kitchen. Her green chef's apron was dusted with flour.

"Hi." Mary-Kate smiled. "We booked you to cater our party on June thirteenth. I'm Mary-Kate Olsen, and this is Ashley."

"Of course!" Margo nodded. "You're having the sweet sixteen party at your house, aren't you?"

"Right . . ." I began. "At least, that *was* the plan."

"Oh, really? What's changed?" Margo asked.

"Well, we can't have it at our house any more because we changed the number of guests. We were scheduled for a sit-down dinner for fifty, but now we have a *hundred* people coming to our party. We can't spend any more money on the food. So we're here to ask – do you think you'll still be able to cater the party for us?"

"Are you joking?" Margo said.

I held my breath. Was Margo going to cancel on us?

"Of course we can," she finished. "People's guest lists change all the time."

I let out a huge sigh. "Even though the party's less than two weeks away?"

"Sure. We'll just change the menu around to make it work. We're very flexible here – we have to be," Margo said. "Would you mind coming into the kitchen with me to talk about it? I'm on a tight deadline today."

Mary-Kate and I followed her to a large counter, where she was decorating a collection of tiny cheesecakes – each one with a different pattern on top. She was using orange and green icing to draw a carrot on one of them. "So, we've still got a couple of weeks, which is plenty of time. I've had people completely change their parties two *days* ahead of time. For now, you're thinking about a hundred, though?"

Mary-Kate nodded. "We hope it won't be bigger than that."

"Right. And is the party still going to be at your house?"

"No," I told her. "We haven't found a place to have it yet."

Margo stopped decorating the cheesecake and turned to us. "Now, that *is* a problem."

I cringed. "We're working on it."

"My staff and I need to know as soon as possible, so we can be prepared," Margo said.

"I understand," Mary-Kate said. "And we'll get it locked up really, really soon – we promise."

Margo nodded. "Good. In the meantime, let's think about the menu." She started decorating another mini-cheesecake. "For a big party it's fun to have different food stations, each decorated to go with the theme of the food. Your guests could travel between, say, a Mexican beach hut, where we'll be grilling chicken and veggie fajitas, and a Japanese sushi bar, and a New Orleans carnival stand with Cajun crawfish and gumbo – like that."

"Cool," I said, my mouth watering at the thought of all the food she'd just described.

"That really sounds like fun!" Mary-Kate commented. "And way too nice for the Pizza Pals banquet room," she added.

"Pizza Pals? What's that?" Margo asked.

"Just this place we're considering having the party," I said. "We don't like it that much, though."

"You know, if our friends invite too many guys, Pizza Pals won't be big enough for the party," Mary-Kate said. "There won't *be* a place big enough. We'll just have to pitch a tent on the beach and hope for the best!"

My eyes widened as I pictured the scene. A bonfire in the sand, dancing by the surf, the sunset over the ocean . . . "Mary-Kate – that's a brilliant idea! We can have the party in a tent on the beach!"

"We can?" Mary-Kate asked.

"Sure. We'll rent one of those giant white tents, and we can set it up right near the ocean. And if there are too many people to fit under the tent, then they'll just spill out on to the beach," I explained.

Margo nodded. "Your sister's right. It's an excellent idea – if you can pull it off in time."

"Do you know how much it would cost?" I asked her.

"Well, the beach is public property, and the tents are not that expensive. We might even have a few brochures from a tent rental company out front," Margo offered. "Now – I hate to cut this short, but I've really got to focus or I'm going to have ten very burned chickens. Keep in touch, girls – give us the location as soon as you can!"

"We will, I promise. Thanks so much!" I told her.

Mary-Kate and I couldn't get home fast enough. Our new party plan was ultracool. We couldn't wait to let everyone know about it. We had to send out the next party update!

"Give me another line from the brochure," I told Ashley.

Ashley peered at the tent rental flyer Margo had given us. We'd called them and found out that renting a tent was well within our budget. "'There's no better party decoration than the sun setting over the ocean.'"

"Hmm." I stared at my computer screen. I was writing an e-mail giving more details about the party. I wanted to whet everyone's appetite without giving too much away.

"Mary-Kate and Ashley Party Update," I typed. "The official location is a very cool place. Music: the sound of the crashing surf. Decorations: a view of the sun setting over the ocean. Stay tuned for exact location at a later date!"

Ashley read the e-mail over my shoulder. "That's good," she said.

I sent the e-mail to everyone on our list. "There. Everyone will be so psyched when they find out the location is the beach!"

Ashley leaned back on my bed and rested her head against the pillows with a contented sigh. "Isn't this great?" she said. "We're so close to being done. And everything's finally working out."

I rested my chin on the back of my desk chair. "We can just relax and start thinking about the easy stuff now."

Ashley raised her eyebrow. "Like passing our driving tests next week?"

I sighed. "And getting Jake back. I guess things aren't exactly easy yet." The phone rang, and I grabbed it from my dresser. "Hello?"

"Mary-Kate, is that you?"

"Hey, Wilson," I said. "How are you? *Where* are you?"

"Flying over Vegas, but never mind about that. Did you figure out—" he started to ask.

"Wilson, you won't believe it," I interrupted, "but we figured out *everything*." I explained about meeting with Margo, and how I'd got the idea to have the party on the beach. "We checked into renting a tent, and it's totally within our budget. Isn't that awesome?"

"Yeah, it sounds great," Wilson agreed.

"We thought so, too! So we sent out another update and—"

"But it would have been better if you'd thought of it a month ago," Wilson interrupted me. "Then we would have had time to get the permit you need to have a party on the beach."

"What?" I yelped.

"I'm sorry, girls. It's too late. We can't have the party on the beach, no matter how cool it would be."

I quickly tossed the phone to Ashley and sat back down at my computer. "Isn't there some way to unsend messages?" I asked. "Delete! Stop! Return to sender!" I cried as I clicked the mouse in every possible place.

But the message was gone.

And what was worse, we already had a reply from Melanie Han. "Sounds great – I love the surf – keep me posted!"

Ashley hung up the phone. "Wilson told me about the permit. He also said we should take another look at Pizza Pals because we'd be surprised at how much could be done with decorations." She groaned. "If we end up at that Pizza Pals place after we sent that e-mail . . ."

"We won't," I said. "We *can't*. We have thirteen days to find somewhere else. That's what we're going to do!"

chapter nine

"What did Ben think of the whole tent-on-the-beach fiasco?" Mary-Kate asked me on Saturday afternoon. We took our change from the Starbucks cashier and headed for a table.

"Ben?" I stopped in the middle of the room. A tall woman brushed past me. "What do you mean?"

"Didn't you tell him about it?" Mary-Kate asked.

"No," I replied. "I haven't spoken to him since drivers' ed last Wednesday."

Mary-Kate gave me a funny look. Then she pointed out an empty table and headed for it.

"Why?" I asked, taking a seat. "Do you think that's weird?"

"No," Mary-Kate said. "It's just . . . I don't know. When I was with Jake we talked or e-mailed about ten times a day. I wanted to tell him every little thing that happened. But maybe it's different, since

Ben doesn't go to the same school as we do . . ."

"I tell Ben lots of things," I said. "I'll get around to telling him all about it eventually."

But at the time it happened, it never occurred to me to tell him, I realised. When things happened to me, good or bad, Ben usually wasn't the first person I thought of calling.

Does that mean I'm not crazy enough about him? I wondered. *Does it mean I shouldn't be going out with him?* I considered asking Mary-Kate what she thought, but she changed the subject.

"I hate to bring up another decision we have to make," she said. "But what shoes are we going to wear with our cool new dresses?"

She carefully draped the dresses over an empty chair. We'd just picked them up, with the final alterations done. They looked better than ever now that they fitted us perfectly.

"How can you worry about *shoes* at a time like this?" I said. "We don't even know where we're having the party!"

"Maybe not, but we can't go barefoot," she joked. "We've already been through the beach concept, remember?"

I smiled, glad that Mary-Kate could keep her sense of humour about it. I reached into my bag and pulled out my glittery purple notebook. I glanced through the appointment section.

"I have a day set aside in our schedule next week to get all our accessories," I announced. "And in the meantime, we need to go over something more important – the final guest list. That way we can stop by Margo's on the way home, and confirm the total number of guests."

The day before was the final RSVP date. We'd spent the evening reading e-mails, answering the phone and opening mailed replies.

"Well, the good news is that it looks like we're coming in right on target," I said.

"Which target is that?" Mary-Kate asked. "Because let's face it, we've missed a lot of them lately." She unwrapped her straw and stuck it into her grande Frappuccino.

"Almost everyone has sent their RSVP, and we have a total of ninety-eight guests. Which leaves room for a couple more people," I said.

"Hold on – how did *that* work out?" Mary-Kate asked. "What about Rachel inviting the entire boys' basketball team?"

"Oh, she still invited them," I told her. "But a lot of girls decided *not* to ask a guy. Some people are totally happy coming without dates – which is very cool. Especially at a girl power party." I smiled as I reached for my coffee drink.

"And some people are totally *unhappy* coming by themselves," Mary-Kate said glumly. I followed her gaze to a couple sitting at a small table by the window. The girl had long blonde hair, and her boyfriend had short brown hair. They looked a lot like Mary-Kate and Jake – except for three things: (1) They were together, (2) they were holding hands as they talked and sipped from their mugs, and (3) they looked happy.

"Come on, Mary-Kate. Don't give up yet," I said.

"I know you're still upset about Jake, but I think we have a lot to celebrate," I said. "We have our dresses, and they look completely awesome. We have everyone at school talking about our party. We have our final guest list—"

"Ashley!" she interrupted. "Don't you understand? None of this matters if we don't have a place to hold the party!"

"I know," I said, a little hurt. I guessed she hadn't kept her sense of humour so well after all. "I'm just trying to think positively, that's all."

She sighed, pushing her cup in circles on the table. "I'm sorry. I'm just feeling stressed out today."

"I'm stressed, too," I confessed. "But I'm even more worried about my driving test next week."

"What do you mean? Getting our licences is going to be so cool!" she said.

"Easy for you to say. You're totally great at driving." I stirred my coffee. "I'm not. You should have seen me at my lessons this past week. And we get only one more!"

"I'm sure you're better than you think," she told me. "And we'll be there together, so don't worry."

"Don't worry about what?" someone behind me asked.

I turned and saw Theresa standing with Todd Malone, her boyfriend. I'd met Ben at one of Todd's parties. And Mary-Kate had danced with Jake for the first time at the same party.

I glanced at Mary-Kate's face, wondering if she was thinking about that night.

"Ashley's worried about her driving test," Mary-Kate told them. "We're taking it next week."

"It'll be easy – don't sweat it," Todd commented.

"Did you guys get my RSVP?" Theresa asked.

"Yeah, we did – thanks," I said. "And you're bringing—"

"Well, I'm not totally sure who's coming with me," Theresa said, glancing at Todd.

"What?" Todd asked. "What do you mean? *I* am."

"Don't count on it," Theresa said. She laughed and put her arm around Todd's waist. "I haven't asked you yet."

"Ha-ha," Todd said, rolling his eyes.

Theresa and Todd totally like each other, I thought, watching them. *Do Ben and I look that way when we're together?*

"Are you guys inviting dates?" Theresa asked

Mary-Kate and me. "Let me guess – Ashley's bringing Ben, and Mary-Kate . . ."

Her voice trailed off, and her face went red. I could tell she'd suddenly remembered that Jake and Mary-Kate had broken up.

"I don't have a date yet," Mary-Kate said. "But that's okay." She tried to smile, but I knew she felt miserable about it inside.

"Yeah. Well, we should probably get going," Todd said. "We just wanted to say hi."

They turned to leave, but then Theresa stopped. "Mary-Kate, I'm really sorry about you and Jake breaking up," she said. "I know for a fact that he still likes you."

"See you guys around!" Todd called. He gently pulled Theresa out of Starbucks and on to the sidewalk. She turned around to wave at us.

Mary-Kate looked shocked. "What is Jake's problem?" she asked to me. "If he still likes me, the way Theresa says, then why won't he talk to me?"

"I don't know, Mary-Kate," I said. "But we have got to find out."

chapter ten

"So, thanks for the movie." I looked into Ben's dark brown eyes on Sunday night. *He's going to kiss me,* I realised.

For some reason, I found myself edging away from him. "I'll . . . umm . . . see you tomorrow."

I moved towards my house. *What are you doing?* I asked myself. *Don't you want Ben to kiss you?*

"It's my mom, isn't it?" Ben asked. I peeked over his shoulder. His mother was waiting in the car. She had dropped us off at the movies and picked us up afterwards. "She kills the mood, right?" Ben continued.

That must be it! I thought. *I just don't want to kiss him in front of his mother. Of course!*

I peered at Ben's mother sitting in the driver's seat, trying not to look as if she was watching us. "Yeah, it *is* kind of a problem," I said.

"That's cool. I understand. Well, good night, Ashley." Ben gave me a quick hug and walked away..

"Good night," I said. "And thanks for going out tonight – I had a really nice time!" I smiled and waved as he and his mother pulled out of the driveway.

I *did* have a nice time with Ben – so why didn't I want to kiss him good night? The first time we'd kissed, at the party on the houseboat, it had felt amazing. What was my problem?

His mother was watching us! I reminded myself as I unlocked the door and walked into our house. Who would want to kiss under those circumstances?

I headed for the kitchen to get myself a glass of milk. I tossed my denim jacket on to the back of a chair and opened the refrigerator.

Once I had poured my glass of milk, I turned off the kitchen light and headed for the stairs. Then I noticed something bobbing on the hallway wall, by the closet at the bottom of the stairs. It looked like a flashlight beam.

Wait a second, I thought. *Why is someone walking around my house with a flashlight?* There was only one answer that came to mind – and I didn't like it. Were we being *robbed*? I knew Mom and Dad had gone out to a work function, which meant Mary-Kate should have been home by herself.

"H-hello?" I said. Then I cleared my throat and tried to sound older – and bigger. "Who's there?"

I crawled out from behind a stack of boxes in the storage closet. *Nope. Nothing here, either!* This entire present search was turning out to be yet another bust.

"I said, who's there?" a voice demanded.

I gasped and pointed my flashlight in the direction of the voice. The beam landed right on Ashley's face! "Ashley, it's me!" I said.

Ashley shielded her eyes from the light. "Mary-Kate, stop shining that in my face!"

"Oh – sorry." I hopped out of the overcrowded closet and flicked on the hall light switch.

"What were you doing? You scared me," Ashley said.

"I was bored, so I started looking for our presents again."

"In the dark?" Ashley asked.

"In case Mom and Dad came home," I answered. "I didn't want them to see the light on in the storage closet and find out what I was doing."

"And?" Ashley said. "Did you find anything?"

I shook my head. "Not unless you count dust bunnies. How was your date?"

"Okay." Ashley shrugged and took a sip of milk from the glass she was holding. She didn't seem all that thrilled, which was strange. I decided she was just tired. Or maybe she needed to talk.

"Hey, that looks good." I pointed to her glass. "Want to hang out with me while I get some?" I asked.

"Sure," she said.

We went into the kitchen, and Ashley sat down at the kitchen table. "So. What did you do tonight?" she asked.

"Not much. Before Mom and Dad left for their party, I helped Mom make some cookies to take to the day care centre tomorrow. Then I asked Dad where our presents were hiding," I said. "And he blushed a lot, and said there weren't any, and then after they left I searched every room. Hey, it's better than doing homework."

"You seem like you're in a good mood," Ashley commented.

"I'm trying," I said. "But the problem is that every time I try to do my geometry homework, I think about how Jake helped me study for my last test and how much I like him." I sighed. "It's a vicious circle, which is why I'm not even *looking* at my geometry book tonight."

"I know it's not the same thing, but I can help you with geometry later, if you want," Ashley offered.

"Thanks," I said with a smile. "But you're right. It's not the same."

"I know you feel really bad right now – about Jake." Ashley sighed. "But at least you *know* how you feel about him."

"What do you mean?" I asked.

Ashley tucked her hair behind her ears. "It's Ben. I've been thinking. I've noticed the way you talk about Jake."

"And talk and talk and talk . . ." I joked.

She laughed. "Well, sort of. But that just shows how much you like him. Me, on the other hand . . . I like seeing Ben, when I see him. But I don't get all woozy, like you're supposed to when you fall in love."

"Good thing, because who wants to pass out on a date? Very embarrassing," I joked, wrinkling my nose.

"Come on, I'm serious!" Ashley pleaded. "There are ways you're supposed to feel when you're going out with someone – and I don't feel them. Isn't that weird?"

"Not really. Everyone's different," I said.

Ashley frowned. "I don't think that's it."

"Come on, you'll get used to being weird," I teased her. "I have."

"Mary-Kate, I'm serious." Ashley looked at me.

"Okay. Sorry," I apologised. "I am taking this seriously." I took a deep breath and let it out. "I guess I would say that everything you've told me could mean that Ben's not the right guy for you. Maybe he seemed like it at first, so that's why you went out with him."

"This is embarrassing, but to be honest? I think I might have started going out with Ben because I wanted to have a boyfriend – at the same time *you* had one," Ashley said.

"Really?" I was surprised. It wasn't like Ashley to do something just because I was doing it. Not at all. "But I remember when you met him – you really liked him."

"I still do. He's funny, and he always makes me laugh. He's cute. He's smart," I said.

"So what's the problem?" I asked.

Ashley shrugged. "It's fun. But it's not like you and Jake. There are fireworks when you and Jake are together."

"Correction – there *were* fireworks," I said. "Now there are ashes."

"Yikes," Ashley said.

"Sorry. I don't mean to be so dramatic." I looked across the table at Ashley. "But, if you really think you don't like Ben that way . . . you should tell him. And you should tell him soon, before he gets more attached to you."

Ashley nodded. "Okay."

"Because the worst thing in the world is when someone strings you along, when they're not really interested in dating you, but they pretend to be. And you fall really hard for them, and then suddenly they're just, like, not there any more." I stared out at the streetlight, my eyes blurry with tears.

I knew Mary-Kate was talking about my situation, and she was right. I had to talk to Ben, and tell him that even though I liked him a lot, I just wanted to be friends – nothing more.

But I also knew that Mary-Kate was talking about herself. And even though she was trying to hide it by making jokes, she was still really hurt. I could see her trying not to cry, too.

I'd heard more than enough. I couldn't stand seeing Mary-Kate so unhappy for so many days in a row just because Jake wouldn't listen to her apology or explanation. He wasn't acting like a nice guy. He was acting like a jerk. And if he wouldn't listen to Mary-Kate, then he was going to have to listen to me!

chapter eleven

If Mary-Kate knew what I was doing, she'd probably kill me, I thought.

It was first thing Monday morning, and I was searching the halls for Jake's locker. My plan was to talk to him about Mary-Kate. *I don't know what I'm going to say,* I thought nervously. *But I'll come up with something.*

I hate confronting people. I almost never do it – I avoid arguments whenever I can. But there was a lot on the line here – namely Mary-Kate's happiness! I didn't want her to look back on turning sixteen and remember how Jake hurt her. She deserved better than that.

There he was – closing his locker and about to walk down the hall, away from me. I hurried up to him, glad that he was alone and not with a bunch of his basketball buddies.

"Jake, can I talk to you for a second?" I asked as I caught up with him. "It's really important."

His eyes widened when he saw me, but then he smiled. "Oh. Hi, Ashley."

"Hi. I'm . . . well . . . I wanted to . . ." I stammered. *Spit it out, Ashley!* I thought.

"Look, Jake. Do you or do you not like my sister?" I asked.

Jake stopped walking and stared down at me, his face registering confusion. I had sort of blurted out what I wanted to know – but there was no other way to get to the point. I was always teasing Mary-Kate about being too blunt, but maybe it wasn't such a bad thing.

"What are you talking about?" Jake asked. "Why are you asking me that?"

We stepped out of the way of the crowds in the hallway and into an empty classroom.

"Mary-Kate feels terrible," I said. "I mean, she has felt nothing *but* terrible ever since the day you found out from Ben that he was invited to our sweet sixteen."

"Yeah. Well," Jake said.

"Look – I know it's all messed up, but I also know Mary-Kate still really likes you," I said. "Here's what happened, and some of it's my fault, and some is Mary-Kate's, and . . ."

Focus! I told myself. *Stop rambling!*

"First of all," I said, "we did plan on having an

all-girl party at first. But then Mary-Kate wanted to invite you, so she did, and she was sure she could convince me to change the party to include boys. But I said no," I explained. "I still wanted it to be a girls-only party. That's why Mary-Kate uninvited you."

"Okay . . . " Jake said slowly.

"But, at the same time, I met Ben. And I really liked him, and wanted to invite *him* to the party. So I did, because I decided that we should invite guys. I got home and told Mary-Kate that the party should include boys, after all. But before she got the chance to tell you about it in person, you heard from Ben that he was invited and you never heard Mary-Kate's side of the story!" I finally stopped to take a breath. Jake was standing there with a stunned expression. He might have heard enough, but I wasn't done yet.

"You really hurt her because you won't listen to her," I said. "She's been totally honest with you, and you won't even give her a chance."

Jake shifted from one foot to the other. "Okay. What can I say? I'm sorry."

"Thanks. But I'm not the one you should be apologising to," I said. "You should be talking to Mary-Kate." I started to walk away, but then I turned around. "I don't think you're a bad guy. It's just . . . Mary-Kate's my sister."

The bell rang, and I rushed out of the

classroom, eager to get away from Jake. I couldn't believe I had just laced into him like that!

I hope it works, I thought. *I hope I didn't just make things worse for Mary-Kate!*

"So, ready for your final spin before the big test?" Ben asked.

I had just walked out of school on Monday afternoon, and I was totally surprised to see Ben standing outside. He didn't even go to our school! "What are you doing here?" I asked with a laugh.

"I figured we should go to our lesson together," Ben said. "I mean, this *is* a special occasion when you think about it."

"It is?" I said.

Ben nodded. "This is the last time we'll ever see Ms. Junger again! Our life's going to be so empty without her telling us to check our mirrors."

"Yeah, I don't know how I'll handle it," I joked as we fell into step beside each other.

Mary-Kate's words from our conversation the night before suddenly came back to me. *If you really think you don't like Ben that way you should tell him. And you should tell him soon, before he gets more attached to you.*

I looked over at Ben. Should I tell him now? But that would be awkward – we were going to drivers' ed together. We'd have to sit in the same car for an hour.

But there wasn't going to be a good time. And if I didn't tell him soon, we'd end up going to my sweet sixteen together, and then he might get even more attached to me. . . .

I sighed. Why had it been so easy for me to be honest with Jake earlier? And why was it impossible for me to be up front with Ben now?

"Since this is our last lesson, I thought we'd practise some specific skills for the test," Ms. Junger said as Janine, Ben and I stood outside Columbus High School on Monday afternoon. She glanced my way. "Ashley, why don't you go first?"

Because I don't want to? I thought as I got behind the wheel. *Because I'm completely afraid of taking the test?*

"Now, don't be nervous," Ms. Junger instructed.

Easy for her to say! I thought.

"Just remember everything you've already learned."

"Right," I said as I adjusted the rearview mirror.

Ben was sitting in the back seat. I caught his reflection in the mirror, and he gave me a big smile. That made me feel better. "Okay, so where are we going?" I asked Ms. Junger.

She glared at me. "Nowhere, unless you put on your seat belt!"

"Oh – whoops. Sorry. I never forget that," I said as I quickly clicked the buckle.

"I guess you can't say *never* any more," Ms. Junger stated. "If you make that mistake during your test, you'll fail without even driving away from the Motor Vehicle Department!"

"I know, I know," I said quickly. "Sorry!" I always put on my seat belt whenever I got into *any* car. So why did I have to forget now? Was it just the mention of the test that had me flustered?

"All right. We're ready. Please pull out and take us over to Hanover Street," Ms. Junger said. "You remember, we've practised driving there before."

I nodded and turned the key in the ignition. Hanover Street was a very quiet street, so it was a good place to work on turns. I checked to make sure no cars were coming, and pulled out on to the street. I waited at the stop sign, then took a left. I glanced over at Ms. Junger to see how I was doing.

"Keep your eyes on the road at all times!" she commanded.

"I am, I am!" I insisted.

"Really, Ashley. Have I taught you nothing?" Ms. Junger complained.

"Actually, you've taught us all a *lot*," Ben piped up from the back seat. "I'm sure Ashley's just off to a slow start today, that's all."

"Hmm," Ms. Junger grunted.

"And, hey, slow starts are good. I mean, you taught us all not to jam on the gas pedal, right?" Ben joked.

Ms. Junger let out a little snort that sounded slightly like a laugh.

I was really grateful for Ben coming to my rescue. He could even make Ms. Junger laugh, which was amazing. *I really do like him*, I thought. *He's a great guy. Maybe I won't break up with him – at least, not just yet.*

I started to relax as we pulled on to Hanover, and I practised my three-point turn. Now, if only Ben could be in the back seat when I had to take the test!

"Ashley! The curb!" Ms. Junger suddenly warned me.

I braked just as the wheels tapped the curb. "Sorry," I said.

"Don't apologise," Ms. Junger coached me. "Just relax and do it again. You're a good driver, Ashley. You can do it."

I felt grateful that she wasn't yelling, but no matter what she said, I couldn't relax. My hands clutched the wheel as I started another turn.

I couldn't help feeling that I wasn't ready for the test – or my party – or turning sixteen at all!

chapter twelve

The big day had finally arrived. Wednesday afternoon. My driving test.

You can do it, Ashley, I chanted to myself all the way to the Motor Vehicle Department. *You can do it, you can do it, you can do it . . .*

I was so nervous I hardly remembered getting into the driver's seat. But somehow I must have buckled my seat belt, checked my mirrors, started the car, and driven off with a motor vehicle officer sitting next to me.

"Okay, Ashley. Take the next right turn available," he instructed.

My hands were a little sweaty as I gripped the wheel more tightly. So far, I seemed to be doing okay. I hadn't made any major mistakes, anyway. Ms. Junger had told us the tests would take only about five to ten minutes, so I couldn't have too much left to do.

"Now pull over under that big tree," the officer told me. "And complete a three-point turn."

I gulped. This was one of the parts of the test that I hated – but that was why I'd practised it endlessly yesterday afternoon with Mom and Dad!

Remember, Ashley – it's all just angles, I told myself as I turned the wheel to the left. I backed up carefully, without hitting the curb. Then I turned the wheel again and completed the turn.

"Nice job," the officer said. "Now proceed out on to the street to the lights and take a left."

Ms. Junger's words came back to me. "Just relax. You're a good driver, Ashley. You can do it." When we turned back into the motor vehicle office lot, the officer told me to park right in front.

I carefully put the car in Park and turned off the engine. There was a moment of silence while the officer completed some paperwork. It felt like the longest two minutes of my entire life!

"Congratulations, Ashley. You passed!" the officer finally said. He handed me a sheet of paper.

"Yes!" I cheered. "Thank you, thank you, thank you!" I gave the officer a big hug. His face turned bright red. "Ummm, you can take this inside and we'll finish up now – or we can go ahead with your sister's test and complete the process when you're both done."

"Thanks! I'll wait," I said as I unclipped my seat belt. When I got out of the car, Mary-Kate and Mom were waiting for me. "I passed!" I said in a whisper.

Mary-Kate gave me a quick hug. "That's so awesome!"

"Your turn. Good luck!" I told her. "And remember, if I can do it, you can do it."

I stared at the paper in my hand. I couldn't believe it! I actually had my driver's licence!

I was almost done with my driving test. I felt good behind the wheel – confident. Seeing Ashley pass the test had definitely helped.

I had done everything right so far, or at least I thought I had. I'd obeyed all the street signs correctly. I'd parked on a hill. I'd backed up in a straight line and done a three-point turn.

"Okay, please turn right here, into the parking lot," the officer said as he made a check mark on his clipboard.

Check marks are good, I thought. That had to mean that I was doing things right!

I turned into the Motor Vehicle Department lot. I was done! I had passed!

"We need to park this at the back, so please go past that Jeep," the officer said.

"Okay." I glanced over at the Jeep. It was red – just like Jake's Jeep! I looked more closely.

Wait a second – it *was* Jake's Jeep!

The door opened and Jake climbed out. *What is he doing here?* I wondered, glancing at him in the rearview mirror.

"Watch it!" the officer said as I ploughed into an orange pylon cone set up for a motorcycle test.

"Sorry!" I said, jerking the wheel to the left. I ran over another cone, and slammed on the brakes. There was a loud screech.

The officer cleared his throat. "Okay, that'll be enough."

"I'm sorry!" I said. "I just got distracted. See, I know that guy, so – I'm really sorry, I don't drive like that usually and—"

The officer shook his head. "I'm sorry. This test is over. If you'd please just pull over there and park, we'll go inside and we can talk about a retest." He made some more notes on his clipboard.

"Retest?" I yelped.

"I'm sorry," the officer said as I quietly parked the car. "But you failed the test."

My heart sank as I got out of the car. "Well?" Ashley asked, jogging over to me.

I shook my head.

"What? You didn't pass?" she asked.

"No. Didn't you see how I took out those cones?" I asked. "It was awful."

"Maybe so. But your day is taking a turn for the better," Ashley said. She pointed to the left.

I turned and saw Jake walking towards us. My stomach jolted. I strained to see if he was smiling or frowning. Was he glad to see me?

"What are you doing here?" I asked him.

He's smiling, I realised now that he stood in front of me.

"Mary-Kate, you wrote it in my day-planner in capitals," Jake said. "Four o'clock – Mary-Kate and Ashley get their licences. And I think there's a 'Yahoo' on there, too." He glanced at Ashley and smiled.

My stomach was full of butterflies. It was the old Jake, the *nice* Jake. What was going on?

"I know you probably have to get going, but could you come sit down with me for a second?" Jake asked.

"Um . . ." I glanced over at Ashley, who for some reason looked like she knew more than she was letting on.

"I have to go in and do all the paperwork," Ashley said. "Mom and I will meet you inside."

"Yes, don't forget – you'll need to come in, too," the officer said to me. "To schedule another test."

"Okay – I'll be there in two minutes," I promised.

"Another test?" Jake asked.

I grimaced. "I failed. Can you believe it?"

"Well, I did see the way you mowed down

those cones!" Jake laughed. "It was kind of ugly."

"It's all your fault. I was passing until I spotted you!" I said.

"Sorry. But you know what? I failed my driving test the first time, too," Jake said with a grin.

"Really? No way! You're such a good driver."

"*Now* I am. But on that day? Forget it. I was so hyper that I made about five mistakes." Jake led me to a bench outside the brick building. "Just reschedule the test. You'll do fine next time."

We sat down. "I'll try to be quick, so I don't hold you up too long."

He turned to me and put his hand over mine. "I'm really sorry for the way I've been acting."

I bit my lip, waiting for him to go on.

"The reason I was so mad is that I thought you came up with the all-girl party idea as an excuse not to invite me," Jake said. "I thought you didn't want me there."

I nearly fell off the bench. "What? But why wouldn't I?"

"I don't know! It's the only thing that made sense to me," Jake said. "But someone explained that I was wrong."

Really? I thought.

"It was just a huge mix-up all along," Jake said. "You were trying to change the party because you wanted me to be there – not the other way around."

"That's what I tried to tell you," I said. "But you wouldn't listen!"

Jake nodded. "I know."

"It really hurt my feelings that you didn't believe me," I confessed. "Why would I lie about something like that? Why would I lie to you at all? I wouldn't."

"I know – I mean, I realise that now," Jake said. "And I'm sorry." He squeezed my hand. "Do you think you could maybe think about, you know, getting back together?"

I was dying to get back together with him. But after all he'd put me through, I figured he could sweat a little.

"I'll think about it," I said.

"Oh." He stared down at our hands. A look of sadness spread across his face. "For how long?"

"Umm . . . about five seconds," I replied. "Yes, Jake. I would like to get back together with you."

"Really?" Jake asked.

I nodded.

Jake leaned closer and kissed me. I kissed him back, my heart leaping with excitement. A few people walking into the motor vehicle office stopped and glanced over at us, but I didn't care. Finally, I was back together with Jake!

"Wow," I said, scooting closer to Jake. "What made you come here today to tell me all this?"

"Well, I talked to Ashley yesterday. Actually,

she talked – I listened," Jake said. "You know, I think it's been more than two minutes. We'd better go inside."

We went into the building. While Jake went over to Mom and Ashley, .I checked in with the clerk at the desk and told him I wanted to reschedule. Ashley was standing behind the little blue line and smiling for her picture. I was so jealous! I'd even take a *horrible* photo on my licence, as long as I *got* one.

"Let's see. The next possible date is" – the clerk checked his computer – "June thirteenth."

June 13! Our birthday – and the day of the party!

I stared at him. "No way. Aren't there any other openings?"

He shook his head. "Nope. Not until the middle of July."

The middle of July? That was eons away!

"Okay, I'll take it," I said. I glanced over my shoulder at Jake, who was talking with Ashley and Mom. If Jake could pass the test on his second try, then so could I.

Besides, now that we were back together, I felt like anything was possible – even finding the perfect place for our sweet sixteen in the next – gulp! – eight days!

chapter thirteen

An hour after passing my driving test, I was cruising down the highway with the radio on and a smile on my face. Mom let me drive us home in the Volvo. Right now she was on her mobile with Dad. She had called to give him the good – and not so good – news about our tests.

There was nothing like the feeling of being behind the wheel and knowing exactly what I was doing. Why had I worried so much about the drivers' test? I passed with flying colours. I couldn't believe Mary-Kate hadn't.

I glanced in the rearview mirror. Mary-Kate was sitting in the back seat, gazing out of the window with a sort of dreamy smile on her face. She didn't seem to care much about the test now that she was back with Jake. I looked at the road ahead of me. I realised that I'd missed seeing

Mary-Kate so happy. I was just glad I'd had a tiny bit to do with it.

"Excuse me – Ashley?" Mom said. "I don't mean to criticise, but, um—"

"What? Am I going too fast?" I quickly checked the speedometer. "No, I'm going thirty – that's the speed limit."

"It's not that," Mom said.

"Did I miss a sign? Am I swerving?" I asked.

"Honey, all I wanted to ask is – where *are* we? I wasn't paying attention to where we were going, because I was talking to your father. But I don't recognise this area at all." Mom peered out the front window.

"Mom, this is Oceanside Drive," I said. "We take this road almost every day."

"Yes, but we don't live in this direction. You're going south. We need to go north."

"Oh." So maybe driving *and* navigating was a bit too much for me on my first day as an official driver. "Oops."

"Why don't you pull over at the next scenic viewpoint, and we'll turn around there," Mom suggested with a wry smile. "I promise not to get distracted by any more phone calls."

"How did I do that? I mean, I've been on this road a hundred thousand times," I complained.

"Well, it's not like any of us was paying attention. You were too busy having fun driving, I was talking, and Mary-Kate . . ." Mom glanced over the back of her seat. She turned back to me. "I don't think she's with us, if you know what I mean."

"She's on Planet Jake," I said knowingly.

A few minutes later, I spotted a sign, and signalled before turning into it. I pulled into the small parking lot and made a slow, gentle curve to point us in the opposite direction.

"Wait!" Mary-Kate suddenly yelled. "Stop the car!"

I slammed on the brakes, thinking I was about to run into something. "What now?" I asked.

"What is it – a dog? A cat?" Mom looked frantically around the small parking lot.

"No. It's that *house!*" Mary-Kate cried.

I tried to follow Mary-Kate's finger, to see where she was pointing, but I had a bad angle. The house was behind us, to the right, perched on a rocky cliff over the ocean.

"Why don't you pull over and park," Mom suggested to me. "We can get out and stretch our legs and check out the place."

I had barely put the car in Park when Mary-Kate flung her door open and raced towards the large white house. "There's a sign out front, Ashley – come on!"

I didn't realise what she was so excited about until I followed her to the house. Then I saw it: the sign. For Rent : Available for Photo Shoots and

SPECIAL OCCASIONS. CALL FOR INFORMATION.

"Wouldn't this be the perfect place for our party?" Mary-Kate asked me. "It's big enough. It's very glamorous. And it's on the beach, practically, with a gorgeous view, like we promised in our invitations!"

"You're right," I said as we wandered around the front lawn. "This place would be awesome for our party."

"I agree," Mom said.

"You do?" I asked.

She nodded. "The house is beautiful, and the setting is perfect. Imagine the photos you could get. Besides that, all of your guests would be very impressed."

"Then can I borrow your phone to call Wilson and see what he thinks?" Mary-Kate asked excitedly.

"Sure – hold on, and I'll get it for you," Mom offered. She jogged over to the car, which gave me and Mary-Kate another minute to stand and admire the house. It was the best location we'd seen, by far. I hoped it wouldn't be out of our price range. *And* I hoped it would be available eight days from now!

"Here you go." Mom handed her phone to me. "Wilson's number is programmed."

I dialled, then Mary-Kate leaned against my shoulder, and we both pressed an ear to the phone. We waited a few seconds for the call to go through. After it rang twice, Wilson answered. "Hello, Olsens!" he said cheerfully. "Was I supposed to call you today? I knew something slipped my mind – I'm sorry. I'm down here in the Bahamas. So what's up?"

"Wilson, we're calling because we're standing outside the place where we've decided to have our party!" Mary-Kate announced.

"Pizza Pals?"

"No!" Mary-Kate and I both said at once.

Wilson laughed. "Okay, then where are you?"

"We're standing on Oceanside Drive. We just passed the most gorgeous house – it's perched on the cliffs above the ocean," I said. "There's a sign here saying that the house can be rented!"

"Hmm. It sounds wonderful. I think I may know that house," Wilson said. "Is there an address on it?"

"Let's see . . ." We walked closer to the house so I could read the number by the door. "It says 14375 Oceanside."

"Sounds familiar. What's the phone number listed? I'll cross-check it in my database," Wilson said.

I read off the phone number from the sign. A few seconds later, Wilson sighed. "Sorry, guys. It's not available. The owner allows only certain kinds of events there, and I know for a fact her policy is not to rent it out for any kids' events – ever."

"But we're not *kids*," Mary-Kate protested. "We're almost sixteen."

"*I* know that, but I tried to rent it before, and she said nobody under twenty-one," Wilson said. "I'm so sorry, guys. You're right, it *would* be an awesome location. Oh, no – I've got to run, but I'll call you later – we'll get this location thing solved! I promise."

I turned to Mary-Kate as I clicked off the phone. "Well, so much for that idea."

"Wait a minute. If she'll rent only to people twenty-one and over . . ." Mary-Kate tapped her chin as she stepped back to look at the house. She glanced over at Mom, who was sitting on the car's bumper. "Then we'll just have to be twenty-one."

"Do I look twenty-one?" I asked Ashley as I walked into her bedroom right before dinner. I twirled around in my faded jeans, hooded sweatshirt and untied sneakers. "I figured we should call the owner of that house right away to let her know we're interested."

"Good idea," Ashley agreed. "You don't look twenty-one, but maybe you can sound twenty-one." She handed me the slip of paper with the house address and the owner's phone number on it. I quickly dialled, anxious to get this over with. If she said yes, great. If she said no, we needed to get back to Plan B – or rather, Plan Pizza Pals. I shuddered at the thought.

"Hello, McKenzie Real Estate Holdings. This is Bridget McKenzie," a cheerful voice answered.

"Hi," I said. "I'm calling because my sister and I are interested in renting a house we saw – and this number was listed on the sign, 14375 Oceanside?"

"Yes, that's one of our properties."

"Oh, *good*. Well, we were wondering if the building would be available next Thursday – June thirteenth," I said.

"What would you be using it for?" she asked.

"It's our birthday party," I said. At least that much was true. "We're turning twenty-one, and we've been looking for the perfect place to have a big party. We already have the music and the caterer lined up – and our parents would be there, too."

Ashley shook her head. "Don't talk about our parents!" she whispered. "That makes us sound too young."

I shrugged. "Too late," I mouthed.

"Let's see. I just need a little more information," the woman said. "Did you want the house for the entire day?"

"Late afternoon and evening," I said.

"Okay. Well, you're in luck. It looks as though the house isn't booked for that day."

"Great!" I exclaimed.

"However, I like to meet all of the renters in person before I let them use the space. So if you don't mind, could you and your sister meet me at the building tomorrow afternoon? Say, three o'clock?"

Pretending to be twenty-one over the phone was one thing. But convincing someone in person . . .

I bit my lip, wondering if we could pull it off. Then I realised that if we didn't go after this, we'd be stuck at Pizza Pals for sure.

"Yes. Three o'clock would be perfect," I told her. "Thank you so much!" A minute later, I hung up the phone with a smile. "Done!"

"Are you kidding?" Ashley cried. "You mean we have the place?"

"Yup," I replied. "There's just one little thing we have to do first."

"It's so awesome that we both got our driver's licences. I told you that you'd do fine, didn't I?" Ben and I took a seat at a black wire table at the ice cream shop later that evening.

"Yeah, but I didn't believe you," I said.

"You just needed to focus. Which was probably a lot easier to do without me in the car to distract you, right?" Ben joked.

"Right. That must have been it." I smiled.

Come on, Ashley, I thought. *If you can confront Jake Impenna in the middle of a school hallway, you can do this.*

"Ben, I have to tell you something," I began. I was so nervous that my hand was shaking, so I set my dish of ice cream on the table. "And it's kind of hard for me to say, so I hope I don't mess it up or hurt your feelings."

"I know what you're going to say," Ben said. "You really miss our driving lessons."

I smiled. "Not exactly."

"You don't really like mint chocolate chip, right? It's okay, you can tell me. I can take it," Ben joked.

Why was he being so funny and cute? It was making this *so* hard. "Actually, it's about us," I said, looking down at the table. "I was thinking that maybe we should . . . be . . . just friends."

Ben didn't say anything for a minute, and I finally got the nerve to look up at him. He was actually almost smiling. "Yeah. You know, I was thinking the same thing."

"*What?* You were?" I asked. Here I was, agonising over breaking the news to him – and it turned out that this wasn't news at all?

"Ashley, I think you're great – you're so nice, and pretty, and fun to be around. But, um . . ."

"No sparks?" I guessed.

He nodded. "No sparks. Which is a good

thing, because those can really cause eye injuries."

I laughed. "So weren't you ever going to say anything?"

"Sure. I just didn't want to say it before your sweet sixteen party. I know it means a lot to you. And if you were counting on me to be your date, I didn't want to let you down." Ben licked his ice cream cone.

I sat there and took a bite of my sundae. I couldn't help feeling momentarily stunned. Here I'd been afraid to tell Ben I didn't like him as a boyfriend. And he'd been worried about telling me that he didn't want *me* as a girlfriend! So it was true, we really weren't a good match.

Even though I knew it was stupid, I couldn't help feeling a little insulted. Shouldn't Ben be heartbroken about our break-up?

Then again, he was still cool, and good-looking and funny. There wasn't anything wrong with *him*. We just didn't click the way a boyfriend and girlfriend are supposed to. I was glad we'd both decided to be honest with each other. There was just one thing, though . . .

"Ben? I still really like you – as a friend. So if it's okay with you, would you still come to our sweet sixteen, as my sort-of date?"

"Are you kidding?" Ben asked.

I held my breath. Had I said the wrong thing?

Then he grinned. "I would not miss that party for the world. Your e-mails have everyone totally intrigued. But you know, Ashley, you can tell *me*. Where's it going to be? What's this mystery location?"

"You'll just have to wait and see," I said.

And so will I, I thought. It was either a gorgeous mansion by the ocean . . . or a kids' restaurant with a dinosaur out front!

Tomorrow is the day, I thought. Tomorrow we'll find out if we're having the party of our dreams, or a Pizza Pals nightmare!

chapter fourteen

"I *still* can't believe you agreed to do this!" I said to Mary-Kate. I tried not to wobble in my high-heeled pumps as I walked up the sidewalk to the giant white house on Thursday afternoon. I was wearing one of Mom's dresses, stockings and pumps. Mary-Kate was wearing a blazer and black pants. She'd actually told Bridget McKenzie we'd be coming from work! We'd done everything we could think of to look older than we were.

"This is *it*, Ashley," Mary-Kate said as we walked up the steps to the porch. "If we can't get this settled today, we have to call Pizza Pals and confirm our reservation for the Pals Party Room. If that doesn't motivate you, I don't know what will."

"Don't worry, I'm motivated," I said. I knocked on the front door of the house, and a tall woman with long red hair immediately came to open it.

"Hello," she said. "Are you here to discuss the rental?"

"Yes, I am," I said. "I'm Ashley Olsen, and this is Mary-Kate. You must be Ms. McKenzie?"

"Please, call me Bridget." She narrowed her eyes at us for a second. "Come in!" Bridget stepped back to let us into the house.

"Thank you." I walked in and nearly gasped as I glimpsed the house's interior. Three picture windows side by side gave a perfect romantic view of the ocean. There were separate living rooms where people could hang out and talk, and a big open floor space with a high ceiling that would make a perfect dance floor.

Bridget gestured for us to take a seat on the sofa in the largest room. I noticed Bridget examining me carefully.

"So, we're desperately hoping we can rent this gorgeous house for our birthday party," I began. "We drove past this house the other day and it just took my breath away. When we saw your sign, naturally we were thrilled."

"Yes. Most people are," Bridget said. "This house has been in my family for quite some time, so as you can imagine, I'm very protective of it. Very," she insisted.

"Oh, I understand, completely," I agreed.

"So. You mentioned your birthday party. And

you two girls are going to be . . . how old?" Bridget asked.

"Twenty-one?" Mary-Kate said, sounding unsure of herself.

I cleared my throat. "Twenty-one," I said with a little more force.

"Really. That's exciting," Bridget said with a polite smile.

"Oh, yeah. Twenty-one. We're hitting the big time," Mary-Kate said. "Getting old. Moving away from home."

"You still live at home?" Bridget asked.

"Y-yes," I stammered. Why did I feel like were we saying all the wrong things?

"I thought you'd be off on your own by now – didn't you say something about coming here from work?" Bridget asked.

"Uh, yes," Mary-Kate answered. "Summer jobs. Internships, really."

"Oh," Bridget said. "So you're in college?"

"College. Of course," Mary-Kate said. "We're there all the time. Constantly. We – we love college."

"We just live at home to, ah, save money," I added. "Classes and books and all. Very pricey."

"Right. That can add up." Bridget leaned back and looked from me to Mary-Kate and back again. "Do you girls go to the same college?"

"Yes," I said.

"Which one?" Bridget asked.

"UCLA," Mary-Kate said.

"USC," I said at the same time.

Bridget raised an eyebrow. I thought I saw a slight smile play across her lips. I laughed nervously.

"Well, see, we take some classes at UCLA, and some at USC," Mary-Kate added.

Bridget smiled. "So, what are the two of you majoring in?"

"Uh," I mumbled.

"We're majoring in, um, science," Mary-Kate said.

"Science. That's kind of vague, isn't it?" Bridget said. "Which science, exactly?"

I was sitting there racking my brain for an answer: Biology? Chemistry? Astrology? Engineering? What sounded right? What sounded grown-up?

Suddenly I couldn't take it any more. Mary-Kate and I didn't lie like this. I felt really awful about trying to pull this off.

I blinked back the tears that were welling up in my eyes. "I'm sorry," I said, getting to my feet. "I can't do this, Mary-Kate."

Mary-Kate hung her head. "I know . . . neither can I."

"Girls, what's going on here?" Bridget asked.

"Ms. McKenzie, we've wasted your time. None of this is true. We don't go to college. We just really, really wanted to have our sweet sixteen party in this house," I explained.

"So we came here pretending to be twenty-one. But we're really not," Mary-Kate finished for me.

"We didn't want to lie, but we just – well, we're desperate." I tried to muffle a sob, but it didn't help. A tear slid down my cheek.

I rummaged through my bag for a tissue, and blew my nose. "I don't know why I'm telling you this. None of it is your problem." I sniffled. "We'll go now – sorry."

Mary-Kate sighed. "I'm sorry, too. This was really stupid of us. Thanks for meeting with us anyway." She put her arm around me. "It's okay, Ashley," she whispered.

Together, we headed for the door. I couldn't get out of there fast enough. We crossed the porch and sat down on the front steps.

A few more fat, warm tears spilled down my face. "Pizza Pals won't be that bad," I said, trying to convince myself as much as Mary-Kate. "Wilson can put some kind of beach mural on the wall – and we can play a CD of ocean sounds until the DJ starts – right?"

"Right," Mary-Kate agreed. "And we have a really good DJ, so, you know, it'll be fine."

"Yeah," I sighed. "Just . . . fine."

The door opened behind us. Bridget stepped on to the porch. "Girls, come on inside and let's talk. I think I may be able to help you after all."

I stared up at her. "Really?"

"You're kidding, right?" Mary-Kate said.

She smiled. "No, I'm not kidding."

A million thoughts raced through my mind as we walked back into the house. Was Bridget really going to let us use the place? Why? What had changed her mind?

"First, I should tell you that it wasn't cool that you lied to me. But, at the same time, I admire your guts," Bridget said with a smile. "You girls have a lot of ambition. And if you tell me just a little bit more about your party, and what it'll be like, maybe I'll give you my approval."

I nodded, sat up straight, and cleared my throat. "Okay. First, we want to apologise again for trying to fool you. We're really, really sorry." Then I quickly described the party – who was coming, and how our parents would be there to chaperone.

"We promise, it's going to be a *fun* party – but not a wild, out-of-control party," Mary-Kate added. "We're going to have dinner, dancing – with a DJ – and a big birthday cake... and that's it."

"What do you mean, that's it?" Bridget laughed. "Sounds pretty fun to me."

"Maybe you'd like to come?" I offered.

Bridget smiled. "Maybe. I'll have to check my schedule. Now, here's a list of our daily rates for renting the house." She handed a brochure to

Mary-Kate. Mary-Kate's eyes widened as she skimmed the brochure. *Uh-oh,* I thought.

My heart sank as Mary-Kate said, "I'm not sure we can afford this. We have a budget, and we just can't go over it—"

"Hmmm . . . well, we do have special rates for USC students." Bridget winked at us. "What if we cut the rate to . . . a hundred dollars flat."

"Really?" I asked.

Bridget shrugged. "Sure."

"No way. You normally get thousands of dollars for this place. You're being *too* nice," Mary-Kate said, looking guilty. "We don't deserve this."

"Let's just say I have my own reasons for helping you girls out. I mean, I was your age not that long ago," Bridget said. "I know how important it is to have big events work out the way you want them to. If you didn't have the party here, where were you going to have it?"

"Pizza Pals. You know that kids' restaurant on Highway Twelve where they have rollerskating waiters and clowns?" I said.

Bridget started to laugh. "Do you think I could let that happen? You know, this is a very funny coincidence. When it was time for my high-school graduation party? My parents decided they would plan the entire thing. I kept trying to tell them what I wanted, but no. They rented out a pizza parlour, and hired a cheesy magician." She shuddered. "Do you have any idea how long it took to live *that* down?"

I giggled. "I'm so sorry. That's awful."

"Tell me about it," Bridget said. "So, I think we're all set here. You can get in touch with your caterers. They'll want to know where to bring the food, and they may need to speak to me about arrangements. Which caterers are you using?"

"Menu by Margo," Mary-Kate said.

"Oh! Perfect. You won't be disappointed," Bridget said. "She's been here before, so she knows the set-up. I'm going to get myself a glass of water – would you girls like some?"

"Thanks, that would be great," I said. "Can I help?"

"Oh, no – I'll get it," Bridget said. "You just call Margo and I'll be right back."

"Wow, she is *so* nice. This is working out perfectly," Mary-Kate said once Bridget had left the room. "Ashley, how did we ever pull this off?"

"All it took was hard work, dedication, and about a ton of luck," I admitted.

"Now there are only two things left to stress about," Mary-Kate said. "My driving test. And the actual day of the party!"

chapter fifteen

"What colour should we pick?" I asked Mary-Kate. We were standing by the wedge-shaped nail polish display at Salon 21 on our birthday. There had to be a hundred colours to choose from!

"Here's the question. What looks perfect for our birthday *and* matches our dresses *and* will show up nicely in pictures?" Mary-Kate's eyes sparkled with excitement as she studied the different colours.

I knew how she felt. This was the most thrilling day of our lives – so far, anyway. It was hard to focus on nail polish!

"If I were you," Mom said, "I'd go with something that picks up your dress. Which would be . . ." Her fingers skimmed the top of several bottles, searching for the right shade. "Ah-ha! Here it is." She lifted a bottle of a rich royal blue-black with sparkly silver flecks mixed into it. "Night Magic."

"I love it," I said. "What about you, Mary-Kate?"

"The little sparkles in it will catch the light," Mary-Kate observed as she held up the bottle. "Let's do it. Thanks, Mom!" Then she handed the bottle to the manicurist who was politely waiting for us.

"Night Magic it is," she said. "Everyone can use a little magic, right?"

"You go first," Mary-Kate said to me.

"Actually we can take both of you at once," the manicurist said. She gestured to another table, where a different manicurist was waiting.

"Thanks – that's great!" I put my hand over my mouth as I yawned. "Sorry, I was so excited about today that I couldn't sleep last night," I told the manicurist as I sat down.

"Neither could I," Mary-Kate said, sitting at the next table along. "I kept worrying about taking my driving test, and if the DJ will play the songs we requested, and if everyone who says they're coming will actually show up, and if they'll like the party, and if it'll rain—"

"What? It almost never rains here." I laughed. "And you almost never worry that much!"

"What can I say? Turning sixteen has changed me dramatically," Mary-Kate joked.

"Yeah, right," I said as the manicurist rubbed lotion into my hands. "Sure it has."

Being pampered like this wasn't something that happened very often – I was totally loving it.

First Mom and Dad had woken us up by bringing us breakfast in bed – complete with fresh strawberries and whipped cream, Dad's famous French toast, and cappuccinos. They'd both taken the day off from work to spend with us, and we'd all gone for a walk on the beach together.

When we got home, we had at least ten birthday voice-mail messages waiting for us, from Brittany, Lauren, Jake, Ben and some of our other friends. The day was perfect so far. And it could only get better!

"You know what? While you're doing this, I'll go get you two something to drink," Mom said. "I'll be back in twenty minutes or so, okay?"

"That's so nice," I told her. "Thanks!"

"Any idea what your mom's giving you for your birthdays?" the manicurist working on Mary-Kate's nails asked us.

Mary-Kate glanced over at me, and we both shrugged. "*No* idea," we said at the same time.

"Whatever it is, they're saving it for our party tonight," I said. Unless the gift *was* our party, as they kept insisting!

"What do you think, Mary-Kate? Will this work for you?" Sonja, the hairstylist, swiveled my chair and held a mirror up behind my head to show me her work.

My eyes lit up as I saw the detailed weaving of

my hair into a smooth, sophisticated style. In the front, a few tendrils of my long blonde hair curled as they fell against my cheeks. After our manicures, we'd had our make-up done by the beauty artist at the salon. I hardly recognised myself in the mirror. I mean, I couldn't remember the last time I looked so put together. And we didn't even have our killer dresses, accessories, and shoes on yet!

"It looks incredible – you're amazing!" I told Sonja. "How did you do that?" I glanced over at Ashley, who was sitting next to me and having her hair styled by Ruben, the salon owner.

"Ashley, what do you think?" I swirled around in my chair to show her the complete look.

"Wow!" she said.

"Nice work, Sonja," Ruben said with admiration. "One of your best. Tell you what – when we both finish, let's take a picture of Mary-Kate and Ashley for our book."

"Your book?" I asked as Sonja unclipped the cape around my shoulders and brushed a few stray hairs off my collar.

"We keep a photo book of our clients," Ruben explained. "So we can show off our best work. Not that we had *that* much to do with it. You girls are naturally beautiful."

I got out of the chair and shook out my arms to stretch a bit. "Did you *see* me when I walked into this place? I hardly slept last night and I looked like a zombie."

"But a zombie with potential," Ashley joked, smiling at me.

"Right. We'd love to be in your book!" I said. "So when Ashley's done, you can take our picture . . ." I glanced at the clock to see how we were doing on time. I gulped. "Uh-oh. Ashley, my driving test is in an hour!"

"Then you'd better get going," Ashley said.

"Wait a minute – you did all this for a driving test?" Ruben joked.

"It's a long story," I said. I hurried over to Mom, who was reading a book in the waiting area. "Mom, we have to get going to the Motor Vehicle Department."

"Sorry, I got completely caught up in this story!" She got to her feet and studied me for a moment. "Mary-Kate, you look beautiful! More beautiful than usual, that is."

I laughed. "Do you think I could come here every week?"

We quickly stopped to say goodbye to Ashley. I wouldn't see her until we met at the house just before the party. "Good luck on your test – I know you can do it, Mary-Kate," she said.

"Thanks." I grabbed my bag. "Come on, Mom."

"Don't worry, honey – Dad will be here to pick

you up, cover the bill, and take you home to change," Mom told Ashley.

I leaned over and squeezed her hand. "See you later! And don't worry, I'll be there on time. Thanks, everyone!" I called over my shoulder as we dashed out of the door.

Two minutes later, Mom and I were completely stuck in traffic. We weren't moving at all. We'd never make it to the test, and have time to get home for me to change into my dress!

"Mom, if we take this next exit and drive on the back roads instead, won't that take us right past our house?" I asked. I stared out of the window at the endless line of cars and trucks ahead of us.

"Well, I suppose, yes," she said.

"And if we did that, couldn't I run in and get dressed and *then* go to the driving test?" I asked.

"Hmm. I don't know." She glanced at the clock on the Volvo's dashboard. "It's about ten minutes to our house if we jump off here."

"And we could get to the motor vehicle place on the back roads, too, which wouldn't have this major traffic jam," I reasoned.

"Sounds like a plan to me. Except – can you get dressed in ten minutes?"

"Mom, for this, I can get dressed in *five*," I said.

Of course, I might have my shoes on the

wrong feet, I thought. But I could always fix that later!

I slid into the driver's seat and clipped the seat belt around me, careful not to wrinkle the fabric of my dress.

Then I reached up to check the rearview and side mirrors. I wasn't making any mistakes today – not one!

"You're a little more formally dressed than you were last time," the motor vehicle officer said, giving me a curious look.

"Yes. I have a big party right after this, and it's my birthday," I said. I hoped he didn't think I'd dressed up just for the test!

"Well, happy birthday," he said in a formal tone. "Now let's proceed with the test."

I nodded and waited for his instructions. When I started the engine, I realised driving in heels wasn't going to be the same as driving in my usual shoes. But no problem – I could handle it.

I checked over my shoulder before pulling out of the parking space. A curled strand of hair fell in my face and blocked my vision.

"Oh, come on," I groaned. I blew the hair away from my eyes and pulled on to the street.

I squirmed in my seat a bit to make myself more comfortable.

"Ouch!" I yelped. My skin was stuck to the vinyl seat because of my backless dress.

"Everything okay?" the motor vehicle officer asked.

"Fine! Just fine!" I insisted. I pushed the stinging sensation out of my mind. Nothing would stop me from passing this test today!

Suddenly another car pulled into traffic from a side street, right in front of us! I backed off the accelerator and slowed down, avoiding the car.

"Nicely done," the officer said. "You reacted very well."

I heaved a sigh of relief as we proceeded to the traffic light. I waited until we had the green Turn arrow, then drove on to the quiet street we'd used before, as instructed.

I slowly made my three-point turn, being careful not to step on my long skirt as I worked the pedals. As I turned around from backing up, I caught a glimpse of my hair in the rearview mirror. So far I hadn't made any mistakes, and I hadn't ruined my hair.

So far, so good!

"You're doing much better today," the officer said as we returned to the parking lot at the Motor Vehicle Department.

Don't blow it now! I told myself. *Don't even look at any other cars – or any other people, not even Mom!* I slowly pulled into the spot, put the car in Park, and shut off the motor. I glanced nervously at the officer's clipboard, holding my breath.

He looked up at me. "Congratulations, Mary-Kate. You passed!"

The best thing about taking your driving test just moments before your sweet sixteen party is that you're pretty much guaranteed to take a great photo for your licence.

"Okay!" the official photographer said. "Smile!" He snapped the picture. I raced around to his monitor to check how I looked.

I sighed. Perfect. Absolutely perfect.

The photographer chuckled. "We'll send you your photo licence in about two months. You know, it's a little fancier than most people's pictures, but for you, it works."

I grinned. "Well, I was worried I wouldn't look good so I thought, you know, I'd dress up."

He laughed. "Really? Just for this?"

"No, I have a big party to go to," I admitted. "So, am I done?"

"You're done here," he said.

"Great! Thanks a lot!" I called as I ran outside to meet Mom. "All finished," I told her. "You know what? It was much easier the second time around. So, shall we head to the party?" I held my arm out, expecting Mom to take it. She had changed at the house during our brief pit stop and was all dressed for the big event.

"I'm sorry, Mary-Kate. I can't drive you to the party," Mom said.

I stared at her and felt all the colour drain out of my face. "But, Mom! Why? I have to get there – Ashley's going to freak out. We have to leave – now."

Mom shook her head. "No, *I* have to leave now. I have a last-minute errand to run."

I protested. "But—"

"And besides, that nice-looking boy over there said he could give you a lift." Mom pointed across the parking lot.

I turned and spotted Jake striding towards us. He was wearing black chino pants, a blue button-down shirt, and a patterned tie. I'd never seen him so dressed up before. He looked so handsome, it took my breath away. I couldn't think of what to say.

Fortunately, that didn't last *too* long. "I did it, I did it!" I called as I ran towards him.

He wrapped his arms around my waist and lifted me into the air. I squealed with happiness. "All right," Jake cried. "You passed! And happy birthday!"

"Thank you!" He set me down and I hugged him tightly. "Thanks for encouraging me to take the test again!"

"You're welcome. Now, come on, Mary-Kate," he whispered in my ear. "We have a party to get to." He took my hand and slipped his car keys into my palm.

"Really?" I asked. "You're going to let me drive?"

"Of course. It's your birthday, isn't it?" He put his arm around my waist as we walked towards his car. So far this was the most awesome birthday ever – and the party hadn't even started yet!

chapter sixteen

When I walked up to the party with Jake, Ashley was standing on the front porch, looking at her watch.

"What took you so long?" she asked. "I was starting to worry you wouldn't get here in time."

"Sorry – I was busy passing my driving test," I replied.

"You passed?" Ashley asked. "Awesome!" She gave me a high-five.

I stepped inside the house and glanced around. "Ashley, this place looks amazing!"

"I know!" Ashley said excitedly. "And everyone's starting to arrive."

"Can you believe our sweet sixteen is actually here? About to happen?" I asked.

"I can," Jake said. "She talked about it the entire way over." He smiled at me. "Hey, I think I'll go inside and see if there's anything your parents want me to do. You guys will be okay, right?"

I nodded. "Thanks for letting me drive!" Once Jake was inside, I grabbed Ashley's hand. "Can you believe this day? Can it get any better?"

"I think it's about to," Mary-Kate said as the DJ started to play some music.

"Can you see – is everyone here?" I asked Mary-Kate as she peered down at the first floor from the top of the stairs.

"I hope so," she said. "I don't think many more people can fit in the door!"

"Oh my gosh – I can smell the food cooking. It's the fajitas. Mary-Kate, my stomach is growling – can't we go downstairs yet?" I asked.

"How can you think about eating? My stomach's doing nervous flips," Mary-Kate said. "Do you think everyone's going to have a good time? Do I look okay?"

"You look great," I said. "How about me?"

"Perfect," Mary-Kate said. Then she turned to look down the stairway again. "Mom and Dad are talking to the DJ!"

A few seconds later, the music stopped. I held my breath. Now I had butterflies in my stomach, too. This was it. Our big introduction!

"Whatever you do, please, please, please do not let me trip down the stairs," I said to Mary-Kate.

"Here – take my hand," Mary-Kate said.

"Hello, everyone, and on behalf of Mr. and Mrs. Olsen, I'd like to welcome you to Mary-Kate and Ashley's sweet sixteen," the DJ said into the microphone. "Without further ado, I'd like to introduce the birthday girls – the girls everyone is here to celebrate . . . may I present Ashley Olsen and Mary-Kate Olsen!"

He clicked on one of our favourite dance songs as Mary-Kate and I walked down the stairs together. Everyone was cheering and applauding and yelling as we descended the staircase. I was so happy I didn't know whether to laugh or cry!

"Isn't this incredible?" I said to Mary-Kate, almost yelling to be heard above the crowd and the music.

"This place is packed!" she said. "And it's all for us."

"We could never have pulled this off if we didn't work together," I told her. "Thanks for being the best sister in the world – and my best friend!"

We hugged each other at the bottom of the stairs, then headed straight for the dance floor.

Our sweet sixteen was just the way I'd always imagined it – only better!

"Having fun?" Jake asked as I put my hands on his shoulders. The DJ was playing the first slow song of the evening, and Jake and I were dancing together.

"I think I can say without exaggerating that this is the best night of my entire life," I told him. "And it's partly because of you."

"Well, thanks. But I think your family gets *most* of the credit!" Jake said.

"I know," I said, blushing. "I'm just really glad you're here to share this with me."

"So am I. And if I haven't said this before, you look incredible tonight." He brushed my cheek with his fingers.

"You've said it a few times, but a few more times would be okay, too," I said. "Thanks."

When the song ended, Jake and I headed over to the refreshment station to get some punch. When I turned around, I saw Dad standing at the microphone instead of the DJ.

"Attention, everyone. Could I please have your attention? We'd like to give Mary-Kate and Ashley their birthday presents now," Dad announced. "If they wouldn't mind coming up here?"

Ashley and I walked forward, and Mom reached into a bag and took out two envelopes. She handed one to each of us.

I reached into the envelope and pulled out a very official-looking piece of paper, from the U.S. Treasury. "What's this?"

"A savings bond?" Ashley said. She looked up at Mom and Dad and smiled. "Gee, thanks. This is great."

"Yeah, thanks!" I added. It was sort of a boring present, but I didn't care – not when our party was so great.

"You know what?" Dad shook his head. "This is stupid, but I left the paperwork that goes with your savings bonds out in the car. Would you two mind going outside to get it? Should be right on the passenger seat, or in the glove box."

"Uh, okay," I said.

"Savings bonds, huh?" Ashley mumbled as we headed outside. "I guess that's why we never found anything in our present hunt. I mean, they're pretty thin – easy to hide—"

"Ashley, look!" I cried. There, in the parking lot, in the closest spot – where Dad's car *had* been parked when I showed up – was a vintage pink Ford Mustang convertible. There was a huge red bow on the hood, with a poster-sized card that said *Happy Sweet 16, Ashley and Mary-Kate*!

"*What*? Is that for *us*?" Ashley squealed. Together, we started to race over to the Mustang.

"Of course it's for you!" Mom said.

I turned around and realised Mom and Dad had come outside behind us – and so had every single guest at the party!

All our friends were crowded on to the porch and the front steps.

"Like we'd really get you some boring old savings bonds for your sweet sixteen," Dad said.

He tossed me a set of keys. "Happy birthday!"

Everyone started to cheer and clap as Ashley and I opened the Mustang's doors and jumped into the car. "This is so awesome!" I said. "Can you imagine us driving around town in this? No wonder we couldn't find our present in the house!"

"We'll take turns driving," Ashley said. "Where do you want to go first?"

I leaned on the horn and waved to the party crowd. "Thanks, Mom and Dad!" We jumped out of the car and ran over to hug our parents. "This is the most generous gift ever. Thank you so much!" I said as I hugged Mom.

"Thanks, Dad – how did you know we wanted a Mustang?" Ashley said.

"Doesn't everyone?" Dad joked. "But there's something else. Only we need to talk to you about it in private, if that's okay."

I glanced at Ashley. This sounded even more intriguing than the car. "Sure thing. You guys go back inside and get dancing – we'll be there in a second to cut the birthday cake, okay!" I called to everyone.

"Don't take too long!" Brittany yelled.

"We want cake, we want cake!" a couple of guys chanted as everyone drifted back into the house.

"What was so important that you needed to

talk to us in private?" Ashley asked as we perched on the front steps.

"You know the big summer music festival I've been organising," Dad said. "With some of your favourite bands."

I nodded eagerly. "Of course."

"Well, you're sixteen now. And that means you can try new things, take on new adventures," Mom said.

"Right . . ." Ashley glanced at me to see if I knew where this was headed.

"I've arranged jobs for both of you this summer," Dad finally said. "Working at the music festival!"

"*What?*" Ashley and I both screamed.

"It's not as glamorous as it sounds," Dad said. "You'll be working very, very hard – with long hours doing set-up, and selling T-shirts and things like that. But you'll be paid, and when you're finished with whatever work you're doing, you'll get to see the bands perform. And hanging out day after day around the bands means you'll meet some of the musicians."

"Dad, thank you so much – working at the festival sounds incredible!" Ashley said.

"You guys are way too generous. You've given us this great party, plus the car, plus got us these jobs . . ." I looked at both my parents and smiled. "This has been the most amazing party, the best night of our life – and now this summer's going to be even *more* exciting!"

Ashley looked at me and smiled. "I can't wait to hit the road!"

mary-kateandashley

Sweet 16
THE PERFECT SUMMER

Kieran Scott

📖 HarperCollins*Entertainment*
An Imprint of HarperCollins*Publishers*

A PARACHUTE PRESS BOOK

chapter one

"Ashley! Have you seen my purple tank top?" I shouted. I yanked open my bottom dresser drawer and emptied the entire contents onto the floor.

"No! Sorry!" Ashley shouted back, her voice muffled. She was obviously in the back of her closet, doing the same thing I was – last-minute emergency packing for our summer away.

I sifted through the tangle of clothes, then looked around my room and sighed. The place was always a wreck, but today it was ten times messier than usual. My suitcase sat open in the middle of my bed with clothes spewing out of it. All the rejected items were strewn on the floor. My make-up case was packed to the brim and my backpack overflowed with magazines, hair products and pictures of my friends.

1

The tank top, of course, was nowhere in sight.

"I can't believe we're leaving today!" Ashley gasped. She ran into my room, her big blue eyes sparkling.

"I know!" I said. "This time tomorrow, we are going to be chillin' with rock stars."

"Living on our own!" Ashley added.

"Living on our own surrounded by *rock stars*," I added.

Ashley perched on the edge of my bed. "I still can't believe Dad is letting us work at MusicFest."

"Yeah, tell me about it." I frowned with mock concern. "Do you think he's going senile?"

"Mary-Kate!" Ashley rolled her eyes. She picked up a piece of clothing from the floor and tossed it at me. It landed on my head, covering my face. I peeled it away. Oh, wow! My purple tank top.

"You found it!" I cheered, shoving it into my bag. "Now I'm almost ready."

"Good. I'm going to go put my stuff in the car. I'll meet you downstairs!" Ashley nearly skipped out of the room.

I went back to packing. I was totally kidding about that senile comment – but it really *had* come as a shock when Dad announced that he'd found summer jobs for Ashley and me at a huge music festival.

Dad works for a record company and constantly

2

hangs with all these way cool people, but he's never let Ashley and me within three miles of anyone famous. He makes a point of keeping his family separate from his job.

But I guess when he heard about this MusicFest opportunity, he realised it was too good to pass up. Ashley and I would be spending a month living in the dorms at Trager University, going to free concerts, meeting new people . . . and, oh, yeah, working a little.

Satisfied that I finally had everything, I zipped my suitcase shut, grabbed all my bags and lugged them downstairs.

My parents were outside, leaning on the Mustang convertible they had given Ashley and me as a sweet sixteen gift. Looking at the shiny pink car still gave me goose bumps. I couldn't believe it was ours!

"Have I mentioned recently that you guys are the coolest parents ever?" I said. I struggled to lift my bags into the backseat next to Ashley's.

"No, not recently," Dad joked. He gave Mom's shoulder a little squeeze.

"I mean, first you let us throw the biggest, most amazing sweet sixteen party ever, then you get us a car, and now you're letting us go away for an entire month." I put my hands on my hips. "I really think there should be an award for this kind of behaviour."

"Well, you're about to think we're even cooler," Dad said. He reached into the passenger seat of our car and pulled out two brand-new mobile phones – one was shiny silver. The other one was metallic purple.

"Are you kidding me?" I exclaimed. I grabbed the silver one. I knew Ashley would totally love the purple.

"We weren't going to let you leave without a way of contacting us in an emergency," Mom said.

"Thank you, guys, *so* much!" I cried. "Now I can call Jake and Brittany and Lauren—"

"I said emergencies," Mom corrected me. She gave me a big bear hug. "I'm going to miss you!"

"I'm going to miss you, too!" I answered.

"Mary-Kate!" Ashley called from the house. "Telephone! It's Jake!"

My heart gave a little flop. I ran back to the house, slipping my new mobile in my pocket.

Jake Impenna was this amazing, gorgeous, sensitive, athletic, soon-to-be-senior whom I started dating last spring after a ton of misunderstandings. First I invited him to our sweet sixteen party. Then I uninvited him and he thought I didn't like him. Then I invited him again... It was a huge mess! But it ended with Jake and me totally happy together.

"Wait till you see what Mom and Dad got us!" I whispered to Ashley as I took the phone from her. She grinned and jogged outside.

"Hey," I said to Jake. I tucked my long blonde hair behind my ear as I walked into the living room.

"Hey," he said quietly. The sound of his voice made my skin tingle. I could tell he was already missing me. I had to admit I was missing him, too. "I just wanted to call to say good-bye again and . . . you know . . . wish you luck."

"Thanks." I walked slowly around the couch. "I'll call you as soon as I get there."

"Cool," Jake said. "So listen, don't fall in love with any rock stars while you're there, okay?"

"I promise I won't," I answered. "Unless, of course, I meet Gavin Michaels. Then I can't be responsible for my actions."

Gavin was the eighteen-year-old lead singer of my favourite band, Glowstick, and everyone knew I had a massive crush on him.

"Ha ha," Jake said dryly. "Well, I'll miss you, Mary-Kate."

"I'll miss you, too, Jake." I squeezed my eyes shut, hard, to keep the tears back. "Bye."

"Bye," he whispered.

I hung up and just stood still for a second, feeling sorry for myself. Jake and I were so happy. It would have been great to spend the whole summer with him, going to the movies, hitting the beach, having picnics...

"Mary-Kate!" Ashley called from the front door. "Let's go! The rock stars are waiting for us!"

I laughed and snapped out of my funk. It wasn't like I was going to Alaska. I could talk to Jake as much as I wanted. And in the meantime Ashley and I would be living on our own, meeting fabulous people, and having the time of our lives.

I put the phone back in the kitchen and rushed outside to the car.

Let the fun begin!

"Oooh! We are so going to be late!" I glanced away from the road to check my watch.

"Ashley, can you please stop being Miss Responsible for one second and appreciate the tremendousness of this moment?" Mary-Kate said, tipping her head back to look up at the clear blue sky. "We're in our own car, cruising up the coast, heading for the coolest summer ever!"

"I know! I know." I gave myself a moment to savour the feel of my hair whipping around in the wind and the sun on my face. But it didn't last long. "Still, a lot of people have already been there for a week. This is the last day to check in, and if we're late—"

"We're not going to be late," Mary-Kate said, cutting me off. She pushed her purple-tinted sunglasses up on her head and grinned at me. "Come on, let's talk about something else. What do you think our jobs are going to be?"

"Maybe we'll get to be personal assistants to the stars," I said dreamily.

"Or maybe we'll both get to work in wardrobe, picking out costumes for all the acts," Mary-Kate suggested. "Whatever we do, I'm sure we're going to get to hang out with famous people."

"I know! And they're going to pay us to do it!" I added.

"What are you going to do with all the cash we're making this summer?" Mary-Kate asked.

"I am going to buy the Kentmore 2000 surround-sound stereo with ten-disc changer, dual-cassette deck and four remote speakers," I told her.

Mary-Kate stared at me as though I had just announced that I was going to buy myself a mail-order boyfriend.

"What?" I asked. "You can programme it to play forty hours of continuous music. I have the ad." I pointed at my crocheted bag, which sat at her feet.

Mary-Kate laughed as she leaned forward and pulled out the folded-up clipping. "Wow. You've put a lot of thought into this, haven't you?"

"I guess," I answered with a shrug. "I mean, I have wanted a stereo upgrade *forever*. So I'm going to sock away as much money as I possibly can this summer."

"Excellent," Mary-Kate said. "It's good to have a plan."

I cast her a sly look out of the corner of my eye. "You have no idea what you're going to buy, do you?"

My sister's attention span is a bit on the short side. Like last summer, one second she wanted to learn to surf and the next second she was all about scuba lessons, and the next second she moved on to horseback riding.

"I have some ideas." Mary-Kate adjusted her sunglasses. "I'm thinking of a new wardrobe, or maybe a DVD player for my room, or one of those new portable music players ... or maybe I'll get something for Jake..."

She trailed off with a little sigh. I could tell she missed her boyfriend already. What was it like? I wondered. What was it like to miss someone so much you could hardly bear to go away? Aside from my parents and my friends, I didn't have anyone special to miss this summer.

"Oh, no! Ashley!" Mary-Kate suddenly yelped.

"What?" I asked. I glanced in all of my mirrors. Was there a tractor-trailer bearing down on us?

"I think you just missed the turn-off!" Mary-Kate said. She grabbed the map and the directions from her lap and studied them.

"Oh, no." I gripped the steering wheel harder. "What do I do, Mary-Kate? What do I do?"

"Hold on... hold on..." She slapped the map with the back of her hand and moaned. "Yeah. We were supposed to take exit eighteen. We just passed exit twenty."

I tried not to panic. "I don't believe this. Our first big road trip and we're lost!" I thought of the new mobile phone nestled inside my bag. "Maybe we should call Mom and Dad."

"No way. This whole summer is supposed to be about us being independent!" Mary-Kate objected. "We can't call them for help when we've been away from home for only one hour!"

"Well?" I asked. "What do you suggest we do?"

"Stay calm," Mary-Kate said, looking over her shoulder. "We just have to turn around. Here! Take this exit! Maybe we can get back on the highway going in the other direction!"

"Okay . . . okay," I said shakily. I changed lanes. A car horn blared at us. I glanced in the rearview mirror.

"Sorry!" I called out. I had accidentally cut up an SUV behind me! A huge knot formed in my throat, but I managed to get on the exit ramp. At the top of the exit, all the signs were for unfamiliar towns.

"Now what?" I said. Cars were lining up behind us. One of them honked again and I yelped in surprise. "This isn't happening," I said, my palms starting to sweat.

"Okay, make a left," Mary-Kate said. "We have to get back on the highway. Maybe the entrance is over there."

I hit my blinker and made the left, but again, there were no signs for the highway. We were on a two-lane road, driving farther away from the road we wanted to be on.

"How far am I supposed to go?" I asked, glancing at Mary-Kate. She was starting to look a bit pale herself.

"There has to be a gas station somewhere." I could tell she was trying to sound calm. "We'll just stop and get directions."

"Okay." I forced myself to breathe evenly, but the road was lined with nothing but weeds and rocks as far as I could see. There were no signs of life anywhere!

"Oh! Stop there!" Mary-Kate cried out. She pointed at a little run-down building up ahead on the right.

I slowed down to check the place out. "You have to be kidding," I said. One of the windows was broken, the wooden door was all rotted, and it was marked by a hand-painted sign that simply said BAIT.

"That place has 'danger' written all over it," I insisted.

"Ashley, come on! We have to stop somewhere!" Mary-Kate argued.

"Not there," I said, hitting the gas.

"What are you doing?" Mary-Kate shouted as we sped by.

"There has to be another place," I replied.

Of course I was wrong. Fifteen minutes later the road we were on grew rocky, then it turned to dirt. Finally we saw a worn-down sign for a state park.

"Well . . . there you go." I smiled weakly. "People have to be in the park, right?"

The road opened up in front of us into a small parking lot. Along the far side was a rickety wooden fence, and on the other side of the fence was a sharp drop. I had driven us right to the edge of a cliff.

"Uh... nice view," I said, putting the car in park.

"This is a state park?" Mary-Kate asked, looking around at the deserted area. "I think Mom and Dad should check on where their tax dollars are going."

I groaned and buried my face in my hands. I couldn't believe this was happening. We were lost, we were late, and we had no idea how to get back on the main highway.

The best summer of our lives was definitely off to a not-so-promising start.

chapter two

"Look, Mary-Kate!" I cried. "We're saved!" As we drove away from the park, I spotted a little old man walking along the side of the road. He carried a tackle box and a couple of fishing rods. "Let's ask him how to get back to the main highway."

I pulled over near the old man. "Excuse me," Mary-Kate began. "Can you tell us how to get on" – she picked up the directions and looked them over – "Route 57 north?"

The man stared blankly at us for a moment. A *long* moment.

"Uh... sir?" I said.

"Well... sure, I can tell you that," the man said slowly. He pointed down the road. "Now... you want to go down here... and you'll see a left-hand turn just after a big rusted-out barrel—"

"Left-hand turn after a barrel," Mary-Kate said. "Now… you don't want to take *that* turn—"

Mary-Kate looked at me. I shot her a glance that said *be patient*.

"And you don't want to take the *next* turn… but when you come to a fork in the road, you'll want to turn… *left*. Yes, left."

"Okay… " Mary-Kate said.

"Now, once you make that left, you're going to go about two… no… five… no… make that six or so miles and . . ."

I checked my watch. This could take all day. We were never going to get to MusicFest.

Ten minutes – ten *excruciating* minutes – later Mary-Kate had clear directions from the fisherman. We found our way back to the highway and I carefully merged into traffic.

"Okay, everything's going to be fine now," Mary-Kate said.

"Right," I answered. "How much longer until we get there?"

Mary-Kate looked down at the directions and then glanced at the clock.

"Another hour." She bit her bottom lip.

"And we're already an hour late," I said, shaking my head. "Let's just hope they don't fire us on sight."

"There it is!" An hour later, Mary-Kate pointed out the entrance to the Trager University campus. I was in a seriously bad mood. I was tired, I was hungry, and I was still upset over getting lost. I took a look around the campus. "Hey... this place is—"

"Totally cool?" Mary-Kate finished.

"Exactly." I grinned. Mary-Kate twisted around in her seat, taking in the huge stucco buildings, the winding paths and the beautiful flowers. Kids our age were everywhere, walking and talking, stringing up banners, and hauling instruments and amplifiers. The air buzzed with excitement.

"Whoa, Ashley, look at those guys!" Mary-Kate said under her breath. She grinned past me at a couple of cute older guys playing their guitars on a sprawling lawn.

"Hello? Have you already forgotten about Jake?" I joked.

"I meant for *you*!" Mary-Kate said quickly. "Look at those guys for *you*!"

I pulled the car into a parking space. Mary-Kate and I quickly unloaded our bags.

We hurried up a little hill, following the handwritten signs that read "MusicFest staff! Check in here!" I couldn't wait to find out where we were going to be living, not to mention what our jobs were.

The check-in table was set up in the middle of a huge lawn. But a bunch of workers were already packing it up. Oh, no! What if we were really in trouble? What if they gave away our jobs – or fired us or something? Mary-Kate marched right up to one of the girls and introduced herself.

"Hi! I'm Mary-Kate and this is Ashley." She put her bag down at her feet and lifted her hand in greeting. "Sorry we're late. We got a little lost."

The girl, who was Asian and really pretty, looked us over and smiled.

"Don't worry about it." She pushed her extremely long braid over her shoulder. "I'm always late for everything."

I sighed, relieved. We still had our jobs!

"I'm Akiko," she said, reaching out to shake hands with us. "Welcome to MusicFest. It's insane here. You're going to love it."

Mary-Kate and I laughed as Akiko looked up our names and housing assignments. An electric guitar blared out of an open window somewhere nearby. A few kids gathered in a circle on the grass, singing and dancing as a guy beat on a set of bongos. This place was definitely charged with musical energy!

"Okay, you guys are in Murray Hall," Akiko finally told us. She handed us a couple of keys and entry cards. She pointed over her shoulder. "Just follow that path up the hill halfway and you'll see it on your right. When you get there, find your dorm monitor, Mary-Beth. She's in room 105 and she'll give you your work assignments and all the other info."

"Thanks, Akiko," I said. I took the key with a smile, and Mary-Kate and I started up the path.

"Have fun!" Akiko called after us.

Don't worry – we plan to! I thought.

"Look at this place!" Ashley exclaimed as we walked into the lobby of our dorm.

There was a huge bulletin board across from the entrance with colourful lettering that read "Welcome All!" Beneath the letters were dozens of pictures of concerts and parties from last year's MusicFest. My jaw dropped when I saw all the cool people who had attended.

"Isn't that Spike from Jupiter Jones?" Ashley gasped, stabbing a finger at one of the photos. It showed a punked-out guy with a blue mohawk.

"It is," I confirmed, staring at the pictures. "And that's Melissa Ryan!" She was one of my favourite singers. "I've died and gone to heaven!"

"Come on," Ashley laughed. She headed for the door that led to the rooms. "We have to check in with Mary-Beth. I hope she's as nice as Akiko was."

The hallway was carpeted with newish blue rugs and the whole place smelled like fresh paint. I looked down at my key.

"We're in 122," I said.

"It should be right around this corner," Ashley

answered. "Yikes!" She stopped dead in her tracks – so quickly that I almost smacked right into her.

"Oh, hi," Ashley said tentatively.

An older girl with straight red hair and a serious scowl on her face stood in front of our room.

"*Finally,*" she huffed.

I shot a wary glance at Ashley.

"I'm guessing you're Ashley and Mary-Kate," she snapped.

"And you must be Mary-Beth." I flashed her my sweetest smile. "Is that our room?" I asked, moving to get around her. I was dying to put my stuff down.

"Yes." She glared at me as she blocked my way. "Aren't you a little late?"

Ashley began to apologise. "Yeah, sorry about that. We got lost and we—"

"Whatever," Mary-Beth interrupted. She shoved a stack of papers at each of us. "Here are your assignments, info on the cafeteria, the schedule, and everything else you'll need."

I dropped my bags and grabbed the papers excitedly. Mary-Beth can be as rude as she wants, I thought, scanning the papers. Just tell me what my work assignment is! Maybe I'll be a backstage make-up artist or coordinating costumes or—

"Food service?" Ashley asked.

I blinked down at my own assignment. "Stagehand? What does that mean?"

Mary-Beth smirked. "Basically it means you'll be lugging equipment around," she said. "And *you* will be working at the pizza stand," she told Ashley.

Ashley and I looked at each other, dumbfounded. So much for our glamorous summer jobs.

"Well, you better report to your assignments right away," Mary-Beth said, squeezing between us and starting off down the hall. "They were only expecting you two *hours* ago."

Ashley shot me a desperate pleading look. I knew we had to speak up about this now.

"Uh, Mary-Beth?" I said. She stopped and turned slowly to face us. "About these assignments, is there any way we can switch with someone else? We just thought—"

Mary-Beth laughed. "Maybe if you'd arrived here last week like the rest of us did... or if you'd even arrived on time *today*, you would have had some say in your assignments," she said. "But you didn't. So sorry but you're stuck."

With that, she walked around the corner. A couple of seconds later we heard a door slam.

"Yuck. Stuck with the Wicked Witch of the West as our dorm monitor," I said flatly.

Ashley sighed. I suddenly felt exhausted and disappointed. These jobs... and Mary-Beth... weren't exactly what we expected.

"Oh, well," Ashley said, trying to cheer us both up. "It can only get better from here – right?"

chapter three

"That girl is a serious downer," Mary-Kate said as I unlocked the door to our room.

"Well... maybe she's just having a bad day," I reasoned. I tried hard to stay optimistic, even though I was going to be selling pizza all summer.

I swung the door open and Mary-Kate's eyes immediately brightened.

"Check it out!" she cried, running past me into our room.

The room was spacious with two big closets and even bigger windows. The place was absolutely gleaming with sunlight. There were two beds, two large dressers, and a couple of desks with built-in bulletin boards.

"Hey! We have our own kitchen!" Mary-Kate said.

Along the back wall were a couple of cabinets, a tiny stove and a small fridge. She opened one of the cabinets and found a few plates, pots, pans and other random cooking equipment.

"This is so great!" I dropped my stuff in front of one of the closets and checked out the fridge. "We can keep water and juice and stuff—"

"And we can make our own meals!" Mary-Kate said, holding up one of the pots.

"We're going to have to hit the grocery store ASAP!" I added.

"Definitely," Mary-Kate said. She flung herself on to one of the beds and crossed her legs, looking up at the ceiling. "Home sweet home."

"I guess we should get ready for work." I opened one of my suitcases.

"Ugh!" Mary-Kate propped herself up on her elbows. "Hauling equipment around all summer? Well... maybe I can develop some muscle tone."

"There you go!" I said as I unfolded a T-shirt and started to change. "Try to look at the positive side. Our room is great and we are going to get to see all those performances for free."

"Exactly." Mary-Kate rummaged through one of her smaller bags. "We are the bright-side girls."

She pulled out her phone and sat down again, clicking it on.

"Ummm... bright-side girl?" I pulled the T-shirt over my head and lifted my hair out. "What are you doing?"

"I'm calling Mom and Dad to tell them we got

20

here okay," Mary-Kate said innocently. "And… *maybe* I was thinking about calling Jake."

I laughed as I grabbed my crocheted bag and my work assignment. "Just make it quick," I told her. "You don't want to be late on your first day… again!" I headed out of the door.

As I made my way across campus to the pizza stand, I couldn't believe what was going on around me. There was a whole shopping area with little vendors set up in canvas tents. They sold everything from concert T-shirts to beaded jewellery to pottery and bumper stickers. Out on the main lawn, little groups of people sat around, playing guitars and singing.

Everyone seemed so sophisticated. *And here I am,* I thought. *I'm one of them! All of these people are staff here, just like me. So that means I must be just like them – free to do what I want, cool, and…* mature! *Who cares about the pizza stand and the crazy drive and our even crazier dorm monitor. I'm here to have fun, and no matter what, I'm going to have it!*

I slowed my steps as I walked between the rows of food vendors, looking for the pizza stand. There was a kiosk selling hot dogs, another called "The Veggie Spot" with all-vegetarian meals, and a bunch of other places selling ice cream, lemonade, burgers – you name it!

By the time I found the pizza stand, I was sweating. It was really, really hot out. I reached up to push my hair away from my face and found my forehead dotted with sweat. Ugh! Just the way I wanted to look when I met my boss and co-workers!

Still, there wasn't much I could do. Two people were working the counter – a tall guy with jet-black hair and a pretty, petite, brunette girl who was helping a customer. I walked up and the guy greeted me with a bright smile.

"Can I help you?" he asked.

"Actually, I'm supposed to be working here," I said. "I'm Ashley."

"Oh! Nice to meet you! I'm Dennis," he said. "Come on in."

I walked around the counter and he opened a little half-door to let me in. The moment I stepped behind the counter, the already soaring temperature sky-rocketed. The heat coming off the pizza ovens was enough to make my hair frizz. I pulled the front of my shirt away from my stomach, hoping to cool off a little.

"It's not that bad. You'll get used to it after an hour or two," Dennis said kindly. "Listen, since it's your first day, you can just hand out the slices and sodas. I have to head out to a managers' meeting, so I'll teach you the register on your next shift. Okay?"

"Sounds good," I said.

"Penny!" Dennis called to the other worker. "This is Ashley. She's going to fill orders, so you ring while I'm gone."

"Sure," Penny said quietly. I smiled at her, but she quickly turned her attention to wiping down the counter.

"Good luck, Ashley," Dennis said. He walked off and disappeared into the crowd.

I looked around uncertainly, not sure where to stand or what to do.

"Wow. This place is like a sauna, huh?" I grinned at Penny, trying to break the ice.

She looked me over and didn't crack a smile. My grin faded. This girl wasn't giving me much to work with.

"So... where are you from?" I asked.

"I'm sure you've never heard of it," she said. Her tone told me she wasn't going to volunteer anything else.

Stung, I turned away. Penny was obviously not the Miss Congeniality of MusicFest. I looked down at my watch and sighed. Only three hours and fifty-six minutes left in my shift.

After I talked to Jake and changed my clothes, I jogged toward stage B.

"Hey! Do you know who's in charge around here?" I asked a short guy with dreadlocks.

"You found him!" he said, holding out his

hand to me. "I'm Theo, supervisor of this fine stage area. And you are… ?"

"So sorry I'm late," I answered, shaking his hand. "I'm Mary-Kate Olsen."

"It's a great pleasure to meet you, Mary-Kate." Theo smiled at me. "Olsen? That name sounds familiar. I know!" Theo snapped his fingers. "Are you related to the Olsen at Zone Records?"

"Yes, that's my dad," I explained. "He arranged for me and my sister to work here."

"Excellent." Theo nodded. "I've heard of your dad – the musicians like working with him. Anyway, I'm glad you're here, and don't worry about being late. Chris and Melinda over there will tell you what to do." He pointed at a truck next to the stage, where a guy and a girl were manoeuvring a large amp down to the ground.

"Thanks, Theo!" I said. I jogged over to the truck, glad that my boss was so nice.

"Hey! I'm Mary-Kate," I said. "You guys need help?"

"Yeah, actually," the girl answered. She had curly blonde hair that was pushed back from her face with a colourful scarf. She wore a pink tank top and denim shorts. "I'm Melinda," she said. "And this is my brother Chris."

"Hi there!" Chris said. "I would shake your hand, but I'm pretty grungy." He held up a sweaty palm and laughed.

"That's okay," I said. "So, what should I do?"

We spent the next half hour or so unloading equipment for a heavy metal band called Killer Turtles. I had never heard their music or even seen pictures of them. Heavy metal isn't my thing.

There were tons of people walking around the stage area. "So… which of these people are in the group?" I whispered to Chris and Melinda as we made our way from the stage back to the truck on one of our runs.

They laughed. "It's hard to tell," Chris said, running a hand over his shaggy blond hair. "Killer Turtles fans all dress just like the band!"

After about an hour of unloading, Theo walked by and told us we could take a break. There was a refreshment table set up behind the stage, and we attacked it. I was totally thirsty from all that hard work!

Chris, Melinda and I kicked back under a tree with some sodas and snacks. "So, Mary-Kate," Chris said. "How did you end up at MusicFest?"

"My dad," I replied, taking a sip of my soda. "He works for a record company, and when he heard they were looking for workers up here, he filled out applications for me and my sister as a surprise."

"Wow! That was so cool of him!" Melinda said. "My parents actually laughed when I showed them the application I got off the Internet."

"So how did you get them to let you come here?" I asked.

"We convinced them that a summer working away from home would look good on our college applications," Melinda said.

"It was definitely one of my better moments," Chris put in, leaning back on his elbows. "I knew that debate club practice would come in handy one day. But we're huge music fans, and we weren't going to miss seeing all these bands play. This is like, history in the making."

"Cool," I nodded. "What are your favourite bands?"

"Well, my sister is obsessed with a new pop band every week." Chris rolled his eyes at her. "Right now it's Glowstick, right? Or was that yesterday's pick?"

"I'm not *that* bad." Melinda whacked his arm. "At least I'm not a heavy metal fiend."

Chris hooked his arm around Melinda's neck and gave her a serious noogie as they both laughed. "Let's just say we have different tastes."

"Well, I'm going to have to side with Melinda and Glowstick," I told Chris. "I hope we can still be friends," I joked.

"Oh… I guess so," Chris replied. He held his hand up to shield the sun from his eyes as he looked at me. "So, are you going to come by the beach house tonight?"

"The beach house?" I asked, raising my eyebrows. "What's that?"

"It's so totally cool," Melinda gushed. "There's this old abandoned house on the shore, and the staff goes there every night to hang out."

"Yeah, there's usually a bonfire and music and dancing . . ." Chris added. "Plus tons of food."

"Sounds amazing!" I said with a grin. "My sister, Ashley, and I will definitely be there."

"Excellent!" Melinda said. "You'll love it!"

I sighed happily as I lay back in the grass. This beach-house thing sounded perfect. I couldn't wait to tell Ashley about it.

I hope the people Ashley's working with are as nice as Chris and Melinda, I thought. *I'm sure they must be. . . .*

"Here's your cola and here's your slice," I said, smiling. My brain had become kind of foggy in all the heat from the pizza stand.

"Thanks," my customer said before walking off.

I pushed a few wisps of hair away from my face and took a deep breath. In another half an hour I was out of here. I could not wait to take a shower and call it a night. It was hard staying energetic and customer-friendly when I was rapidly wilting. Not to mention that the person I was working with hadn't said a word to me in the last three hours.

"Hey, Penny!" someone called from behind me. "Plate delivery!"

Startled, I turned around to find a guy – an incredibly *cute* guy – coming in through the back of the stand with a few bags of paper plates and cups. He opened one of the cabinets and started putting stuff away. I couldn't help noticing his perfect tanned arms and sun-lightened brown hair.

When he stood up, he wiped his hands on the back of his jeans and smiled politely.

"Hi, I'm Ashley," I said.

"Hi," he said a bit timidly. "Brian."

He returned to organising the cabinets. I turned back to the counter with a huge grin plastered to my face. Apparently Brian was the strong, silent type!

"So, Penny," I said, suddenly feeling a bit more upbeat. "I never asked you... how did you end up working here?"

"I needed a job, so here I am," she said flatly.

I felt my face flush. Why didn't she want to talk to me?

It didn't matter. I wasn't ready to give up yet. "Are you... into music?"

"I have to refill the ice," Penny told me. She disappeared behind the ovens to raid the cooler.

For the first time in my life I wanted to yell at someone I didn't know. What was wrong with her? Couldn't she be just a little nice?

I glanced at Brian to see if he noticed our exchange. He shot me a sympathetic look. Still, I had to get out of there. I walked out of the back, behind the stand.

Whew! The air outside was about ten degrees cooler. A breeze hit my face and I began to feel better. Brian came out and stood beside me.

"Hey," he said. "Just hang in there. Penny will come around. It's your first day at a new job. It's supposed to stink."

He cracked a smile that I felt all the way down to my toes.

"Thanks," I said.

"It'll get better," he told me.

I smiled. He sounded so sure of himself that I believed him on the spot.

"See you around," Brian said as he headed off.

"Bye," I called after him.

As he walked away, I noticed that I was grinning – majorly grinning. Brian definitely had an effect on me.

Maybe there *would* be some upsides to this job!

chapter four

"I'm starving. I can't wait for dinner!" I said. Ashley and I walked into the dining hall. "Wow, it's practially empty in here," I noted.

There were a few people scattered at tables around the room. Otherwise, the place was dead.

Where was everybody? I wondered.

"So, meet any rock stars yet?" Ashley asked me as we grabbed a couple of trays.

I peered at the menu, checking out my choices. Shepherd's pie – no. Fried fish – double no. Meat loaf – yuck. "I met the Killer Turtles," I told her, taking a plate of pasta with tomato sauce.

"Who?" Ashley asked.

"Exactly," I replied.

Ashley laughed. "Well, I'm never going to meet anyone famous selling pizza all summer."

"Sure you will!" I told her. "We're the bright-side girls, remember? Besides, all those superstars eat nothing *but* pizza. Really. And you're going to be their supplier."

"Maybe," Ashley said.

Her shoulders were slumped and she was definitely dragging as we made our way across the dining hall to a table. She obviously hadn't had the best day. I felt bad for her, but at least I had some news that would cheer her up.

"So, guess what?" I said as we sat down at an empty table. "I met these really cool people, Melinda and Chris. They're brother and sister. They told me about this old beach house that the staff hangs out at every night. We *have* to go."

"Really?" Ashley's face brightened a bit. "What's it like?"

I twirled my fork into my pasta. "They said there's music and dancing and food and drinks. You know, standard party central."

"Sounds exactly like what I need," Ashley said.

"Didn't you meet anyone you liked today?" I asked.

"Well, there was this one guy, Brian." Ashley smiled slightly. "He seemed nice, but we barely got to talk."

"Cute?" I asked.

"Definitely," she said.

"So why so mopey?" I asked.

"The girl I work with, Penny, completely blew me off," Ashley explained, resting her cheek on her hand. "I don't think she likes me at all."

"Not possible," I said, taking a bite of my spaghetti.

The moment I tasted it, I frowned and grabbed my water. The pasta was cold and the sauce was terrible.

"What's wrong?" Ashley asked, scrunching her face up as she watched me try to swallow.

"No wonder there's no one here," I said. "It's just like the food back at school."

Ashley pushed her plate away and picked up her water bottle. "How about that grocery-store run?" she asked.

"I have a better idea," I said. "Let's hit the beach house, pronto."

Leaving our trays behind, we made a break for it. *Beach house, here we come!* I thought.

"Wow!" I gasped when I saw the beach house that night. Ashley, Chris, Melinda and I climbed out of Chris's Jeep Cherokee and checked out the scene. "This is *not* standard party central."

Fifty or sixty people were milling around a huge bonfire on the beach. A little farther down the beach loomed a hulking, boarded-up house. A band played on a makeshift stage, lit by the headlights of five parked cars. Everybody was dancing.

"What are we waiting for?" Ashley said. "Let's get in there!"

We headed down the beach towards a huge cooler. I reached in and grabbed drinks for everybody. Chris rummaged through one of the brown bags filled with snacks.

"S'mores, anyone?" he offered.

"I'm in!" I answered.

Chris snagged some chocolate, marshmallows and graham crackers. A pile of thin sticks was lying on the ground near the snack bags, obviously meant for toasting marshmallows. We each grabbed a stick and headed for the fire.

"Chris is an expert s'more maker," Melinda explained, handing her stick to her brother.

"I like to think of it as an art form," Chris said with mock seriousness.

"Will you make mine?" Ashley asked. "I don't think I've ever toasted a marshmallow without setting it on fire."

"No problem." Chris speared four marshmallows with our sticks and took them over to the fire. Minutes later he returned and handed us each a stick.

"The key is proper graham cracker placement," Chris explained. He brought a chunk of chocolate and two grahams over to me, sandwiched my marshmallow between them, and pulled the whole thing off the end of the stick. *"Voilà!"*

I took a small but messy bite of the little sandwich. "It's perfect," I declared as the chocolate melted in my mouth.

Chris beamed at the compliment, then made three more for himself, Ashley and Melinda.

"Let's go check out the band!" Melinda said, licking a bit of marshmallow off her lip.

"They're really good. Who are they?" Ashley asked as we approached the stage.

"That's Dan, Justin, Chico and Rick," Chris said, pointing to each of the guys. "They haven't named their band yet."

"You know them?" I asked.

"Sure. They're all working security," Melinda said. "A lot of the people working here this summer are aspiring musicians."

"Yeah, at the end of the summer they have this contest," Chris said, popping his last bit of s'more into his mouth. "There's a huge concert and one of the amateur acts gets a record contract."

"You're kidding," Ashley said, her eyes wide. "So these guys came here to get discovered?"

"And to see all these other acts play," Melinda said. "It's a great place to hear new styles of music and meet all kinds of people—"

"Of course, they do all want to win," Chris interjected.

The band finished their last song and everyone applauded. Then they took their instruments off the stage and came right down into the crowd to watch the next act.

"How cool!" I whispered to Ashley. "Someone here could be a star by the end of the summer!"

"Hey! That's Akiko!" Ashley pointed to the stage.

I turned. Sure enough, the girl who had checked us in that afternoon was walking to the mike with a guitar.

"Go, Akiko!" I shouted, and everyone clapped.

"Thanks... whoever that was," Akiko said, squinting at the crowd.

She started to play and I looked at my friends, impressed. She had a cool, slightly rough-sounding voice. There was obviously going to be some major competition for that record deal. I couldn't wait to find out who would win!

I shivered in the stiff wind blowing off the ocean. Akiko was just finishing her set. I pulled my sweater tighter around my body. How could I be so hot and so cold in one day?

"You guys wanna go for a walk?" I asked Mary-Kate and the others, hoping it would warm us up a little.

"Okay. Let's check out the rest of the beach," Mary-Kate agreed.

The four of us turned away from the stage

and walked along the water's edge together.

A few notes from a guitar floated along on the breeze. I grabbed Mary-Kate's wrist.

"Do you hear that?" I asked her.

"What?" She stopped to listen.

Our ears picked up the guitar again, louder, and accompanied by a voice. A girl's really pretty voice.

"It's coming from that cove," Melinda said.

"Come on," Chris whispered.

He jogged over to the rocks and we followed quietly. We crept around the rocks and peeked into the cove.

Penny and Brian were sitting next to a small campfire. Brian was playing the guitar and Penny was singing.

I watched them, stunned speechless. Penny – the girl who never talked – had the most angelic voice I'd ever heard. And Brian was amazing on his guitar, too.

"Who are they?" Mary-Kate whispered.

"Brian and Penny," I answered her.

"Brian and Penny from the pizza stand? Brian, the guy you thought was cute?" Mary-Kate asked.

"Yeah," I said. I studied the scene – a boy, a girl, a moonlit beach. It was all pretty... romantic.

"Oh, no." I lowered my eyes. Were Penny and Brian boyfriend and girlfriend?

chapter five

"Wow. Brian and Penny are really good together," Melinda whispered.

"They are," I agreed.

Mary-Kate nudged me with her elbow. "You're dying to know – just ask," she said.

I swallowed hard. "Are Brian and Penny... you know... a couple?"

"Penny and Brian? Nah," Melinda said, waving off the suggestion. "They're friends from home, actually. They came down here from Seattle."

"Just friends. That's cool," I said. I let out a sigh. I couldn't believe how relieved I felt!

"Whoa!" Chris shifted his feet and lost his balance. He grabbed at the rocks for support and loosened a bunch of pebbles, causing a mini-avalanche. Brian and Penny stopped playing, startled, and looked up at us.

"Uh, hi!" Melinda said with a little wave.

"Hi," Brian returned. His eyes darted to me and he smiled.

Penny stood up. "How long have you been standing there?" she demanded.

"Not long," I said quickly. "Really. We were just walking on the beach and we—"

"I can't believe you were spying on us!" Penny cried.

"Sorry, Penny." Melinda bit her lip. "But I never knew you were such a great singer!"

"Yeah! You guys should talk to Mary-Kate and Ashley here," Chris added. "Maybe their dad can pull a few strings and get you a record deal!"

"What do you mean?" Brian asked.

"Their dad's a big record exec," Chris explained. "That's how they got their jobs here." He turned to Mary-Kate, all excited over his brainstorm. "You guys should totally call him and—"

"We don't need any help, thanks," Penny snapped. All the colour drained from Chris's face as she brushed right by us and stormed up the beach.

"Penny! Wait!" Brian called. But it was too late. She was already out of earshot.

"Sorry, you guys," Chris said, hanging his head. "I thought I was helping."

"Hey, don't worry about it," Mary-Kate said, touching his arm. "You didn't do anything wrong."

The beach got a little darker. I turned around to find that Brian had kicked sand on the fire, killing the flames.

"Don't mind Penny," he said through the darkness. He walked over to where we stood at the edge of the cove. He looked incredible in an oversized blue sweater and well-worn jeans. He was holding his guitar by the neck. "We usually practice without an audience."

"That's okay," I told him, even though I was still flustered by Penny's reaction. "Brian, this is my sister, Mary-Kate."

"Hi," Brian said. Then he did a little double take.

"Yeah, we're twins," Mary-Kate said. "Don't worry, the moonlight is not playing tricks on you."

"Good to know," Brian said with a smile. "So, your dad works for a record company, huh? That's cool."

"Yeah," Mary-Kate replied. "But it's not like we'd ever know it. These jobs are the closest we've ever come to 'the biz'. To be honest, I don't even think we could help you guys *buy* a record, let alone make one."

"Don't worry. I wouldn't ask you to," Brian said as we followed Penny's footprints in the sand. Chris and Melinda marched along ahead of us. "We're planning to enter the contest, so who knows? Maybe that record deal will work out anyway."

"You guys are really amazing," I said, tucking my hands inside the sleeves of my sweater. "Do you have any favourite guitarists... you know... influences?"

"Sure," Brian said. "I learned a whole lot from listening to some older stuff – you know, from the seventies. But lately I've been really into Glowstick. Gavin Michaels is one of the best guitarists out there."

Mary-Kate and I exchanged a look.

"We love Glowstick," I told Brian. "You definitely have good taste."

"Hey, thanks," Brian laughed.

The noise began to pick up as we walked closer to the party. Penny was standing at the top of the beach near the cars, kicking at the sand. She looked so dejected, I decided to try to apologise again.

"Hey... Penny," I called when I was a few yards away. She looked up and her face paled a little. "I'm really sorry for sneaking up on you guys like that, but I have to tell you, you really have the most unbelievable voice. I—"

"Brian," Penny interrupted, staring past me.

I stopped, confused. I looked over my shoulder to find Brian and Mary-Kate coming up behind me.

"Yeah, Penny?" Brian said.

"I'm kind of tired. Could you take me back to

the dorms?" she asked. She was already clutching the door handle of a nearby VW Bug.

"Sure." Brian shot me an apologetic glance.

Penny climbed into the car and slammed the door. I felt a little surge of anger. What was Penny's problem? How many times was I going to have to try with her?

Brian walked around to the trunk of his car and put his guitar inside.

"What is with her?" I whispered to Mary-Kate, turning my back to the car.

"I'll give you a four letter clue: s-n-o-b," Mary-Kate whispered back.

I sighed and shook my head. I wanted to give Penny the benefit of the doubt, but at this point it seemed like Mary-Kate was right.

"Listen," Brian said as he came back around the car. "Don't mind Penny. She just has a lot of *stuff* going on."

"It's okay," I said uncertainly. But my mind started racing. What did Brian mean by "stuff"?

"Well, I'll see you later, Ashley," he said. "It was nice meeting you, Mary-Kate."

"You, too!" Mary-Kate called as Brian climbed into his car. In a moment he pulled out of the space and was gone.

Chris, Melinda, Mary-Kate and I headed down the beach. I wanted to get back into party mode, but it bothered me when I thought people

41

didn't like me. Especially when they had no reason to feel that way.

"What do you think Brian meant when he said she had a lot of stuff going on?" I asked Mary-Kate. The wind whipped my hair around my face.

"Who knows?" Mary-Kate said. She paused. "But I bet you're not going to feel better until you get her to talk to you."

"Am I that obvious?" I asked.

"Yeah. But don't worry – it's not a bad thing. You just want everyone around you to be happy," she said. "Come on. Let's go and dance."

"Sounds like a plan," I said.

We ran down the beach towards the stage area. Even though I wanted to let the Penny thing go, Mary-Kate was right. I couldn't stop thinking about her. Exactly what kind of "stuff" could she be dealing with? What would make her act so mean?

chapter six

The next morning I woke up early and couldn't get back to sleep. Mary-Kate, of course, was snoring away, and wouldn't wake up until she hit the snooze button exactly three times. When I finally couldn't stand staring at the ceiling any more, I got up, grabbed my bathroom supplies and headed for the communal bathroom down the hall.

The hall was empty, but I heard someone talking in the lounge. A girl's voice. Whoever she was, she sounded upset. Curious, I passed the bathroom and kept walking towards the lounge. I turned the corner and peeked around the door. I froze.

It was Penny. She was talking to someone on the pay phone.

"Yeah, I know. I miss you, too," she said.

I ducked back around the corner. Hmmm... I wondered. Does Penny have a boyfriend back home?

I crept closer to the door. I felt a little guilty about listening in on her conversation, but I couldn't pull myself away. Maybe I could find out more about the mysterious "stuff" she had going on.

"Don't worry about it, Mom," Penny said. She gripped the phone and looked down at her feet. "We'll figure it out. It'll be okay."

So it wasn't a boyfriend. But what were she and her mom talking about? Maybe her parents were having trouble. That could definitely put a person in a bad mood.

Penny started to turn in my direction. I quickly ducked back into the hallway. I knocked my basket of bathroom stuff against the wall and it crashed to the floor.

"Mom, I've got to go," Penny said in a tense voice.

I crouched down to pick up my things as quickly as I could. But I knew it was too late.

"Spying again?" Penny snapped as she hovered over me. "Don't you have anything better to do?"

"I... I'm sorry," I stammered out. I slowly rose to my feet. "I didn't mean to—"

"Forget it," Penny said. Her face was almost purple with anger. She stalked off down the hall. I leaned back against the wall and closed my eyes, wishing I had never peeked into the lounge.

I wasn't any closer to understanding Penny and her problems than before. And now she had even more reason not to like me.

At the pizza stand that afternoon, Dennis taught me how to use the cash register. "How do you like the job so far, Ashley?" he asked.

"It's fun," I replied. "Much better now that I know how to dress for it!"

Dennis laughed. I was wearing a tiny tank top and short shorts and had my hair up in a loose bun. It made the conditions behind the pizza counter much more bearable. Luckily, Penny and I weren't scheduled to work together that day, which totally helped. I couldn't handle seeing her after the argument we'd had that morning. My stomach churned every time I even thought about it.

"Well, I think you have the hang of everything," Dennis said. "I have to go if I'm going to make it to my other job. Tammy will be along in a little while to help you."

"You have another job?" I asked. "I'd think running the pizza stand would be enough work for one MusicFest."

"Oh, it's not for MusicFest," Dennis explained, hoisting his backpack to his shoulder. "It's my regular job. I live in town and work at a day-care centre. I hired this guy to perform for the kids today and I have to be there when he shows up."

"Cool! Well, I'll see you tomorrow!" I said.

"Bye!" Dennis replied, turning to go.

When he was gone, I stared down at the register, reviewing everything that Dennis had shown me.

"Working hard?"

I glanced up to find Brian leaning against the counter. He held a large piece of paper rolled up like a poster in one hand.

"Not really," I replied. "It's a slow pizza day. Do you want a slice?"

"No, thanks. I just ate," Brian said. "Actually, I wanted to apologise again for last night. Penny doesn't exactly like to perform in front of people."

My brow furrowed. "I kind of figured that. But why?"

"She has this weird stage fright thing," Brian explained. "She kind of freaks when she knows people are watching."

"Then… how are you going to compete in the contest?" I asked.

"I'm not sure," Brian said with an embarrassed little laugh. "We're working on it. Penny is so talented, and I love playing with her, but she has to get over her fear or… well… we're never going to make it. And all I've ever wanted to be is a professional musician."

"Wow," I said. "That must be hard."

Now everything began to make sense. Penny wanted to be a musician – but she was terrified of performing for people. And she was holding Brian back, too. That was pretty scary. It probably explained her attitude. That and whatever was going on at home... I glanced at Brian. Should I ask him about the phone call I'd overheard? No, I decided. I didn't know either him or Penny well enough to pry.

"Anyway, I didn't mean to get all serious." Brian shook his head. "I... uh... I hope you don't think this is weird, but I made something for you."

He cleared his throat as he rolled the paper open on the counter in front of me. I gasped. It was a beautiful charcoal drawing of the beach house.

"You drew this?" I asked.

"Yeah." Brian stuffed his hands in his pockets and shrugged. "It's just something I do when I can't sleep, and I was up last night, so . . ."

I picked up the paper and held it out in front of me. My mind was racing in a million directions. I couldn't believe how talented Brian was. First the guitar and now this!

"This is incredible, Brian," I said. "Thank you."

"You're welcome. Listen, I was wondering if... you might like to go out with me sometime?" he asked.

Wow! For a few seconds I was too stunned to

speak. "I-I would love to," I finally managed to answer.

"That's great!" Brian's face lit up. "How about Wednesday at around five? We can meet in the quad."

"Perfect," I told him.

"Good," Brian said. "I'll see you then."

I swear there was an extra little bounce in his step as he walked off. I laughed and looked down at the drawing again. I knew exactly how Brian felt. I couldn't stop smiling myself!

"Let's just stack all the rigging backstage," Melinda suggested. We stared down at the huge pile of metal rods we had to move. "I don't know what any of it is for, so we might as well just keep it all together."

"Sounds good to me," I said.

We had just bent to pick up one of the larger pieces, when I spotted Chris walking towards us with a bunch of envelopes in his hand.

"Mail came." He handed a couple of things to Melinda. Then he ripped open a big red envelope and pulled out a colourful card. He read it and sighed sadly.

"What's up?" I asked. "Someone send you an 'I don't miss you' card?"

Chris laughed. "No. It's just a birthday card from my parents."

"Aw! Chrissy is all sad and weepy because he won't be with Mommy and Daddy for his birthday!" Melinda sing-songed in a sappy voice.

"Whatever," Chris said, whapping her arm with the envelope. "You'd be upset, too."

"I know." Melinda rolled her eyes. "Our parents really do it up on our birthdays," she explained to me. "Dad makes our favourite meal—"

"And our mother is, like, a cake genius," Chris added.

"It's kind of a big deal," Melinda finished.

"So?" I said. "*We* can do something special. We'll go to lunch, have cake, sing the birthday song. It'll be fun!"

"Hey, thanks, Mary-Kate." Chris brightened a bit. "That would be cool."

"What are friends for?" I asked.

"Here you go, people! Performance schedule for the summer!" Theo shouted, coming up behind us. He thrust one sheet of pink paper in each of our faces, then moved on.

I grabbed the page and quickly scanned the list of bands and acts. Some of my favourite bands were going to be there! Rave was scheduled to play in a couple of weeks, and Melissa Ryan was coming as well. But what really knocked the wind out of me was one word, right at the top of the page: *Glowstick!*

I looked at Melinda and we both screamed at the exact same time. We ran up to Theo, who was talking to some other supervisors. We each grabbed one of his arms.

"When is Glowstick getting here?" Melinda asked.

"They should be arriving tomorrow," Theo said in his usual laid-back way. "I take it you're fans."

"I can't believe it!" I shrieked. "Gavin Michaels is going to be here tomorrow! We may actually get to meet him!"

"You probably will," Theo said. "Gavin's cool."

"You *know* him?" I gasped.

Theo nodded. "I went to high school with Dave, Glowstick's drummer."

We both let out a squeal and ran back to Chris. I felt like an idiot, but I didn't care. It was too exciting!

"Oh my *GOD*! Oh my *GOD*!" Chris shouted, jumping up and down like an insane person. "Gavin Michaels is *so* hot! I'm just going to *faint* if I get to meet him!"

I looked at Melinda and she nodded. Before Chris could defend himself, we both picked up our water bottles and squirted him.

The attack didn't stop him. He darted away, shouting, "Gavin! I *love* you, Gavin!"

Melinda and I chased after him, laughing the whole way.

chapter seven

When I walked into our room that afternoon, Mary-Kate was on the phone. I waved at her frantically until I got her attention, pointed at my poster, and whispered: *"I have to talk to you!"*

"One sec," Mary-Kate whispered back. "Don't worry! I will not fall in love with Gavin Michaels!" she said into the phone.

My jaw dropped open. Gavin Michaels? Was he coming to the festival? Had she *met* him? Now I *really* wanted her to get off the phone.

"Okay, Jake," she finished. "I'll talk to you soon. Bye!"

"Gavin Michaels?" I blurted out the second she hung up.

"Yeah, he's coming here... tomorrow!" she exclaimed, tapping her feet on the floor.

"I can't believe it!" I cried. "Glowstick is

playing the festival?"

"And not just them," Mary-Kate said. She handed me a list of all the performers for the summer.

I scanned the list. "Melissa Ryan, Rave, DJ Diamond... this summer is going to be even cooler than we thought!" I said.

Then I put the list down and waved the rolled-up paper in my hand. "Speaking of which," I added, "check out what Brian made for me."

I unrolled the paper and held it up so that Mary-Kate could see it. She jumped to her feet and took the drawing from my hands. Her eyes were practically popping out of her head.

"Ashley, this is so sweet!" she said.

"I know!" I grabbed a roll of tape off my desk and hung the picture up next to my bed. I stood back to admire it. "And that's not even the best part." I flopped down on my bed. "He asked me out on a date!"

"Excellent!" Mary-Kate said. She lay down on her bed and rolled on to her side. "When are you guys going out?"

"Wednesday," I answered. "I can't wait."

"Whatever happened with Penny?" Mary-Kate asked. "Did you work with her today?"

"No. But I saw her this morning," I said, my stomach turning. "We got into a fight."

"You're kidding! Why?" Mary-Kate asked.

"I overheard her on the phone in the lounge and she lost it," I explained. "I think there's something going on at home, but I'm not sure what. Whatever it is, she didn't want me to hear about it."

"Wow. This is not good," Mary-Kate said.

"I know," I agreed. "And there's something else. Brian told me she has major stage fright. He's not even sure she'll be able to perform at the concert."

"Wow." Mary-Kate frowned. "I guess that explains why she got so upset when she saw us watching her at the beach."

"Yeah. It's so awful," I said. "This contest could really help Brian get noticed – and Penny, too. But if Penny won't even go onstage, they don't have a chance!"

"Well, we'll just have to help them." Mary-Kate's eyes flashed.

"But how?" I asked. "It's not as if we can help Penny get over her stage fright. She hates me."

Mary-Kate sighed. "Yeah, that could be a problem. But don't worry, Ash. We'll figure something out."

I was glad that she felt so confident, but I couldn't make myself believe it. I just wished there was something I could do to make Penny like me… or at least trust me. Then we might be able to help her and Brian.

But after our fight this morning, I didn't see how that was ever going to happen.

• • •

That evening, Melinda and I were backstage at the Killer Turtles' sound check, trying not to cover our ears. We had to be there to set up some of the equipment, but listening to their screeching music was torture on my eardrums. Still, Chris was out front with a bunch of the staff, banging his head and moshing. To each his own, I guess.

"Mary-Kate!" Melinda suddenly grabbed my shoulder. "Look!" She pointed out the backstage door.

I felt as if someone had yanked the floor out from under me. A bus was pulling up in the parking lot with the word "Glowstick" painted on the side in huge gold letters.

"Come on," I said.

Melinda and I sneaked away from the stage. We walked over to the break table, where Theo and some of the other workers were munching on cookies. Excellent! Now we had a much better view of the bus.

"I think I'm going to throw up," Melinda whispered. She picked up a plastic cup and tried to look busy. People started to file out of the bus. I recognized the drummer, Dave Aikens, and the bassist, Mark Passaro.

And then Gavin Michaels stepped down from the bus. He stretched out his arms and yawned. His T-shirt rose to expose a tiny little strip of his flat stomach. I couldn't take my eyes off him.

Melinda and I tried not to stare as Gavin chatted with some of the other guys. Theo wandered over to them and gripped Dave's hand. Gavin said something and Theo pointed over to the snack table – and *us*. Gavin nodded and headed in our direction.

"He's coming over here!" I whispered, grabbing Melinda's wrist. "Gavin Michaels is coming over here!"

Melinda turned white as a sheet. I was afraid she really was going to throw up. Before I knew it, Gavin was standing right next to us! I could barely breathe.

"Hey there," Gavin said to me.

"Hi!" I answered. My knees felt as if they had turned into marshmallows.

"I'm Gavin Michaels." He held out his hand.

I smiled. As if we didn't know!

I shook his hand. I couldn't believe it! I was touching Gavin Michaels! His tousled brown hair fell in a messy-stylish way over his forehead, and his eyes seemed even bluer than they were in the posters I had back home.

"I'm Mary-Kate," I said. "And this is Melinda."

"Hi," Gavin said.

Melinda just nodded. She looked petrified.

"So, what do you guys do around here?" Gavin asked, grabbing a couple of crackers. "Do you mind? I'm starving."

"Please, go ahead," I told him. I was surprised he would ask. I thought rock stars pretty much took whatever they wanted. "We're stagehands," I said.

"Oh, that's cool," Gavin said. "I bet you get to see all the bands."

"Yeah," I answered. "But, I mean, you're probably *friends* with everyone in the bands."

"Nah," Gavin said. "Sometimes I come to these things and I feel like I don't know anyone. It's like being the high school geek all over again."

Melinda laughed. "*You* were a geek in high school?"

I smiled at her, happy that she had finally found her voice.

"No. I was *the* geek in high school," Gavin said. "I was the music nerd who talked to no one."

"That's hard to believe," I said.

"But true!" Gavin returned with a grin, popping a cracker into his mouth.

"Hey, Gavin! Let's go! They're going to show us around!" one of the guys by the bus shouted.

"I have to go," Gavin said. "But it was nice meeting you."

"You, too!" Melinda and I said in unison.

"Hey, do you want to hang out again sometime soon – when you're not working?" Gavin asked me.

Was he kidding?

"Uh... sure," I stammered. "That would be cool."

"Great," Gavin said, backing away. "I'll see you around, Mary-Kate."

As soon as Gavin was far enough away, Melinda let out a squeal. "Did Gavin Michaels just ask you out on a date?" she gushed.

I couldn't even answer her. I was too busy gripping the edge of the table, trying to process what had just happened. I couldn't believe it. Gavin Michaels, my favourite rock star, had just picked me out of a crowd! And he wanted *me* to hang out with him! This was quickly becoming the greatest summer in all of history!

chapter eight

"So? How do I look?" I asked Mary-Kate. I turned away from my reflection in the mirror so she could see me.

She smiled. "When Brian sees you, he is going to go nonverbal."

"You think?" I asked.

I studied my light blue linen sundress and matching sandals, wondering for the millionth time if I should have worn my black minidress instead. But it was still light out and I didn't want to go overboard.

"You look amazing. Trust me," Mary-Kate insisted. She picked up my bag and handed it to me.

"Thanks." I took a deep breath and let it out slowly. I *had* to calm down. I'd been nervous and jittery since I'd woken up that morning. It had got worse all day long. It was kind of silly, but I really liked Brian. And I wanted our first date to be perfect.

"Now go." Mary-Kate grabbed my shoulders and turned me towards the door. "He's probably out there waiting for you already."

"Okay," I said as I left the room. "Wish me luck!"

"Good luck!" Mary-Kate called out. "Not that you'll need it!"

I saw Brian in the distance and hurried across the quad towards him. As I got closer, I went from nervous to mortified. Brian was wearing cargo shorts, hiking boots and a well-worn T-shirt. And he was holding a backpack. He definitely did go nonverbal when he got a look at me. His whole face fell, in fact.

"Uh… I guess I should have dressed down, huh?" I felt like a complete moron in my heeled sandals and glossy lip balm.

"I'm sorry," Brian said, scratching at the back of his neck. "I was planning on taking you on this hiking trail so . . ."

I wanted to disappear. But I lifted my chin, smiled, and said, "Don't worry about it. Just give me two seconds."

Then I turned and ran back to my room as fast as my little heels could carry me.

"I'm glad I changed my clothes," I said to Brian. "It was worth it!"

We'd been hiking for about an hour. The shady woods felt great on a hot evening, and the scenery was gorgeous.

"This is nothing," Brian told me. "Wait till you see what's coming up over this hill..."

We hiked to the top of the hill and stepped into a beautiful clearing. It was bordered by a stream and an amazing shimmering waterfall.

"This is unreal!" I gasped. "How did you find this place?"

"I came up here for a hike the day after I checked in," Brian explained. "I kind of stumbled across this spot." He pulled a blanket out of his backpack and laid it out on the ground near the stream. "I guess I was hoping to meet someone who would want to come back up here with me," he added with a shy smile.

"Thanks for bringing me," I said.

"Here. Sit down." Brian kneeled on the blanket. He produced a slim box of crackers, a little round of cheese and a thermos of iced tea out of his bag, along with a few napkins.

"This is great." I sat and tucked my legs under me. "It's like a date in a bag."

Brian laughed. "Yeah. Maybe I should sell them down at the vendors' market."

"Definitely the next big trend." I poured iced tea into two plastic cups. "So... you're a great musician, how long have you been playing guitar?" I asked.

"Forever," Brian answered. "My dad's a music teacher and he started teaching me as soon as my hands were big enough."

"Have you and Penny always played together?" I asked.

"Only for the last year," Brian replied. "We played a duet for a music class at school and it just clicked, you know? We knew it was right. I hope the contest works out. It would be unreal if we got a record contract."

I shifted my legs uncomfortably. This contest clearly meant a lot to Brian. I hoped Penny would come through for him.

"Is Penny... I mean, is everything okay with her? Besides the stage fright?" I asked tentatively.

Brian looked away.

"I'm sorry," I said. "Did I say something wrong?"

"I know you guys got off on the wrong foot, but Penny really is a cool person," he told me. "She's just... complicated."

"Oh." I wondered what he meant.

Brian's face softened and he smiled at me. "Okay, listen. Let's not talk about Penny. This is *our* date. Let's kick back and have fun. Okay?"

"Okay," I agreed.

"Oh! I forgot something!" he said suddenly.

He got up, walked over to the edge of the

woods and crouched down with his back to me. What is he doing? I wondered. As I gazed at the lush scenery, a warm, fuzzy feeling settled over me. Brian put so much effort into this picnic, I realised. Every detail is just right. I think I've met the perfect guy!

"These are for you." Brian returned to the blanket with a tiny bouquet of wild flowers.

I laughed as I took them from him.

"What?" Brian asked. "Something wrong?"

"No," I answered. "I was just thinking that I've never met anyone like you before."

And it was true. Guys back home were always trying to impress girls with their cool cars or with expensive dinners and gifts. But where was the romance in that?

"Is that a good thing or a bad thing?" Brian asked, sitting across from me.

"Good." I gazed into his warm brown eyes. "Definitely good."

"Good," Brian said with a smile.

Suddenly I knew that he wanted to kiss me. A tingle of anticipation rushed down my spine. At that moment, Brian leaned in ever so slowly. Just as I closed my eyes, our lips met.

It was the perfect kiss in the perfect place with the perfect guy. I knew it was a moment I would remember for the rest of my life.

• • •

"T-shirts! Get your Glowstick T-shirts!"

I smiled at the cute guy behind the souvenir counter in the vendors' area, wondering if he had to shout like that all day. It was Thursday afternoon, the day after my perfect date with Brian. I had a little extra time before I had to be at the pizza stand, so I decided to browse on my way there. I stopped at one of the accessory stands. Something immediately caught my eye.

"These are so cool," I said under my breath, pulling a pair of sunglasses from a rack. They had slim, dark blue lenses and almost no frame. Definitely rocker-worthy sunglasses. Maybe I could use a *little* of the money I was making this summer . . .

I checked the price tag and winced. They were seriously expensive. I guess you pay a certain price for the cool factor.

Still, there was no way I could afford them *and* have enough money for my stereo. I put the glasses back on the rack and hurried off to work.

When I got to the pizza stand, Penny was already there. We hadn't spoken since our argument earlier in the week. I took a deep breath and walked behind the counter, wondering if she'd say anything. Then I noticed a single red rose lying on the counter.

"That's for you," Penny said tonelessly.

"Oh," I said. "Thanks, Penny."

"It's not like it's from me," she snapped.

"I know. I meant thanks for telling me," I said.

Penny turned away. I ignored her rudeness and picked up the flower. I brought it to my nose. I imagined Brian leaving it for me.

Penny slammed a cabinet shut, startling me out of my mushy thoughts. I knew I had to talk to her. We were stuck behind a pizza counter together. We had no choice. But we'd never make it through the summer like this.

I set the flower on the counter. "Listen, Penny, I'm sorry about the other day. I didn't mean to eavesdrop."

Penny sighed. "How much did you hear?" she asked, crossing her arms over her chest.

"Nothing, I swear," I said.

"Well, I don't have a *mobile* or anything, so just... try not to walk in on me again, okay?" she asked.

"Okay," I replied. I was about to ask her why she'd said *mobile* like that when Brian came jogging up to the pizza stand.

"Hey, guys," he said, out of breath.

"Hey! Thanks for the rose," I told him. "It's really pretty."

"I'm glad you liked it." His eyes darted to Penny. "Actually, I'm here to see you," he said to her. "I have big news!"

"What's going on?" Penny asked.

"Well, these big record-exec guys stopped me a minute ago to ask me where stage B was, and I walked them there," Brian explained. "And while we were walking I told them about us and they said they would love to hear us play!"

"Brian! That's awesome!" I said.

All the blood rushed out of Penny's face. "Are you kidding?" she asked quietly.

"This could be huge for us!" Brian said. "But you have to come with me now."

"Right now?" Penny asked shakily. "I... I can't. I'm working a double."

"I'll cover for you!" I offered.

"You will?" Penny asked, obviously shocked.

"Yeah. This is your big chance," I said. "I'd be happy to help."

Penny reached out and braced her hand against the counter. She was shaking.

"Come on, Pen," Brian said softly. "It's just a few people. You won't have to perform in front of a big crowd... like you would at the end-of-summer concert."

Penny darted a glance at me.

"He's right," I said. "If you impress the record executives, you might not have to enter the contest."

Penny looked at the ground and took a shaky breath. "Are you sure you can cover?" she asked.

"Absolutely. No problem," I told her.

She lifted her head slowly and glanced at Brian. She was still pale, but she managed a stiff smile. "Okay. Let's do it."

"Yes!" Brian cheered, clenching his fists.

Penny brushed by me and out of the side door to join him.

"Good luck, you guys!" I called.

"Thanks," Brian said. He took my hand and gave it a little squeeze. "Hey... do you want to have dinner tonight after your shift?"

"I'd love to," I replied.

Then the most amazing thing happened – Penny smiled at me for the very first time. "Thanks, Ashley," she said. "You didn't have to offer to do this so... thanks."

"Any time," I told her. "Really."

Penny and Brian hurried away. I crossed my fingers as I watched them go. Excellent! Not only did I finally have a little breakthrough with Penny, but Brian and I had a second date! And any minute now all of Penny and Brian's dreams could be coming true!

"I *really* have to go," I told Jake that night, pulling on a sandal with one hand while clutching the phone with the other. "I'm meeting Melinda for dinner in about two minutes and I haven't even changed yet. We're going to plan a birthday party for her brother Chris."

"Where's Ashley?" Jake asked.

"She had to work a double," I replied, walking over to my closet and pushing a few hangers around. "So I'll call you tomorrow, okay?"

"Okay. Have fun," Jake said. "Bye, Mary-Kate."

"Bye!" I replied.

I clicked off the phone and tossed it on my bed. "Okay, just put something on," I muttered to myself. I yanked my favourite red sweater on over my head, fluffed out my hair and grabbed my bag.

"Perfect," I told my reflection. Then I grabbed my keys and swung open the door. I sucked in a breath. Someone was standing in the doorway!

"You scared me!" Gavin Michaels said with a laugh, bringing a hand to his chest.

"You? I'm the one who's having a heart attack," I told him. My pulse was racing. Not only had Gavin startled me, but he was looking perfect in battered jeans, a grey T-shirt and a worn suede jacket.

There's a rock star standing at my door, a little voice in my head squealed. *A real live rock star!*

"I came by to see if you wanted to go grab some dinner with me." Gavin pushed his hands into the back pockets of his jeans. A little lock of hair fell over his eye, reminding me of the poster I had hanging over my bed back home.

"But... you were on your way out, weren't

you?" he added. "Great timing, Gav," he said under his breath.

"I was," I said, my face falling.

Then it hit me. The perfect solution!

"What if you come out to dinner with me and my friend Melinda?" I suggested. "I'm sure she would love it."

Gavin took a deep breath and shrugged. "That would be cool," he said. "But I was kind of hoping to spend some time alone with you, to... get to know you."

My knees went weak. Me and Gavin Michaels. Alone. Having dinner together. Was I dreaming? This was too amazing to be real! This *definitely* sounded like a date.

But how could I go on a date? I had a boyfriend – a boyfriend I was crazy about. And, anyway, this was *Gavin Michaels*. He dated supermodels and Hollywood actresses. How could he be interested in me?

"Hey, are you okay?" Gavin asked.

"Sorry," I said. "Can you just... wait here for one second? I need to call Melinda."

"Sure," Gavin said.

I rushed back into my room, quickly dialled Melinda, and explained the situation. She laughed so loudly I had to hold the phone away from my ear.

"Are you kidding?" she asked. "Of course you

should go with him!"

"You wouldn't mind my cancelling?" I said, almost hoping she would hold me to our plans and give me an easy out. "What about Chris's birthday?"

"Please," she said. "We can plan that later. What kind of friend would I be if I didn't let you go out with Gavin Michaels?"

"See, there's the thing that's freaking me out," I whispered into the phone. "The words *'go out'*. I can't go out with him. I have a boyfriend!"

"Okay, girl, chill," Melinda said. "Jake is not an issue here. No one has said the word 'date', right? So it's not like you're cheating on him!"

"I guess not," I said, glancing towards the door.

"So go. Have fun. And don't forget to give me all the details," Melinda said.

"Okay." I took a deep breath and sat up straight. "Thanks, Melinda."

We hung up, and before I could think it through for another second, I walked out of the door and locked it behind me. Gavin grinned.

"We're all set," I told him.

"Perfect," Gavin said.

As we set off down the hall I pushed the last little bit of guilt aside and started feeling utterly, completely cool. I was going out to dinner with one of my favourite stars!

chapter nine

"This is definitely the best burger I have ever had," Gavin told the waitress. She kept coming over to our table every two minutes to ask if everything was okay. She was about my age and giggled uncontrollably. I had a feeling she was another Glowstick fan.

"Really?" she said. "Thanks!"

She scurried over to the other waitresses and they all squealed when she told them what Gavin had said.

Gavin dipped a fry into his ketchup and glanced at the monstrous, half-eaten burger on my plate. His face fell.

"What's wrong, Mary-Kate?" he asked. "Don't you like the food here? Do you want to go someplace else?"

"No! I loved it!" I said. "I just couldn't be any more full."

Gavin leaned across the table, his blue eyes glittering. "Want to hear a confession?" he asked.

My heart skipped a beat. A confession of a rock star? Did I ever!

"Sure," I said.

"I'm kind of a burger-obsessive," he told me. "Every place the tour takes us, I try every burger in town until I find the best one. That way, if I ever come back, I'll know exactly where to go."

"Wow!" I raised my eyebrows. "So is this one really the best?"

"Best burger for miles around," he announced. "So far."

I smiled. I was having an amazing time with Gavin. He was so easy to talk to, and he didn't babble on about his fame. He just talked about normal stuff, like... burgers.

Plus I didn't mind the fact that every girl in the restaurant was eyeing me enviously. I had to admit it was kind of fun.

Of course, the moment I had this thought, a prickly feeling of guilt settled in. I was out alone with another guy, having a great time. And after Jake and I had joked about me getting together with Gavin. How would he feel if he knew where I was at that moment?

I thought of Jake being out with another girl, and the feeling intensified. It made me feel awful.

But it's okay, I told myself, twirling my straw

around in my soda. *This isn't a date. You and Gavin are just going to be friends.*

"Are you sure you're full?" Gavin asked. "Because the dessert menu looks killer."

"Killer?" I echoed, laughing.

"Well, one of the cakes *is* called 'Death by Chocolate'," he said, pointing it out to me.

We decided to split one. As Gavin placed the order, the waitress finally got up the nerve to ask him if she could have his autograph. Gavin didn't even flinch. He was totally sweet about it and even wrote her a personal message.

Gavin was a nice, sensitive, funny, cute guy. Scratch that. A nice, sensitive, funny, cute *rock star*.

Suddenly I realised that it was a good thing that this *wasn't* a date. Because I could really end up liking Gavin. A lot.

"One sec!" I called out when Brian knocked on my door that night. I took a last look in the mirror, pressed my lips together and smiled. Second date, here I come!

I opened the door. "Hi, Brian!"

"Hey," he answered. He was wearing a clean, pressed white shirt and a pair of khakis. It was the first time I had ever seen him dressed up. He looked amazing.

Then I noticed the expression on his face.

"What's wrong?" I asked. And before he could answer, I remembered the audition. "Oh, no. What happened?"

"Penny couldn't do it," Brian said flatly as I stepped into the hall. "She froze up, told me she couldn't go on, and then ran."

I felt terrible for them. If Penny couldn't perform in front of a few people, how was she ever going to become a professional singer?

"That's awful," I said. "I'm so sorry."

"It's okay." Brian shrugged. "I just wish I could get her to see that performing for people isn't that bad. I thought a small group would help, but it obviously didn't."

I thought about that for a few minutes. "Maybe you have to find an audience that won't scare her," I suggested. "Maybe, if she could just get through one performance, she'd snap out of her stage fright."

Brian sighed. "Yeah, but where are we going to find a group of people that won't scare her?"

A thought nagged at the back of my mind. Hadn't I just heard someone mention hiring performers. . . ?

"That's it!" I exclaimed. "I think I have an idea."

"Turn left here," I told Mary-Kate as she drove us through town on Monday afternoon. "We're almost there!" I called out to Brian and Penny in the backseat. I glanced at them in the rearview mirror of the convertible. Penny did not look happy.

"Almost where?" she demanded. "Where are you guys taking me?"

"Just trust us," Brian said.

"Trust you? Are you kidding?" Penny asked, turning to Brain. "You tell me we're going out to lunch and then five minutes into the car ride you tell me you're kidnapping me and taking me somewhere to perform? Why should I trust you?"

"Hey! Turn in here!" I told Mary-Kate.

She made a quick right and pulled into the parking lot of the Lollipop Day-Care Centre.

"This is it?" Penny asked.

"This is it!" Mary-Kate and I announced.

"Your manager, Dennis, works here," Brian explained. "It was Ashley's idea."

I winced. I'd just got Penny to *smile* at me two days earlier and now he was telling her I was responsible for setting her up. But it was true, so what could I say?

"We figured you could practise performing for four-year-olds," I explained, unbuckling my seat belt. "It might help you start to get over your stage fright."

"You guys are lucky I know some kiddie songs." Penny shook her head as she climbed out of the car. At least she wasn't demanding that we take her home, so that was a start.

Inside, Dennis introduced us to a roomful of colourfully dressed, bright-eyed kids. "Hello!" the kids shouted at the top of their lungs.

"Okay, kids. Brian is going to play the guitar and Penny is here to sing for you, so you know what to do," Dennis said.

The kids all scurried to find seats on a big ladybird-shaped rug. Brian led Penny to the front of the room. They sat down on two chairs in front of the kids.

"Okay, I'm going to sing a song for you called 'The Green Grass Grows All Around'," Penny said. "Ready?"

"Yeah!" the kids cheered loudly. She couldn't have asked for a more enthusiastic audience.

Penny laughed and nodded at Brian. They launched into the song, which was fun and fast and had the kids clapping to the beat. When they were finished, the kids cheered. One little girl with black pigtails got up and hugged Penny.

Penny looked up at me as she hugged the girl back.

"Thanks," she whispered.

I grinned. Mary-Kate leaned close to me and said, "You're good, Ash – really good."

"Is this, like, a *normal* Wednesday afternoon for you?" I asked Gavin a few days later. We settled into the box seats at Dodger Stadium with our arms full of food. "Somehow I never imagined you were a big baseball fan."

"I love baseball," Gavin said, pulling out his programme. "But I hardly ever have time to go to a game. I haven't been to one since I was a kid."

"But everyone here is acting like they know you!" I said. Ever since we pulled up to the gate – in a stretch limo, of course – the stadium workers had waited on us hand and foot.

"I'm sure they treat all the celebrities like that," Gavin said. "It's kind of weird, actually. Doesn't it make you feel… I don't know… freaky?"

My mouth fell open. Was he kidding? Perfect seats? Free food? Free souvenirs? All I felt was cool!

"I don't know," I said, leaning back. "I could get used to this."

Gavin smiled. "Well, I'm glad you're having fun."

I took a deep breath as I felt the now familiar wave of guilt wash over me.

What's Jake doing right now? a little voice in my head asked. *You know he'd love to be here with you…*

"It's funny." Gavin cut into my thoughts. "I've been all over the world with the band and no one in other countries is as affected by the whole rock star thing as people are in the U.S."

"Really?" I asked, trying to push aside my Jake thoughts.

"Yeah." Gavin frowned. "One time, in Venezuela, we went to this restaurant and my manager, who is totally high on power, tried to get us a better table by telling them who we were. The guy made us wait *longer* for being so egotistical."

"You're kidding!" I exclaimed.

"Nope. But actually, when we were in Germany, things did get a little weird," he went on. "This one girl snuck on to our tour bus and tried to steal hair out of all of our combs."

"Ew!" I exclaimed, dropping a piece of popcorn back into the box. "Why would she want to do that?"

"People are strange." Gavin shook his head slowly as he stared out at the field. "I get sick of talking about myself," he said. "Let's talk about you."

I shifted in my seat uncomfortably. What story could I possibly tell that Gavin Michaels would find interesting? My tales of evil geometry classes weren't quite as interesting as hair-stealing freaks.

"What do you want to know?" I asked, stalling.

"Well, let's see… what was the most fun you ever had?" he asked.

That was easy – but should I tell him about it? It might sound kind of babyish to Gavin. "Well, it was my sweet sixteen party," I finally said. "It was outrageous."

"What was it like?" Gavin asked, sitting up straight.

I blinked, surprised. He couldn't really be interested in hearing about our party. Still, it *was* a subject I loved to talk about.

"It was... *killer*," I joked. We both laughed. "We had it in this amazing house overlooking the ocean. The decorations were unbelievable and we had this awesome DJ. But the best part was when my parents gave us our car... and my dad told us we were going to MusicFest for the summer."

"Sounds very cool," Gavin said. "It's too bad we didn't meet earlier. I would have loved to have come."

I grinned and returned my attention to my popcorn. I couldn't believe this was actually happening. Gavin Michaels and I were getting to know each other. We were actually becoming friends. Friends with a rock star!

"I'm sure you've been to *really* cool parties," I said.

"Yeah. It's part of the job," Gavin said. "Not that I don't enjoy them, of course."

Gavin frowned and suddenly turned silent.

"Hey, what's wrong?" I asked.

"Sorry." Gavin chuckled. "I guess I spaced out there. I'm just a little worried about something."

"What is it?" I asked.

"Well, Glowstick's contract with Coil Records

is up at the end of the summer and there's a good chance we won't be re-signed," Gavin said. "We're having creative differences."

"You're kidding!" I cried.

"Nope. Not kidding," he said. "So we need to find a new label – the right label – fast!"

Dad could help him, I thought suddenly. *Maybe his label would be interested in signing Glowstick.* I glanced at Gavin. Part of me wanted to cheer him up with that little bit of hope, but for once I made myself bite my tongue. I wasn't about to make a promise that wasn't mine to make.

That night, Gavin and I were making our way across campus, loaded down with Dodger souvenirs, most of which I'd picked up for Jake. As soon as we walked into the quad, I saw Chris and Melinda coming out of their building.

"Hey, guys!" I called out, waving with my free hand. I was psyched to tell them about our day.

But when Chris and Melinda reached us, I realised something was wrong. They both stared coldly at me.

"We've been looking all over for you," Melinda said, glancing at Gavin. "We were supposed to have lunch for Chris's birthday today, remember?"

I felt as if someone had dumped a bucket of cold water over my head. How could I have been so forgetful?

"You guys, I am so sorry," I said. "I can't believe I spaced on—"

"Come on," Gavin interrupted. "What's the big deal? It's just a lunch. This Chris kid has to be a serious baby if he's that upset."

I glanced at Chris, speechless. Obviously, Gavin didn't know that Chris was the guy standing right in front of him. Chris's face darkened.

"Excuse me," Chris spat out. "But I think it's time for my *bottle*."

Melinda shot me an offended look as the two of them stalked off. "Chris! Melinda! Wait!" I called after them. They ignored me. When I looked back at Gavin, his hands were covering his face

"That was Chris, wasn't it?" He groaned. "I'm so sorry, Mary-Kate."

"It's okay," I said. "You didn't know."

We started off for my dorm, but all of my psyched, happy feelings were gone. Chris's birthday had meant so much to him, and I'd completely forgotten about it.

How could I possibly make it up to him?

chapter ten

"Wow! This place is packed!" Mary-Kate exclaimed as she, Penny and I walked through the gates at stage A on Friday night.

"I told you we should have come early," I said loudly enough to be heard over the crazy crowd. "This is *Rave* we're talking about!"

All the shows at the Fest were taking place on huge fields. People brought folding chairs and blankets to sit on. We were hoping for a good view, but there were already so many people in front of the stage, we were at least a football field away.

"Oh, well," Mary-Kate said as she spread out our blanket. "I'm sure we'll still be able to see, right, Penny?"

"Yeah," Penny said. She looked at us tentatively as she sat. "Thanks for inviting me, guys."

"No problem," I said. "Thanks for coming with us."

"I wanted to say . . ." Penny began, picking at a blade of grass next to the blanket. "I wanted to say I'm sorry for being so rude the first week you were here. I just... have a lot of stuff going on."

Mary-Kate and I exchanged a glance. There was that *stuff* thing again.

"It's okay," I told Penny. "I just hope we can be friends now."

"Me, too." She smiled at us. "And thanks for taking me to that day-care centre. It was fun."

"Any time," Mary-Kate said.

At that moment, the stage lights lit up and Rave bounded on to the stage. They launched into the intro for their number one song, "Love Thing". The three of us stood up with the rest of the crowd and cheered. I grinned at Mary-Kate, once again unable to believe that we were actually here.

As Penny started dancing and mouthing the words, I couldn't help noticing there was a little something extra in her eyes. Was she daydreaming about being up there herself someday? I looked back at the band. Maybe the day-care experiment had shown Penny that she had nothing to be afraid of.

"Oh, no!" Penny began searching the back pocket of her jeans. Then she crouched on the ground frantically looking for something.

"What's wrong?" I asked. "Did you lose something?"

"My paycheck!" Penny exclaimed, looking up at me desperately. "I just remembered that I left it in my back pocket. Now it's gone! What if I lost it?"

"It's okay," Mary-Kate said, crouching next to her. "They can void it and write you another one. It'll just take a week or two."

"But I need it *now*!" Penny cried, near tears as she looked around. "I have to send it home to my mother."

I felt the colour drain from my face. "I don't understand," I said.

"No. You wouldn't," Penny snapped, standing quickly. "You've probably never had to worry about money with your record-company dad and your car and your mobiles, but my mom lost her second job, and if I don't send my paycheck home, she's not going to be able to pay the bills this week!"

I was stunned. Mary-Kate stood up shakily and reached out her hand to touch Penny's shoulder, but Penny pulled away.

"I have to go," she said, a tear spilling over her cheek. Before either of us could say anything else, she ran off, disappearing into the crowd.

"I don't believe this," I said as people partied all around us. "Poor Penny."

"Now we know what 'stuff' means," Mary-Kate added. "And it's pretty rough."

"I'm not really in the mood for a concert any more," Ashley said a few minutes after Penny had run off. "I'm going to head back to the house."

"I'm with you," I said, gathering up the blanket. My heart was too heavy to enjoy Rave at the moment.

"I can't believe Penny's family has such serious money problems," Ashley said.

"I know," I replied. "But just imagine... if she and Brian win the contest and get a recording contract, all her troubles will be over. Her mother wouldn't have to work two jobs. And neither of them would have to worry about bills being paid."

"True. But what if she can't do it?" Ashley said. "What if the day-care thing wasn't enough?"

I took a deep breath. "Don't worry about it. We'll figure something out."

We wove our way through the crowd. As we passed by the concession stand, I caught a glimpse of familiar curly blonde hair. My stomach lurched. It was Melinda – and Chris was with her. I hadn't seen them all day, and I still needed to apologise for ditching Chris's birthday.

"I'll be right back!" I shouted to Ashley.

"Where are you going?" she called after me.

I didn't have time to answer. I had to run if I was going to catch up with them. Luckily, Chris and Melinda joined the line at the snack bar. I walked up and slid in behind them.

"Hi," I said tentatively. They ignored me.

"You guys, you have to listen to me." I squeezed in front of them so they had to pay attention. "I'm really, *really* sorry for forgetting about our plans," I pleaded. "I don't know what I was thinking. And I'm just... you *have* to forgive me."

Chris and Melinda exchanged a look and then Chris turned away.

"You know this meant a lot to him," Melinda whispered coldly. "You can't just apologise and make everything okay."

"I'm sorry," I said. "What can I do?"

Melinda sighed and looked me up and down as if *she* felt sorry for *me*. "I'm not sure there's anything you *can* do," she said. Then she turned away from me, too.

Stunned, I trudged back to Ashley, feeling even lower than I had before. "We are not having a good night," I told her.

"They're really mad, huh?" she asked.

"Mad is an understatement," I said. "Melinda wouldn't even tell me what I could do to... Wait a minute."

An idea hit me so suddenly, it felt as if one of those cartoon lightbulbs were lighting up over my head.

Ashley raised her eyebrows. "What? What is it?"

"I think I know something we can do to cheer them up," I said.

The next day I was organising some cables backstage, totally exhausted. Ashley and I had been up half the night making plans, and I couldn't stop yawning. I was in the middle of a huge stretch when Gavin came around the corner, practically bursting with excitement.

"Guess what!" He grabbed my hand and pulled me away from my co-workers.

"What's up?" I asked, a bit flustered.

"A bunch of the bands are planning to have an end-of-the-festival party and it's going to be huge," Gavin told me. "People are coming from all over, there's gonna be great food, music, press."

"Sounds amazing," I told him.

"Do you think you and your sister would want to come?" Gavin asked.

"Are you kidding?" I exclaimed. "Do you even have to ask?"

"Great!" Gavin said. "I would love to introduce you to my friends."

"Do you think I could bring a few other people, too?" I asked. I knew Ashley would want to bring Brian and that Melinda, Penny, and Chris would love to come, too – if our plan worked tonight and we all managed to make up.

Gavin's smile faltered a bit. "You mean like

those kids from the quad the other day?" he asked. "I don't know, Mary-Kate. I doubt the guys would want too many... *staff* people there."

I felt like someone had just punched me in the stomach. Did Gavin think my friends were somehow lower than he was?

"But you can invite your father if you want," he added.

A punch *and* a kick.

"My father?" My mind reeled.

"Yeah. Theo mentioned that your dad worked for a record company," Gavin said casually. "I just figured he might know some people there."

"Oh," I said.

"Or, you know, he may want to *meet* some people there," Gavin added, winking as he quickly rubbed his hands together. "Anyway, I hope you'll come. I have to go and tell some other people, so I'll see you later?"

"Sure," I said quietly. But Gavin was already halfway across the parking lot.

I leaned back against one of the amps and tried to grasp what had just happened. *When,* exactly, had Gavin found out that my father was in the music business? And why hadn't he mentioned it until now?

I swallowed hard, an awful feeling seeping through my veins. Was Gavin interested in hanging out with *me*, or did he just want to meet my dad?

chapter eleven

"Surprise!" Mary-Kate and I shouted when Brian opened the door to our room on Saturday night.

Melinda was so startled, she jumped back, but Chris froze on the spot. His mouth fell open as he took in the room. There was a homemade banner strung from the ceiling that read "Happy Belated Birthday!" and colourful streamers crisscrossed the room. Balloons covered almost every surface.

"You tricked me!" Chris said to Brian. "I thought you had to come over to Ashley's room because you left your wallet here."

"What can I say?" Brian shrugged. "I'm sneaky like that."

"This is amazing." Melinda admired the huge chocolate cake we'd baked that afternoon. She smiled at Mary-Kate.

Mary-Kate clasped her hands together. "Chris, do you forgive me?" she asked.

"That depends." Chris's eyes narrowed. "What do you have for music?"

"Heavy metal only," Mary-Kate replied. She showed him a few CDs. "I borrowed them from Theo."

"You're forgiven," Chris said.

He wrapped Mary-Kate in a huge bear hug. Everything was working out as planned – so far. I was eagerly waiting for Penny to arrive.

"Do you think she's going to show?" I asked Brian.

He glanced at the open door. "I invited her, but I don't know . . ." He sighed. "She said she'd think about it."

Chris turned on the CD player, and loud, screeching guitar music filled the room. He jumped up on Mary-Kate's bed and started playing air guitar like a true rock star. Everyone laughed as Melinda rolled her eyes at him.

"Well, if you can't beat 'em . . ." Mary-Kate said. Then she and Melinda started to dance around to the music, shaking their heads and flinging their hair all over the place.

"This is fun, Ashley! You should try it!" Mary-Kate yelled out.

I had just started headbanging when there was a loud rap at the door.

"What do you people think you're doing?"

I turned around to find Mary-Beth standing in the doorway, red-faced.

She stalked into the room and hit the off button on the CD player. "In case you didn't know, you're supposed to register all parties with the floor monitor."

"Really?" Mary-Kate pushed her wild hair out of her face. "Because I read the dorm handbook – and it said that parties of fewer than eight people don't need to be registered."

Mary-Beth blinked, obviously surprised that we'd actually read the rules. "Well, is this everyone?" she asked, looking around the room.

"Yes," I told her. "It's just the five of us."

"Six, actually." Penny stepped into the room. I grinned. She had come!

"All right, then," Mary-Beth said. "Just... keep it down." She stormed out.

Mary-Kate turned the music on, lower this time, and she, Melinda and Chris went back to dancing.

Penny approached Brian and me. "Hi, Penny," I said.

"Hi." She wrapped her arms around herself. "Thanks for inviting me. After the way I blew up last night—"

"Please," I said, waving my hand. "You were upset. I understand."

"Still, that's no excuse. I shouldn't have taken it out on you," Penny said. "I'm sorry."

"It's okay," I told her. "Just forget it ever happened." I smiled at her, and she stared at me for a second as if she didn't trust me. But then her face relaxed and she smiled back.

"Oh, hey! I have news," Chris announced, jumping down from the bed. "There's going to be a big party at the beach house the night before the contest, and we're going to have a practice concert."

"Kind of like a dress rehearsal," Melinda put in, looking at Brian and Penny. "So you'll get to check out the competition."

Penny forced a smile, but I noticed she paled a bit at the mention of the contest. Maybe the performance at the day-care centre really *hadn't* done the trick.

We had to find some other way to help Penny get over her stage-fright. But how?

"Has Penny tried imagining her audience in their underwear?" Jake asked me over the phone. "That always worked for me in creative writing class."

It was the day after the birthday bash and I had just told him about Penny and her stage-fright problem.

"Wait a minute – you were imagining us in our underwear all year?" I asked. "Everybody in the class?"

"No!" Jake protested. "Just Ms. Trauth."

"Um… ew," I said. I didn't want to imagine *any* of our teachers in their underwear. The whole idea was just gross.

"I'm kidding," Jake laughed. "So what are you doing tonight, anyway?"

I felt a little flutter in my stomach and paused. A few nights ago I told Jake that I was hanging out with Gavin Michaels – and he was totally cool about it. But if he knew I had plans with Gavin again tonight, would he be upset?

I thought about it for a second. It might *sound* like I was spending all my free time with Gavin… but that wasn't exactly true. Gavin had rehearsals every night – and I was usually at the beach house.

Besides, Gavin and I were just friends. Jake had nothing to worry about…

"Mary-Kate?"

"Oh! I'm taking Gavin to the beach house," I told Jake. "He hasn't been there yet."

Now it was Jake's turn to be quiet. I could practically feel his tension through the phone line. My pulse began to race.

"You've been spending a lot of time with him, huh?" Jake finally said.

"I guess, but we're just friends," I assured him.

"So, does this *friend* know about me?" Jake asked.

I held my breath. I hadn't told Gavin about Jake. Why, why, *why* hadn't I told Gavin about Jake?

"I don't believe this," Jake said, guessing the answer from my silence.

"Well, what's the big deal?" I asked, feeling defensive. "It just hasn't come up."

Ten points for lameness, I thought as I squeezed my eyes closed.

"Really? Well, if he's such a good friend, why doesn't he know you have a boyfriend?" Jake shot back. "Or maybe I'm just not important enough to tell your friends about."

"No! That's not true!" I insisted. "I told Chris and Melinda about you!"

The second I said it, I realised my mistake.

"So you told everyone *but* the rock star," Jake said. "What am I supposed to think?"

I had no answer. I hadn't told Gavin, and it looked totally suspicious. So I said the first thing that came to mind.

"Well... just think whatever you want!" I shouted. Then I slammed down the phone before he could make me feel any worse.

"So, how do you like it?" I asked Gavin that night. We paused on the outskirts of the crowd around the bonfire. I wanted to show Gavin how cool the *staff* people were and how much fun we had at the beach house, but after my conversation with Jake that afternoon, I wasn't feeling cool or fun myself.

"It's okay." Gavin folded his arms over his suede jacket. "Is your sister here?"

"I don't know," I answered. I hadn't seen Ashley all day, and I so needed to unload on someone about the Jake thing.

"I can't believe I haven't met her yet," Gavin said.

Just don't bring up my father, I thought. *We can talk about Ashley all you want, but don't bring up my father again.*

"So are we done here?" Gavin asked.

My spirits sank. "Are you bored?" I asked.

"This isn't really my scene," Gavin said. "Why don't we go back and hang out with the band?"

I pulled my sweater more tightly around my body as a stiff breeze chilled me. "I don't know. I'm kind of tired," I told him, disappointed. "Maybe I'll just go back to the dorm."

"Okay," Gavin said. "You can drop me off."

As we started back up the beach towards my car, I couldn't help feeling uncomfortable. He hadn't given the beach house a chance. He hadn't even met any of my friends. Did he really want to get to know me? Or was he a phony?

"So are you coming to the party?" Gavin asked.

I took a deep breath. The party. Right. At that moment I wasn't so sure I wanted to go, even with

all the celebrities and glamour and excitement.
But I wasn't totally ready to give up on Gavin yet.

"Yeah," I agreed. "I'll be there."

"Cool!" Gavin said. "I can't wait for you to
meet everyone."

We got into the car and buckled our seat belts.
Jake's face suddenly flashed into my mind.

This is so wrong, I thought. *There's only one
reason I haven't mentioned Jake to Gavin yet. It's
because I like the idea that Gavin could be
interested in me as a girlfriend!*

And I had to admit, if I didn't have Jake, I
would probably *want* Gavin to be interested.

But I was crazy about Jake – and I knew
what I had to do. "Gavin, there's something you
should know," I said. "I have a boyfriend."

Gavin stared at me, the light from a
streetlamp shining on our faces. What was he
thinking? Was he disappointed?

I gulped. Oh, no. What if he was never
interested in me to begin with? Was I a complete
idiot for imagining that he – a music megastar –
would actually want to go out with me?

I waited to hear what he'd say. My face felt
hot. There was no way this could be good.

At last Gavin grinned at me. "That's okay,
Mary-Kate. I still want you to come to the party…
as my friend."

I relaxed and started the car. I wasn't sure if

Gavin was interested in me as a girlfriend or not, but, either way, it didn't matter.

Gavin wanted to be my friend – and that was cool.

Unlike me, I thought. How could I have hung up on Jake like that?

First thing in the morning, I vowed, I'm calling Jake to apologise.

"Where's Mary-Kate?" Melinda asked.

"She's out with Gavin," I answered. "So it's just the five of us."

I settled down on the edge of my bed with Chris and Melinda and passed them a plate of mini-pizzas I made in our microwave. "Okay, Penny, try to do one song."

"I don't know, you guys," Penny said, shifting slightly on Mary-Kate's mattress. Brian was sitting next to her with his guitar ready. He shot me a pleading look.

"I just want to see if you can do it," I said lightly. "We have to find out if the whole day-care experiment worked."

"Okay. I'll try," she said.

Brian strummed a few chords, and Penny started to sing.

"'There was a time... not so long ago . . .'"

I smiled as I munched on my pizza. She was doing it! But then she glanced over at us and her mouth snapped shut. Brian stopped playing.

"I'm sorry!" Penny covered her face with her hands. "It's like my throat just closes up!"

Mary-Kate walked in and threw her car keys on the desk. She took one look at us and frowned. "What's going on?" she asked.

"We're trying to help Penny come up with a way to get over her stage fright," Melinda explained. She held out the plate. "Mini-pizza?"

"Thanks!" Mary-Kate grabbed a pizza and sat down next to Chris. We all scooted over to make room. "Have you tried imagining the audience in their underwear?" Mary-Kate asked.

"Yeah. That doesn't work," Penny said.

"Ooh! Ooh!" Chris exclaimed, sitting up straight. "What if you don't look at us at all? Like, focus on a spot on the wall behind us or something?"

Penny shook her head. "I've tried it, but I can still see the audience," she said. "This is hopeless!"

"Wait a minute!" I exclaimed, standing up and startling everyone in the room.

I ran to my closet and pulled a flowered scarf off one of the hooks inside.

"Um, what are you doing?" Penny asked as I tied the scarf around her eyes.

"Can you see?" I asked, waving my hand in front of her face.

"No," Penny responded. "I can't see anything."

"Okay. So try it now," I said.

I held my breath as Brian started to play. A few chords in, Penny started to sing and her voice was more confident this time. I smiled at my friends. It was working! It was really working!

Penny got through the whole song, and we all erupted with applause. Penny whipped the scarf off her head, grinning like she'd never grinned before.

"You did it!" I cried. "We found the cure!"

I was so psyched, I jumped up and down. Penny beamed at me, and for the first time I felt like we were actually starting to become friends.

"I can't believe it," Penny said. She gazed at the scarf in her hands as if it were a magic wand. "I knew you were there, but it didn't matter as long as I couldn't see you."

"Not to be the downer here," Melinda said. "But Penny can't exactly perform at the contest blindfolded. The judges will think she's lost it."

"She's right," Penny said, her smile fading.

"Hey, we've come this far," I told her. "We'll find a way."

But inside my mind was scrambling for an answer. There had to be a way to solve Penny's problem. I just couldn't imagine what it was.

chapter twelve

"So... you told him?" Jake asked me on the phone the following morning.

"Yeah," I confessed. "I'm really sorry I didn't tell him before. There was just never a conversation where it naturally came up."

"It's okay," Jake responded. "I overreacted anyway. I just really miss you."

"I miss you, too," I said. "But I'll be home before you know it."

"I can't wait," Jake said. "Well, I have to get ready for work. I'll talk to you later?"

"Definitely," I agreed.

I hung up the phone just as Ashley came back from her shower.

"How did it go with Jake?" she asked.

"Fine." I smiled. "He forgives me."

"Well, that's good news," she said.

"I have more good news," I told her. "Gavin invited us to a huge party at the end of the summer."

"A huge party? You mean a huge rock-star party filled with celebrities?"

"Yep. That's what I mean," I told her.

"You're kidding!" Ashley squealed, her eyes shining. "Why didn't you *tell* me!" She dived into her closet and started shoving hangers around.

"What are you doing?" I asked.

"I don't know if I brought anything I can wear to a rock-star party!" Ashley called from inside the closet.

I laughed, pushed myself off my bed and joined Ashley at her closet. I tried not to show it, but I was just as excited as she was. We were talking about a fabulous, star-studded event here. It was only a moment we'd been waiting for our entire lives.

As Ashley started to lay clothes out on her bed, I thought the whole thing through. It wasn't really that big of a deal that Gavin wasn't interested in my other friends. I hung out with different groups at school. Some of my friends liked one another, and some didn't. So what? And he hadn't mentioned Dad again since that first time... He probably wasn't interested in Dad at all. I'd just overreacted.

"This could work!" Ashley pulled a slim black

dress out of the closet.

"Absolutely!" I told her. "You can never go wrong with basic black."

Ashley held the dress up and stepped in front of the mirror.

"I can't wait to tell Brian!" she breathed. "Gavin Michaels is his idol and now he's going to get to party with him!"

My face fell as I watched Ashley spin in front of the mirror. I didn't have the heart to tell her that Brian might not be welcome at the party. After all, Gavin and the rest of the guys would probably write him off as *just staff.*

"Hey, Gavin!" I called out late that afternoon as I walked on to stage A.

Gavin and the rest of the band were sitting on the edge of the stage, going over their playlist. I walked over to them, determined to convince Gavin to let Ashley bring a date to his party. There was no way I was going to tell Brian that he couldn't come to an event thrown by his idol.

"Mary-Kate!" Gavin exclaimed, tossing his fringe off his forehead. "Hey, guys, this is the girl I was telling you about. Mary-Kate, these are the guys."

"Hi!" I said.

I was flattered that Gavin had told them about me. They all smiled and said hello, and once again I couldn't believe my luck. I was actually chilling out with Glowstick!

Focus, Mary-Kate, a little voice inside my head told me. *You're here for a reason, remember?*

"Gavin? Can I talk to you?" I asked.

"Sure, but let me give you this before I forget." Gavin reached behind him and grabbed a folder. He pulled out a bright blue piece of paper and handed it to me, then jumped down from the stage.

It was an invitation to the party with all the details. I paused when my eyes fell on the date. Why did that day sound so familiar?

"So what did you want to talk to me about?" Gavin asked.

But before I could answer, it hit me. Gavin's party was on the same date as the dress rehearsal party for the contest! Ashley was going to die when she heard about the conflict.

"Um, don't worry about it," I said, taking a few steps back. "I just remembered I have to tell Ashley something."

Then I jogged away, leaving Gavin totally confused.

"So do you know which song you're going to perform at the contest?" I asked Brian as we sat down at a table in the cafeteria. It was fried chicken night – the only night of the week that the food was actually edible.

"We're narrowing it down," Brian answered as he unfolded his napkin. "We wouldn't even be doing that if it weren't for you, Ashley. I think Penny's actually starting to feel like she can do this."

"Well, we're not done yet," I said. "We still have to find a way to blindfold her without actually blindfolding her."

We both laughed, but we *were* running out of time. If we didn't find an answer soon...

"There you are!"

I looked up to find Mary-Kate speed-walking down the centre aisle of the dining hall, her face all flushed.

"What's up?" I asked.

"Big problem," Mary-Kate said, dropping into the seat next to mine. She handed me a piece of blue paper as she struggled to catch her breath.

I put my fork down and read through the invitation, my heart pounding with excitement. I couldn't believe we were actually going to a party thrown by Gavin Michaels.

"Oh." My happiness flitted away the moment I saw the date.

"What's wrong?" Brian asked. He glanced at the piece of paper and his face fell.

"No glamorous party for us," I said brightly. "It's no big deal."

"No, Ashley, you should go to the party,"

Brian insisted. "You want to be there. You were practically drooling when you told me about it," he joked.

"Not gonna happen," I said. "I want to be there for you... and for Penny." I turned to Mary-Kate. "You go without us."

"You're sure?" Mary-Kate asked, looking dejected.

I was disappointed, but my mind was made up. "The stars will just have to wait," I declared.

"Who needs rock stars," I said later that night, "when we've got a whole sky full of *real* stars?"

Brian and I were taking a walk after dinner. Brian had brought along his guitar. We settled under a tall, old sycamore tree in a secluded field on campus. The sky was blazing with stars, and the moon sat low and full on the horizon.

Brian strummed a few chords. "I don't care about rock stars *or* real stars," he said. "I just like hanging out with you, Ashley."

I smiled and leaned back against the tree. The scent of roses floated across the field, carried by a warm breeze. *Brian has to be the sweetest guy I've ever met*, I thought.

"I've been trying to write my own songs," Brian told me. "I wrote this one this morning."

He began to pick out a delicate melody. While he sang, I watched the moon rise in the sky. The air was warm and the field was bathed in moonlight. *This is the most beautiful night in the history of the universe,* I thought.

Then Brian sang the chorus of the song:

"Until I saw your eyes, I never knew
How pretty a pair of blue eyes could be.
Until I saw your face I never knew
That a girl could mean so much to me."

He wrote this just for me! I realised. *It's the most beautiful song I've ever heard, and it's for me.*

"What do you think?" he asked.

"I love it!" I replied. "It's fantastic! You should write more songs. You're really good at it."

"Thanks." He set his guitar on the grass and took my hand. I leaned against him.

Spending the last few weeks with Brian has been amazing, I thought. *I don't think I've ever liked a boy this much before.*

"I can't believe there's only a week left to MusicFest," Brian said.

His words shot through me like a jolt of electricity. He was right – our time together was almost over.

"Brian—" I turned toward him, and he kissed me. For those few seconds, my worries melted away.

I'm so happy, I thought. *I wish this night could go on forever...*

But I knew that it couldn't. Brian would leave for Seattle very soon. I couldn't help but wonder what would happen to us then.

chapter thirteen

"Blindfolds... blindfolds," I muttered to myself. I stalked through the vendors' area on the day of the pre-concert party. We had only a few hours left and we still hadn't found a good way to cover Penny's eyes.

"Why doesn't anyone make stylish blindfolds?" I wondered. Then I caught myself and couldn't help giggling at the silly idea.

Mary-Kate was back at the dorm, trying to decide what to wear to Gavin's mega-party, while I roamed around campus, racking my brain for a solution. Suddenly, something caught my attention and I paused. The sunglasses I had fallen in love with a couple of weeks ago. The cool, fashionable, *rock-star-worthy* sunglasses.

I pulled them off the display and checked the price, then did the maths in my head again. The result was the same. If I bought the glasses, there was no way I would be able to afford my stereo.

"Excuse me," I said to the woman behind the counter. "There isn't an employee discount, is there?"

The woman scoffed at me and rolled her eyes. "Sorry, kid."

I sighed and looked down at the sunglasses. Well, I didn't really *need* the ten-disc changer, right?

Before I could talk myself out of it, I put the sunglasses down next to the register and pulled out my wallet. I could handle having a lesser stereo. This was for a good cause.

The woman eyed the price of the sunglasses. "Are you sure?" she asked.

I slapped the cash down on the counter and grinned. "I'll take 'em."

Gavin ushered me past the tables packed with scrumptious food and champagne glasses. Flashbulbs went off all around us. Everywhere I looked, I saw another famous face. TV stars were chatting with musicians as if they were all regular people. Trina Thurston, the star of my favourite show, *Spencer Academy*, actually asked me to pass her a napkin. I had to bite my lip to keep from screaming.

"So, glad you came?" Gavin asked, handing me a cup full of punch.

"Glad does not cover it," I told him. I did feel a bit guilty about not being at the beach house for Penny, but she had Ashley, Brian, Chris and Melinda. I was sure she was just fine.

"Oh, hey! There's Russell Lawrence, my agent." Gavin waved at an older man with slick, greying hair and glasses. The man made his way through the crowd towards us.

"Gavin! How fabulous to see you!" the man exclaimed.

"Mary-Kate, this is my agent and best friend, Russell." Gavin slung his arm over the man's shoulders. "Russell, Mary-Kate."

"Hey." Russell held up his hand, but he kept his gaze fixed on Gavin. "Well, I'll see you, Gav. Give me a call when you're back in town."

I glanced up at Gavin as his "best friend" disappeared into the throng of people.

Whoa! Talk about rude, I thought. *He could have at least looked at me.* But Gavin didn't seem to notice. He was busy scanning the crowd again.

"Carlos!" he called out suddenly.

Across the room stood Carlos Batista – a huge Latino music star. He saw Gavin and headed towards us. My heart stuck in my throat. Carlos had won about a million sexiest-man-alive awards.

"You have to meet this guy. He's, like, my best friend," Gavin said to me under his breath.

Wait a minute, I thought. *Isn't* Russell *your best friend?*

"Gavin Michaels!" Carlos said, elbowing his way over to us.

"Where ya been, man?" Gavin asked, slapping hands with Carlos.

"Touring," Carlos said. "Europe, Australia, South America . . ."

"I want you to meet my friend Mary-Kate," Gavin said.

I grinned as I looked up at Carlos. "It's a pleasure to meet you," I said. Carlos gave me a mega-watt smile.

"Yeah, well, I'd better go find Melissa Ryan," Carlos said. "My manager tells me I *have* to get her to open for me on the North American dates – so I have to be her new buddy."

Before I knew it, Carlos was gone. I was about to ask Gavin what the deal was with his so-called best friends, but he cut me off.

"I *love* that guy," he said.

What? Hadn't he just heard what Carlos said about Melissa Ryan? He was going to pretend to be her friend – just so he could get her to do something for him!

Gavin pulled some girl over to him and gave her a couple of air kisses. I felt myself growing more and more uncomfortable. What was up with Gavin? Where was the down-to-earth guy I knew?

Had it all been an act? Or was he putting on an act for *these* people?

"We *have* to get together," the girl told Gavin.

"Absolutely," Gavin answered. "I'll have my people call your people."

Okay, that was it. Maybe this snobby, fake Gavin *was* the real Gavin – or maybe he wasn't. But either way I wasn't sure I wanted to be friends with a person who had one real side and one completely different fake side.

Which made me wonder – could Gavin be faking with me? Could he be hanging out with me just because my dad works at Zone Records?

Suddenly, one of the waiters, carrying a tray full of used napkins and cups back to the garbage, tripped and stumbled into Gavin's side. He turned purple when he realised who Gavin was.

"I'm sorry, I—"

"Watch it!" Gavin spat out. "Do I *look* like a trash can?"

A few people turned to stare. I was mortified as the waiter rushed off.

"What is going on with you?" I whispered to Gavin, pulling him towards a semi-quiet corner.

"What are you talking about?" Gavin asked.

"You're acting so different tonight," I told him.

I crossed my arms over the front of the black dress I'd borrowed from Ashley. "Listen, there's something that's been bothering me. Something I have to ask you. Have you been hanging out with me because my father is in the music business?"

"What?" Gavin blurted out, stunned. "Mary-Kate, you have to know me better than that."

I took a deep breath, feeling slightly relieved. Maybe Gavin was just having an off night—

"So, *did* you invite your dad?" he asked, looking over my shoulder.

"Ugh!" I cried out, throwing my hands in the air. "I'm sorry. I have to get out of here."

I turned on my high heels and walked away, paying no attention to the whispers and giggles that followed me. I couldn't believe it! Gavin Michaels was the shallowest and phoniest person I had ever met! And I'd wasted half my summer on him!

It was time for me to get back to what was important. I just hoped Penny and Brian hadn't performed yet.

I clutched the sunglasses as I ran through the crowd at the beach house that night. One of the bands was already playing, and I knew Brian and Penny would be up soon. Thankfully, we had a meeting place, so I didn't have to search for them.

When I came around the back of the darkened beach house, I found Chris, Melinda and Brian standing there, all trying to calm Penny down.

"Ashley! You have to help me!" Penny wailed when she spotted me. "I can't go out there with a scarf around my head! How did I get myself into this? I'm going to look totally stupid."

"No problem!" I cried. I held out the sunglasses to Penny. "I got you these."

Penny took the glasses from me. "How are these going to—"

"Just put them on!" I said.

"Those are totally cool!" Melinda exclaimed when Penny slipped the glasses over her eyes.

In her black tank top and jeans, with those glasses on, Penny looked like a real rock star.

"I can hardly see anything," Penny said.

"That's the idea!" I explained. "The lenses are so dark, no one in the audience will be able to see your eyes, either."

"Hey! You could probably even close your eyes if you wanted to!" Chris suggested.

Penny took the glasses off and grinned. "Thanks, Ashley," she said. "Okay. I'll go on."

Brian let out a whoop of joy and grabbed Penny up in his arms, swinging her around. The rest of us laughed, completely relieved. Penny was finally going to perform!

The band onstage finished up their song to wild cheers from the crowd and then Mary-Beth, who was running the show, stepped up to the microphone.

"Next up are Penny and Brian!" she shouted.

"That's us," Brian said excitedly. He turned to me and gave me a quick kiss. "Thank you," he whispered.

I smiled, chills running all over my body. "Any time," I responded.

Penny and Brian rushed out on to the stage. Chris, Melinda and I hung back. We had a good side view, and I was too nervous to get in the middle of the crowd. Penny and Brian sat down on the two stools in the centre of the stage, and I crossed my fingers.

"It's going to work," Melinda said. "Don't worry."

Chris stood at my other side and I took a deep breath. I felt so much better just having them there with me.

Brian began playing. By now we knew the song by heart. My pulse seemed to quicken with every moment as he got closer and closer to the point where Penny was to start singing.

Come on. Come on, I urged silently.

And then the intro was done. Penny opened her mouth. And nothing came out.

chapter fourteen

A murmur rushed through the crowd as everyone turned to each other, wondering what was up with Penny. Brian stopped and tried starting over, but Penny still didn't make a sound. She was just sitting there, paler than any girl should be in the middle of the summer in California.

And it was all my fault.

"Oh, no," I groaned. "This isn't happening." I reached out and grabbed Melinda's hand. The scene in front of us was horrifying.

"It's gonna be okay," Chris said.

"No, it's not!" I replied as the silent moments crawled by. "I am such an idiot! Did I really think that all of Penny's problems could be solved with a pair of sunglasses?"

As the voices of confusion in the audience grew louder, Brian leaned over and whispered something to Penny. She nodded almost imperceptibly, and Brian, obviously shaken, started to play one more time.

"I can't take it," I said, covering my eyes. "I can't watch this any more!"

But then, when the intro was over, I heard the impossible. I heard Penny start to sing.

"She's doing it," Melinda said, shaking me gleefully. "Look! She's doing it!"

I opened my eyes. Every part of Penny's body aside from her mouth seemed to be frozen. She looked beyond uncomfortable, but at least she was singing. Sort of. Her usually strong voice sounded quiet and strained. I glanced over at the audience and saw that some of them were still squirming.

"Come on, Penny," I urged, trying to send her good vibes. "You can do it."

And gradually it seemed that Penny was realising she could do it, too. The longer she sang, the stronger her voice became. As she and Brian reached the bridge of the song, the audience started paying attention.

I smiled as a few people in the front of the crowd swayed to the music. And I saw Brian smile, too. I allowed myself a little sigh of relief. The ordeal was almost over.

I arrived at the beach house just in time to see Penny singing her heart out on the last few lines of the song. For a moment I couldn't believe it. She wasn't even blindfolded! I jostled my way through the audience until I was as close to the front as I could get. That was when I noticed the sunglasses. They made her look totally glam. She could definitely rub elbows at Gavin's party.

Penny and Brian finished up their song and the crowd went crazy. I couldn't believe I almost missed this just to hang out with Gavin. This was what friendship was really about – supporting one another and being there for the big moments.

And from the grin on Penny's face as she walked offstage, I knew this was one of the biggest moments of her life.

She and Brian headed towards the deserted beach house. I ran after them. Chris, Melinda and Ashley were already there, waiting.

"You were amazing!" I cried as I joined the happy, hugging crowd.

"Mary-Kate! You made it!" Penny exclaimed. She threw her arms around my neck and hugged me so tight, I thought I was going to need an oxygen mask.

"I wouldn't have missed it for all the celebrities in the world," I told her.

"I knew you would come around," Ashley said. "We are *much* more fun than those rich, fabulous, glamorous types."

Everyone laughed. "You have no idea," I

agreed, rolling my eyes. I leaned in towards Ashley's ear and whispered, "I'll tell you all about it later."

"You'd better," she whispered back.

"So they totally loved you!" Ashley exclaimed, clapping her hands together.

"Did they?" Brian asked, scratching at the back of his neck.

"Are you kidding?" Melinda blurted out. She whacked his shoulder to get his attention. "Didn't you hear the adoring applause?"

"I think I'm in a daze," Brian admitted. "A happy daze, of course." He turned his attention to Penny. "You were incredible, Pen. Tomorrow night, we're going to be stars!"

Everyone cheered. But Penny wasn't cheering along with us.

"I don't know, you guys," she said. "Yeah, it worked tonight, but tomorrow we're going to be on that huge stage with all those important people watching. What if I freeze up again?"

"You won't," Ashley said. "Now that you know you can do it, you'll be able to do it again."

Penny nodded, but I could tell that she was scared stiff. I hoped that Ashley was right. I hoped Penny could perform again tomorrow night.

chapter fifteen

"Dad! Over here!" I shouted. I waved at Dad and broke into a grin. I ran over to him and gave him a huge hug.

"It's great to see you, Mary-Kate!" Dad planted a kiss on top of my head. He hugged Ashley, who had run up behind me, and then took a step back to study us. "Is it just me, or do you two look older?"

Ashley and I laughed. We followed the crowd that was streaming towards stage A. One of Dad's co-workers was judging the contest, and Dad had come up to check out the new talent.

"You know, I'm really proud of all the hard work you girls have done this summer," Dad said. "You've really impressed your mother and me."

I glanced at Ashley and we both smiled. "We've kind of impressed ourselves," I said. I thought back to the moment we'd found out what our jobs were going to be – and how I wanted to bail. How stupid I had been! If I hadn't been assigned to that job, I never would have met Chris and Melinda. Or Gavin.

As if my thoughts had conjured him up, Gavin emerged from the crowd and stopped dead in his tracks.

"Hey, Mary-Kate!" he said brightly. I saw his eyes flick to Dad and immediately knew what he was thinking. He wanted me to introduce them.

For a moment, I thought about ignoring him. He was so not worth my time. But then I realised that would be immature. And I wasn't going to sink to his level.

"Hi, Gavin," I said. "This is my sister, Ashley."

"Hello," Ashley said coolly. I was proud of her self-restraint. Even though she was furious when I told her how Gavin had acted at the party, I knew it must be hard for her to be so chill around a superstar.

"And this is my father," I said. "Dad, this is Gavin Michaels. He's the lead singer of Glowstick."

"It's a pleasure to meet you, Gavin." Dad shook hands with him.

"You, too, sir," Gavin gushed.

Somehow Gavin managed to pull Dad aside. I knew he was talking to Dad about the possibility of switching record labels.

"Why did you introduce him to Dad?" Ashley whispered to me. "I thought you were mad at him."

"I am." I shrugged. "But I figure I'll let Dad make up his own mind about Gavin and the band."

"Wow." Ashley arched an eyebrow. "*Did* you get older this summer?"

"Very funny," I laughed.

Dad and Gavin rejoined us. Gavin was grinning broadly. I knew Dad must have set up a meeting with him.

"Do you want to hang out later, Mary-Kate?" Gavin asked, looking pleased with himself.

"Nah. I don't think so," I replied.

His face fell. I turned and walked off with Dad and Ashley. Take that, Mr. Rock Star, I thought.

I sat in the darkened audience next to my dad and Mary-Kate, waiting for Brian and Penny's turn on the stage.

Finally, the MC called their names. The two of them ran out together. Penny was wearing her sunglasses.

Brian and Penny sat down on their stools. I held my breath.

"She looks okay," Mary-Kate said.

I nodded silently. I was too nervous to speak!

Then Brian started to play... and Penny started to sing! She actually looked comfortable. She wasn't stiff or scared or quiet or strained. Finally – she was a performer!

Then, halfway through the first chorus, Penny

took off the sunglasses. The crowd cheered as if she was some huge headliner who got applause every time she moved.

I cheered louder than anyone in the audience. Penny had done it!

The concert was over. We waited anxiously while the judges made their decisions. Mary-Kate, Chris, Melinda and I all managed to sneak backstage so that we could be with Brian and Penny when the announcement was made.

"You guys are definitely going to win," I told them, slipping my hand into Brian's. "I can feel it."

"Yeah? Well, if we do, it's all thanks to you," Brian said. He kissed my forehead and looked into my eyes. I felt a little rush travel from my shoulders all the way down to my toes.

"Okay, enough with the mushy stuff! They're about to announce the winners!" Mary-Kate told us.

All the performers gathered backstage. A hush fell over the crowd. I could feel the excitement and tension in the air as the MC walked to the microphone, an index card in his hand. This was unreal. Someone's life was going to change because of that card!

"The third runner-up is... Akiko Ogiswara!" the MC announced.

Akiko yelped and rushed out onstage to accept her prize. Brian's grip on my hand tightened.

"The second runner-up is... Unnamed!" the MC called out.

The band that had performed on our first night at the beach house cheered and made their way on to the stage.

"I guess when you can't come up with a name, *Unnamed* is an easy choice," Mary-Kate joked.

Everyone laughed, but my heart was pounding harder than it ever had before. This was it. The moment of truth. I looked at Penny and she smiled back at me. She didn't look nervous at all.

"And the winner of the grand prize is... Penny and Brian!"

Suddenly, everyone around me was screaming. Brian hugged me and Penny jumped in, wrapping her arms around both of us. They had done it! They had actually won!

Brian and Penny ran on to the stage. Chris, Melinda, Mary-Kate and I watched them accept their prize.

I felt so happy, I could have burst! Penny's and Brian's faces glowed. They had made their dream come true!

"I'd like to make a toast!" Chris announced at the beach house the following night.

It was our last night at the festival. Mary-Kate, Brian, Penny, Melinda, Chris and I were all sitting a few yards away from the crowd, having a private party. I leaned into Brian's shoulder. We all looked up at Chris.

"To the soon-to-be-biggest music stars in the universe, Penny and Brian!" Chris shouted. He ceremoniously lifted his soda can.

"To Penny and Brian!" we all cheered, clinking our cans together.

"Ashley! Come with me to get some more snacks!" Mary-Kate grabbed my arms and pulled me up off the ground.

"What's up?" I asked.

"Well... Penny told me where she got those sunglasses and I could tell they were not cheap," Mary-Kate said, straightening up. "How did you afford them?"

I flushed a bit and looked down at the sand. "I used some of the money I put aside for the stereo," I said.

"You're kidding me!" Mary-Kate blurted out. "Ashley, you've been salivating over that stereo all summer!"

"So what? Maybe I'll get a part-time job when we get home." I shrugged. "Besides, helping Brian and Penny get that contract was much more important."

"I can't believe you did that," someone behind me said.

I recognised the voice and froze. It was Brian – and he'd overheard everything we said.

"It's no big deal," I insisted.

"Ashley... you're amazing," Brian said, taking my hand in his.

"That's my cue to leave," Mary-Kate joked, jogging away.

"You want to go for a walk?" I asked Brian.

"Yeah," he said.

We strolled down to the water along the surf, leaving the party behind us. For a few minutes, neither of us spoke. I felt happy just being with him.

Finally, Brian stopped. "I don't know what to say... except thank you. I know you really wanted that stereo, and what you did—"

"It's okay," I said. "I wanted to do it."

Brian leaned in and kissed me. It was an amazing kiss, but inside I felt as if my heart were breaking.

Brian was a special guy – the first guy I'd ever really liked. And tomorrow I was going to have to leave him. What if I never saw him again?

"You are such a cool person, Ashley," Brian said. "I've never met anyone like you before." He paused. "I – I like you so much. I don't want to go back home to Seattle." He looked deep into my eyes. "I'm really going to miss you."

"I'm going to miss you, too," I said.

Brian wrapped his arms around me. I felt warm and happy as he hugged me tightly.

"Listen, Seattle isn't that far away," he said. "Maybe I can come and see you. You know – drive down the coast or something? And there's always the phone, and e-mail, and—"

"But it won't be the same," I interrupted. "It won't be the same as having you here with me."

I took a step away from him. "When you're a big rock star, will you send me tickets to all your shows?"

Brian smiled. "Definitely."

We held hands and walked back to our friends. Dad was hanging out nearby with some other record-company people, enjoying the party.

Mary-Kate ran up to me and tapped me on the shoulder. "Dad's leaving right after the fireworks," she told me. "Let's thank him again before he goes."

Mary-Kate and I ran over to Dad. "Hey, girls," he said.

"Dad – we just wanted to thank you again..." I began.

"For setting up the best summer we've ever had!" Mary-Kate finished.

Dad put an arm over each of our shoulders. "My pleasure, girls. I'm glad you had a good time."

"Mark? Is that you?" A tall, grey-haired man about Dad's age approached us. "It's so dark out here, I wasn't sure it was you."

"Don!" Dad reached out and shook the man's hand. "Great to see you! Girls, this is a friend of mine, Don Maneri. We've worked on a lot of music videos together. Don, I'd like you to meet my daughters, Mary-Kate and Ashley."

"Hey, I've heard a lot about you girls," Don said. "Every time I see your dad, he's got new wallet photos of you."

We laughed and shook his hand.

"What brings you here, Don?" Dad asked. "Working with one of the bands?"

"Actually, I've branched out," Don told us. "I'm doing feature-length movies now. I'm casting my next project with unknowns, and I thought MusicFest would be a great place to find new talent." He looked at me and Mary-Kate. Then he blinked and looked harder at us. "How old are you girls?" he asked us.

"Sixteen," I answered.

"I can't believe it. That's perfect!" he cried. "I've got a part for sixteen-year-old sisters. Would you two like to audition?"

Mary-Kate and I exchanged excited glances. "Audition? For a part in a movie?"

"Hold on, girls," Dad said. "I don't know, Don…"

"We start shooting in August," Don said. "Just for a few weeks. It'll be over by the time school starts."

"Please, Dad!" I begged. "It would be so cool!"

"It's a big part, too," Don told us.

"Really?" Mary-Kate cried. "Oh, Dad, this is so exciting! We have to do this!"

"Well, we'll discuss it," Dad said. "But it does sound like a great experience..."

Mary-Kate and I nodded at each other. "Yes!" We knocked our fists together.

"Hold on girls," Dad said. "Don't start celebrating yet. You still have to get through the audition."

"We know," Mary-Kate said. "But we're going to be perfect for those roles. Just wait and see!"

Kaboom! I glanced up. The fireworks were starting.

"See you later, Dad." We kissed him and waved goodbye to Don. Then we hurried across the sand to join our friends for the fireworks.

We all oohed and aahed. I looked at each of our new friends, Chris, Melinda, Penny and Brian, wanting to remember this night forever.

The fireworks ended with the brightest, loudest finale ever. My friends cheered their hearts out.

"I already thought this summer was amazing," I told Mary-Kate. "But it's not over yet."

Mary-Kate nodded. "And it's going to get even better – *if* we can ace those auditions!"

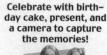

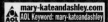

Real Books for Real Girls

b the 1st 2 kno
mary-kateandashley

It's What **YOU** Read ™

REGISTER 4 THE HARPERCOLLINS AND MK&ASH TEXT CLUB AND KEEP UP2 D8 WITH THE L8EST MK&ASH BOOK NEWS AND MORE.

SIMPLY TEXT SS, FOLLOWED BY YOUR GENDER (M/F), DATE OF BIRTH (DD/MM/YY) AND POSTCODE TO: 07786277301.

SO, IF YOU ARE A GIRL BORN ON THE 12TH MARCH 1986 AND LIVE IN THE POSTCODE DISTRICT RG19 YOUR MESSAGE WOULD LOOK LIKE THIS: SSF120386RG19.

IF YOU ARE UNDER 14 YEARS WE WILL NEED YOUR PARENTS' OR GUARDIANS' PERMISSION FOR US TO CONTACT YOU. PLEASE ADD THE LETTER 'G' TO THE END OF YOUR MESSAGE TO SHOW YOU HAVE YOUR PARENTS' CONSENT. LIKE THIS: SSF120386RG19G.

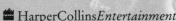 HarperCollins*Entertainment*

 PARACHUTE PRESS

 DUALSTAR PUBLICATIONS

 AOL mary-kateandashley.com AOL Keyword: mary-kateandashley

Order Form

To order direct from the publishers, just make a list of the titles you want and fill in the form below:

Name ....

Address ....

....

....

Send to: Dept 6, HarperCollins Publishers Ltd, Westerhill Road, Bishopbriggs, Glasgow G64 2QT.

Please enclose a cheque or postal order to the value of the cover price, plus:

UK & BFPO: Add £1.00 for the first book, and 25p per copy for each additional book ordered.

Overseas and Eire: Add £2.95 service charge. Books will be sent by surface mail but quotes for airmail despatch will be given on request.

A 24-hour telephone ordering service is available to holders of Visa, MasterCard, Amex or Switch cards on 0141- 772 2281.

Collins
An *Imprint* of HarperCollins*Publishers*